THE PERFECT FIRST

MAYA HUGHES

To anyone who ever wished they were strong enough to change their future. You are.

1

REECE

The icy splash of Gatorade washed over me. I tilted my head back, spraying it all over everyone still standing along the sidelines. If I had to deal with the sticky cleanup of this stuff, so did everyone else. Rivulets of it ran down my back, soaking my jersey and pads. That shit was a bitch to get out of my gear, but damn it felt good to win.

Grabbing hold of LJ's pads, I wrapped my arm around his neck and shook him. His brown hair was half matted to his head with sweat and half sticking straight up. He was our tight end, my roommate, and one of the chillest guys on the team. Maybe only Keyton was more chill, and that was probably why I'd snatched that touchdown pass right out of his grip. A guy who relaxed just didn't get the intensity of the game.

"One of these days your gambles aren't going to pay off, but damn is it awesome when they do." LJ slapped his fist into my chest, but his lips curled up into a smile. His eyebrow with the scar running straight through it lifted.

I grinned and shook out my hair, spraying rain, sweat,

and Gatorade all over him. He shoved me back before running off to celebrate with the rest of the team. Pads and helmets crashed into each other. Arms flew into the air. The Fulton U fans jumped in the stands, shaking the ground under my feet. I basked in their cheers and chants, turning and staring up at all the people, lifting my arm to everyone who'd stuck with us through the rain. The rumble got even louder, filling the stadium. I'd thought after what happened in the offseason, things on the field might have changed, but winning made everyone forget all that off-the-field shit.

My body hummed with the electricity and adrenaline of the crowd and the win. We weren't even halfway through the season and there was already talk of a championship.

I wondered how my dad had walked away from this. It was what made me feel alive, and I wasn't giving it up for anything. I lived for these moments.

"Number 6, baby!" Nix AKA Phoenix Russo AKA my other roommate, team QB, and best friend, screamed into my ear, nearly knocking me over. His bright blue eyes, which the ladies went insane for, practically lit up the place. Girls up in the stands shouted out our names. His cheeks reddened like they always did whenever that sort of attention happened off the field.

"Promise me you'll let someone else catch a pass at least once this season." He smacked against the pads on my back.

"It's what you get for even thinking of passing the ball to anyone else, and if they're too slow, that's not my fault." I shrugged. Wrapping my fingers tighter around the facemask of my helmet, I tugged the sticky neck of my jersey down off my skin. Time for a shower and a party.

The crowd of teammates, coaches, reporters, and officials swarmed us as we rushed into the tunnel. Pads, helmets, and gear banged into the concrete walls and the noise bounced off the tight space. After a win, it was nearly deafening.

Nix tugged open the locker room door. LJ jumped onto us with his arms around our shoulders.

"Press conference first." Coach Saunders grabbed me and Nix by our jerseys, knocking LJ off. Coach's salt and pepper hair would have made him look like a politician, but he'd sooner punt a baby than kiss one. While some former pros let themselves go, he hadn't. He always ran sprints right along with us, mostly to keep the bitching to a minimum. If he could still keep up with us, we had no excuses. He hated everything outside of the plays and practice. His face always looked like he was headed for the firing squad, but his current glare was one reserved for LJ. I had no idea what he'd done to deserve it, but I was just glad I wasn't the one getting the stink eye.

"Hit the showers, Lewis."

LJ didn't have to be told twice and darted inside the locker room. No one knew what he'd done to piss Coach off, but damn had he done a phenomenal job of it. If looks could kill, LJ would've been dead and buried months ago. It had been tense between those two since the beginning of the season, and LJ wouldn't give up the goods on why.

"Can I grab a quick shower first?" The tips of my fingers brushed against the metal handle. Chanting fans I could handle. Pushy reporters shoving microphones into my face? Not my idea of fun. The invasive questions from last spring and the judgment in their eyes had stung after so many years only seeing the adoring side of the media. The backlash had been like a field goal kick to the nuts.

Coach ignored my request, shoving us to the side and down the hall. "Let's get this over with."

Pulling at the front of my slowly drying jersey, I felt its gummy dampness clinging to my skin.

"Don't worry—they'll still think you're pretty," Nix whispered in my ear as he ruffled my sticky hair with his sasquatch hands. He grimaced and wiped it on his pants. "Gross, dude."

"That's what you get."

Coach pulled the door open. The camera flashes temporarily blinded me as we sat down behind the flimsy table on the small stage in front of the reporters. This was something I needed to get used to. Spots danced in front of my eyes. I bit the insides of my cheeks to keep my face neutral. Coach slapped down his playbook and pointed a meaty finger at the first reporter.

The woman stood up and stared straight at me. "Reece, how does it feel, adding another winning touchdown to your stats?" She kept her eyes on me with her pen poised above her notepad. The entire room was hanging on my every word. The tension in my shoulders eased and I lapped that shit up.

I leaned into the mic. "Feels pretty damn good, and I'll be happy for it in every game from here until the championship."

"What about stealing the pass from your own teammate?" A guy leaning against the wall in the back shouted out the question.

Everyone's head turned to him.

"Keyton was lined up perfectly for the interception. You streaked across the field and grabbed it out of his hands."

"Who are you, his dad?" The corners of my mouth darted down. "If he'd been faster he would've gotten to it. End of story." Keyton wasn't exactly the best under pressure. I'd done us all a favor with that snag.

"How do your teammates feel about the drama surrounding you at the end of last season?"

I glared at the smug reporter. There'd been four games this season and not one word about the offseason. Maybe that was why I'd gotten lulled into a false sense of security. "I didn't do anything wrong, and if anyone has something to say about it, they can go f—" The mic was batted off the table and Coach turned to me then grabbed my arm.

"Phoenix, finish up here," he ground out over his shoulder.

The flashes went into overdrive and the shouts followed us into the hallway as the door slammed behind me.

"My office, now," he shouted then stalked off.

Clenching and unclenching my fists, I followed him like a kid being sent to the principal's office. He threw open his door and stepped out of the way to let me in. *Lighten the hell up* was on the tip of my tongue, but I wanted to keep my balls attached to my body, so I decided to keep that sentiment under wraps.

He slammed the door behind him, rattling the glass. "I'm sick and tired of your showboating bullshit. I'd have thought after last season you might have a bit more humility."

After last season, I had a healthy aversion to the opposite sex and even more sureness that my pro career was my first and only focus. "We're winning games, aren't we?" I flopped into one of the chairs in front of his desk. *Have fun scrubbing off this sticky mess when I leave. Should have let me shower first.*

"Winning isn't all that matters." He threw down the playbook onto his desk. The papers all over it blew back and a framed picture of a little girl with pigtails clattered to the floor. I picked it up. The girl looked oddly familiar, but he'd never talked about having a daughter before. I set it back on his desk.

"I'm sure your salary and my draft prospects say differently." I leaned back in the chair and crossed my legs at the ankle.

He turned his back to me and braced his hands behind his head, interlocking his fingers. The big gold championship ring on his right hand glinted in the light.

I shot forward. "And I'm sure you had to do quite a lot of showing off to get that ring."

Turning, he glared at me. "I wasn't out there on the field all by myself, and neither are you. Keyton was there for that pass. He had it and you nearly cost us the game."

"But I didn't." And I hadn't all season.

"If you want to make it in the pros—"

I slammed my lips together and stared up at the ceiling.

He stepped in front of me, right into my line of sight. "If you want to make the pros and actually have a career after, you need to clean up this attitude. No one wants to work with a showoff, and if you don't get your act together, no team out there's going to want to deal with you. I deal with you because you win games, but when it comes to the NFL, they've got bigger prima donnas who can sprint laps around you."

The muscles in my neck strained and my eyes narrowed. I'd like to see someone try to get past me.

"You're a great player, don't get me wrong, but there's more to it than that when it comes to making it long term. That should have been Keyton's play and you know it."

Crossing my arms over my chest, I stared at him, trying to bore a hole through the hair at the top of his head. Maybe it could have been Keyton's play—or maybe he'd have dropped it. He was four out of ten for completions under pressure, and I wasn't going to let him stop the team from getting to the championship.

"I want you to talk to someone."

"I'm not talking to a shrink."

He turned his head and lifted an eyebrow. "I wasn't talking about a therapist, but maybe you should see one. I'm talking about someone to help you handle the media, someone to help you learn how to at least appear gracious in front of a room full of reporters."

Coach sat at his desk, put his glasses on, and began typing on his computer, clicking the mouse now and then. The second hand in his office ticked louder and louder with each passing second. Maybe I shouldn't have done what I'd done out there, but I wasn't going to let anyone get in my way when it came to getting what I wanted, not even my own teammate. This was my time to shine, to show pro scouts what kind of player I could be...but maybe learning to finesse things a bit wouldn't be a bad thing.

"The average pro career is three years, two for wide receivers, but if you're a first-round pick, that goes up to nine. Don't make a team have second thoughts about you because of your attitude." He held out a piece of paper with blue ink scribbled on it.

I wasn't going to be a flash in the pan.

I wasn't going to leave until I was ready.

I wasn't going to end up like my dad.

"Fine, I'll meet with him."

"Her." Coach peered over the top of his glasses. "And I wasn't giving you a choice."

I left his office and went to the locker room. Looked like I'd missed the celebration. Pads, helmets, and bottles littered the floor.

Keyton came out of the showers with a towel wrapped

around his waist and another around his neck. He ran it over his hair, trying to dry his light brown strands. He always kept it short and neat, like the preppy kids who used to tease the shit out of me back in middle school. But he wasn't like them. Keyton had transferred two years earlier, a quiet guy who mainly stuck to himself. He walked past.

"Listen, man, I didn't see you out there or I wouldn't have gone for the ball." I held out my hand.

He stared at me, his fingers tightening around the towel. There was a flash in his eyes, the same kind I'd seen when guys got to their boiling point. He was only half an inch shorter than me, but when people got that look, they could be unpredictable.

"Yeah, you would have." Then the look was gone, blowing right past like a feather on the wind. He smiled and shook my hand, smacking me on the shoulder. "Don't worry about it. I'll beat you to the next one."

I grinned back at him. "I'm sure you will." *Not a chance.*

Rushing into the shower, I blitz-washed myself, scouring my skin to get the remnants of the sticky drink off me then headed back out into the locker room. I dried off and sat in front of my locker. My gaze darted down to the bench, and I glanced underneath it. My heart rate picked up. *What the hell?*

Jumping up, I opened my locker and stood frozen. The blood drained out of my face. The bottom of my locker was empty. Finally able to form words, I bellowed, "Where the fuck are my shoes?"

"What shoes?" Nix sat beside me with his hippie-ass hair and a shit-eating grin.

"Don't screw around with me. Those are limited-edition Adidas." The vintage pair I'd bought over the summer. The same ones I'd begged my parents for, but they had shot me down over and over again when everyone else on the team had had a pair in ninth grade. As a former pro player's son, I'd had a bullseye on my back growing up. Expectations were sky high not just for how I played, but also for how we lived.

"You're worse than a chick, man." Cupping his hand around his mouth, he faced the rest of the room. "Someone hand over his shoes before he passes out."

Berkley strolled out of the shower room with a wide smile showing off his dumbass dimples. His black hair dripped water everywhere because he straight-up refused to use a towel, just free-balling it while air drying.

"You did this, didn't you?" I pointed at him like an evil old witch ready to turn him into a frog.

"What? Did you mean these size 15s that were once again sitting on top of my clothes?" Berk grabbed the pristine pair of sneakers from the top of the lockers behind me and shoved them into my chest.

Recovering from his linebacker attack, I cradled the red and white striped beauties in my arms. "You think I'm putting these just anywhere?"

"Next time you put your shoes on my clothes, they take a Gatorade bath, just like you." He slipped his feet into his beaten and battered sneakers, which no longer had any discernible color other than gray, kind of like the ones I'd worn my last semester of high school. It wasn't that we'd been broke, but my dad had only played pro for a couple years and after that, things weren't easy. If you didn't get a fat contract, you were screwed, which meant first-round draft pick or bust for me.

"And I'll be shaving off your eyebrows while you sleep. I'm not going to set them on the dirty bench."

"But you'll sit your ass on it? You've got some priority

issues." He shook his head, spraying everyone in the vicinity like a dog after a downpour, and tugged a shirt on.

"Just because you've worn the same pair of sneakers since freshman year doesn't mean some of us don't like to look like we didn't drag a pair of shoes out of the dumpster."

"They're comfortable." He shrugged and grabbed his bag. "You headed back to the Brothel?"

I cringed and buttoned my jeans. "Can't you just say the house?" The term was a leftover from the name the frat house had had before they got kicked off campus and we moved in. Theta Beta Sigma, AKA The Bed Shakers Brothel.

We'd spent the last year disinfecting the place, finding condoms crammed into places they had no business being. The name stuck after the previous tenants left and the Brothel was born, whether we liked it or not. It didn't help that our team was the Trojans. The Fulton University Trojans, or the FU Trojans as was often chanted in the stadium, the volume always reaching a deafening point. Being known as a manwhore hadn't been too big of a deal until it was, and I'd learned the hard way that it wasn't easy erasing someone's preconceived notion of you once it settled in.

"Our house has a reputation to uphold." He grinned, reveling in the thought of the almost constant attention he received on and off the field. "But you're right, maybe you should just hole up in the library to study the new plays the coach sent out."

"There's no new play needed, only one—get the ball to me." I swung around, picked up my bag, and followed him out. People hung around the exits like always.

The girls who waited around after the games were always extra eager, sometimes too eager. I'd seen more than a few guys get burned over the past three years. Latest victim—me.

"Hey, Reece."

Smile and wave. That was safest. Not to say I was a monk, I just didn't bang everything that moved, especially not now, and never without making sure she knew I didn't do relationships and I sure as hell wasn't going to be anyone's meal ticket.

There were pieces of paper tucked under my windshield wipers, right alongside a bright pink lace thong with a phone number scrawled across it. *Man, I hope those aren't used.* At least it was better than what had been sitting on my windshield the previous season: fucking onesies and baby bottles. How quickly the pendulum swung. Celeste had left the school, but the rumor mill was still churning under the autographs and high fives.

Opening my trunk, I grabbed my ice scraper and flicked the papers and thong off the front of my car. The numbers written on the papers dissolved as they hit the damp ground.

I laughed and climbed inside. If this was how things were in college, I figured the pros must be insanity. Dad had screwed up by getting married before he was even drafted—not that Mom wasn't awesome. They were disgustingly and embarrassingly in love, but damn he'd missed out. Then again, he'd had more than football going for him. He'd graduated from college with great grades and had taken over my grandfather's business.

My barely bobbing 2.3 GPA wasn't getting me anything other than a greeter spot at a nearby big-box store. Going pro was my chance, and I wasn't going to waste it.

I swung by campus to turn in a paper before driving back to the Brothel, and the party had already started when

I arrived. They'd died down for a while, but they were in full force now. Parking around the block, I sat in the car and put on my other game face. I could be the Reece I'd been before. I needed to be.

Slushy snow and ice cracked and crunched under my shoes. The freaking salt on the sidewalk was going to screw up my shoes. High fives and chest bumps came my way, people milling around, moving from house to house looking for the best party they could get into. Cheers were called out from the houses around us. I waved over my shoulder to everyone hanging off their balconies to welcome me home.

Jogging up the steps, I pushed open the already cracked door. The bass from the music vibrated the floor. I slammed the door shut and the sea of heads turned around.

Pinned against it, I braced myself for the onslaught as partygoers, already more than a few drinks in, showered me with their appreciation, namely in sloshed drinks and bro hugs. The blue lights we'd swapped out for party lights gave the house a club glow.

Beer and alcohol, sweat and girls' fruity-scented perfumes and lotions hung so heavy in the air I could taste it. While other guys struggled to keep their parties from becoming a sausage fest, we'd never had any trouble filling the place up with ladies. The Brothel's reputation made it hard to keep them out, especially when the Trojans inside were on the winningest team in FU history.

Parties literally appeared out of nowhere. Kegs rolled in the front door, red plastic cups handed out by the hundreds. We'd once locked our door during a game weekend and came home to the front window busted out, the deadbolt lock on the door broken, and a party in full drunken swing inside. Sometimes we had to give in to the current of the ocean, and we didn't want to have to pay for new windows and locks after every game.

The wood floors were going to be a bitch to clean, but we gave that job to LJ and Berk since they were juniors. Movie posters hung on the walls. *Die Hard*, *Terminator*, *Kill Bill*, and, of course, *Rocky*. The two couches and chair in the living room were pushed against the back wall to try to protect them from party damage. It wasn't that they were nice or anything; we just didn't feel like sitting on the floor for the next six months until graduation.

Berk and LJ took up their spot at the beer pong table in the dining room, and they shouted and waved me over. Nix held court in the kitchen as Keyton and some of the other guys from the team hung out in the living room with never-empty cups of beer in their hands. I held out my arms in front of me, waving them up and down.

"Who's ready to go to the fucking championship?" I cupped my hands around my mouth for the last word, everyone screamed, and the beer shower began again. I needed to change these shoes or they were going to get drenched.

Playing this part had always been easy, and I hadn't done anything I needed to hide for. I needed to show them there wasn't a reason for me to be ashamed—right after I changed my sneakers. I took off upstairs. More high fives were doled out from people waiting on the steps, in line for the bathroom. Thankfully, I had a single with my own bathroom. Unlocking my door, I slipped inside. We'd learned the hard way to lock our rooms during a party or you'd come back to missing stuff, or worse, people banging on your bed.

A rumpled pile of clothes sat on the center of my bed, the same pile that migrated across my mattress and back onto the floor once it was dirty again. There were string lights my sister had put up when she came to "help" me move in, if by "help" she meant bug the crap out of me and attempt to sneak off to a party on campus.

My desk was stacked with books, and various papers were shoved in between the pages. With two-a-day practices, I hadn't gotten the whole organization thing down before the semester started.

I put my shoes back with the small collection I'd accumulated over the past few years. I wasn't walking into or out of a game with anyone thinking I was less than they were because of shitty shoes ever again.

I swapped for an old pair that was perfect for party mishaps and jogged back downstairs. Hands slipped around my waist and into my back pocket. Someone slammed a red plastic cup into my hand. It was good to be on top.

"You approved me coming here." My violin sat on the couch, teetering on the edge of the cushion. I paced in the living room. Talking to him in my room felt like I was being buried in a coffin. The walls started to close in and I could barely breathe. Our apartment was a study in opposites. My coffee mug was tucked beside the coffeemaker I'd bought, *Be Happy* scrawled across the front in a loopy script.

"I said yes because Dr. Huntsman was teaching there and you said he agreed to look over your studies. Now, Dr. Mickelson is back at Harvard."

Other than a couple of fuzzy pink picture frames with pictures of Alexa my roommate there wasn't much personality in the place. We'd been stuck together for the past seventy-three days, not that I was counting. Her other friends were all studying abroad for the semester, a fact she'd told me at least thirty times since we'd moved in together as a reminder that there was no way in hell she'd have chosen me as a roommate otherwise.

"I've made a commitment to study here. You've always

taught me to follow through with my commitments." Not that I'd ever had a choice.

Alexa's dishes were trying to crawl their way out of the sink as we spoke. I swore one of these mornings I'd wake up and something from the depths of caked-on crap would loop its slimy tentacles around my neck and try to drag me down the drain.

I picked up a pair of her underwear using the tips of two fingers and flung it over on top of the growing pile on the far end of the couch. Her clothes were draped over nearly every surface in the apartment. Nail polish streaks ran across the arm of the couch that had come with the apartment, but losing my security deposit was the least of my worries right then.

"You're being unreasonable, Persephone."

I cringed. My shoulders practically jammed into my ears. No one called me Persephone except my parents, my professors, and tutors...which meant everyone called me Persephone. I could say my friends called me Seph, but then I'd need some friends, wouldn't I?

"I'll barely have two years here. I hardly think it's going to throw my future off track."

"Mickelson is the top of his field. He could have given everyone notice that he'd be coming back to Harvard early."

I was sure that had been at the top of his list when returning from his leave of absence after his wife died.

"This is still a great program. I will finish my degree and then we can talk about studying more. There's time."

"Not if you want to be exceptional." The popping sound his jaw made when he was exceptionally angry sent a shiver down my spine.

I massaged my shoulder with my free hand. "It's an Ivy League school, Dad."

"Do you know which school has had the highest percentage of Fields Medal winners in the last decade?"

"Harvard," I mouthed at the same time he said it. The coveted math prize was all he'd talked about for as long as I could remember, since I was five years old.

"Yes, I know." I sat perched on the edge of the chair like he was there hovering over me. Though he was lecturing me from a few hundred miles away, I still couldn't shake the feeling that his pristinely shined shoes were being pressed harder into the center of my chest.

"You will be the youngest winner."

"I'll do everything in my power to do it, if you just let me graduate from Fulton first."

"I'm glad you said that. I've been speaking with your advisors."

Wasn't that not allowed? I was eighteen now; he shouldn't have been able to speak to them about me at all. "They didn't have a full record of all the college courses and exams you've taken already." There was a slice of censure in his voice. "So it looks like you'll be able to graduate a year earlier than we expected."

The blood drained from my face. It was October. I'd only been in Philly for two months, had barely made a dent in living on my own, and he was already trying to get me back to Boston in less than seven months. The room swam in front of me and I leaned against the arm of the chair.

"Please, Dad."

His disgruntled scoff came through loud and clear. "We didn't dedicate our lives, sacrificing everything so that you could throw away your future. You will be the youngest Field's Medal winner." There was a finality to his words, the same one there'd been when he'd told me in no uncertain terms that I wouldn't be attending public school. Or when he'd said no, I couldn't have a sleepover with a girl in the neighborhood I'd managed to befriend during the short time I'd been allowed to play on our block. Or the time he'd told me violin no longer mattered and I wasn't to play anymore.

Maybe my parents should have checked with me first about what I wanted to do. The door to the apartment opened and Alexa breezed in. She was a bouncing ball of redheaded energy. Green accents in everything she wore brought out her eyes. Today, it was an emerald beret that held back her curls. She looked like a walking cartoon princess. Too bad she'd been cast as my oh-so-real villain.

"You're right. I'm sorry." I dragged my fingers through my hair and squeezed the back of my neck.

"This is valuable time. Records are being broken left and right and you'll be left in the dust if you keep putting things off."

Maybe I didn't want to be the youngest graduate from Harvard's to ever win a Field's Medal.

Maybe I didn't want the math equivalent of a Nobel Prize.

Maybe I just wanted to be normal for a little bit, but those discussions always led to even more uncomfortable and painful conversations.

"I've bought your ticket for Thanksgiving already. Your mother is anxious to see you." Not him. Never him.

"Can I talk to her? I wanted to ask her about something." A little motherly advice about how to make friends, a pep talk like the ones she used to give me when taking me to the playground in our neighborhood before Dad overruled mixing with *those* children. You know, normal kids who ran around, scraped their knees, and made mud pies. Apparently, it didn't provide me with any additional intellectual benefits, so it wasn't allowed. It isn't like playing is something kids *like* to do. It was almost as if he'd never been a child himself. Maybe he'd sprung from the womb as he was now, fully grown and icy cold.

I would stare out the window at the neighborhood kids riding their bikes, playing tag, or just chasing each other with sticks on their lawns while I was learning the quadratic formula. What six-year-old wouldn't love that?

"She's making dinner and I'd rather not disturb her. You know how quickly she can get sidetracked. She burned the potatoes last week..."

As if a call from her daughter couldn't possibly be worth getting dinner on the table a little later than exactly on the hour. I bit back the words. "Of course. I'll try again some other time."

"We have meetings set up for you when you're here over the break. Be prepared."

My fingers tightened around the phone. "I'm looking forward to it." No matter how many times I said no, it was like my words were merely suggestions, or worse, annoyances.

"Goodbye, Persephone."

"Goodbye, Dad." I ended the call and placed my phone down on the counter even though I felt like rocketing it across the room.

"So you're not just an android with strangers? It's with your family too." Alexa's smirk was just like those girls' in the movies, the bitchy ones who ruled the school with an iron fist. Maybe that was why her friends had all run to other countries the second they got the chance. Oh to be so lucky.

I let out a deep breath with my teeth clenched together. "Hi, Alexa." Turning, I kept my face neutral. Weren't college roommates supposed to be friends you had for the rest of your life? The people you'd call up to be in your wedding, or a godparent to your kids?

She flopped down on the couch, nearly knocking my violin to the floor.

I dove for the instrument and grabbed my bow, which was halfway stuck under her ass.

"Dan is coming over in a bit, so why don't you scamper off to your room and lock up tight? Wouldn't want you exposed to any of my bad habits." She flicked her fingers at me, not even looking up from her phone. I'd been dismissed.

This wasn't how things were supposed to be. College was supposed to be the greatest time of my life, a chance to make lifelong friends. Turned out the people left over in the housing lottery for a last-minute addition probably weren't best friend material.

"I don't mind. He seems really nice."

She snorted, glanced up, and rolled her eyes. "He's not interested." Her laugh was like nails on a chalkboard, her gaze trained on her phone.

I stood there with violin and bow tucked under my arm, my hands clasping and unclasping in front of me before I gave up, packed up my instrument, and went to my room. Why was this so hard? Why couldn't I just say something to her? *Alexa, you're a real bitch and it wouldn't hurt if you could be a bit nicer. Why don't* you *go to your room when you have a guy over?*

Her boyfriend was a constant around the apartment, and their sexual escapades had become my sleep sound-track over the past couple of months. The ugly green-eyed monster reared its head more than once during those moments. It was so easy for her, for them—hell, for everyone to make connections.

The little potted plant on my windowsill was the only color in the whole room, violets I'd picked up from where they'd been discarded under a bench on campus. They'd given them out to celebrate new student orientation. The lone plant, half knocked over with soil spilled out on the ground, was the only thing I'd gotten to personalize my room. It was the first new thing I'd added to my room other than books.

I stared at the stark place. Blank white walls, white comforter thrown over my bed, everything neatly arranged on my desk, nothing out of place. Picking up a stack of color-coded notecards, I threw them up in the air. There was a rainbow shower around me as they fluttered to the ground.

Squeezing my hands together, I resisted the urge to pick them up. The next day, I would buy something colorful. I didn't care what it was, but there was a new ban on anything white, gray, beige, or black. No more neutral. It was time for color. It was time to be bold.

I sat in front of my laptop and logged into the student portal. Navigating to the discussion forum, I checked out the different subject lines. *Tutors Needed. Study Groups. Lost Items.* Then there was the more personal section. Sometimes people would post about someone they'd seen on the quad and wanted to find again.

Anger at my dad and Alexa—and myself—boiled in my veins. Maybe there was an easier way, something that would kill a few birds with one stone. I could do something completely out of character, as staying in character hadn't done me any favors. I needed to get proactive. If I wanted to finally start living, I needed to jump-start my life.

Clicking the link to the personals, I opened a new anonymous topic. *Friends Needed.* My finger jammed into the backspace key. How stupid did that sound? Pathetic. *Go big or go home, Seph.* Preferably big because going home as the exact same person I'd left as would be beyond depressing.

The front door to the apartment opened and Alexa's squeal indicated that her boyfriend, Dan, had in fact arrived.

His heavy footsteps down the hallway were accompanied by the sounds of them pawing at each other. I braced myself. Within minutes they were usually banging against the wall like we were in the middle of a blackout and their bodies would provide echolocation to escape the building.

"Hey, Seph," he shouted while passing my open door. I ducked my head. Alexa's muffled voice didn't hide her displeasure. He was the only person who called me Seph.

With my fingers poised on top of my keyboard, Dan and Alexa's sounds blared through the thin wood of her door. I jumped up and closed mine. I banged my head against it and then stared at the computer screen.

Dan and Alexa were right back on that horse, riding it until its dying breath. Closing the door hadn't helped. If anything, the wood was conducting the sound straight into my brain. Pushing off the door, I walked back over to my computer.

The loneliness that hit when I was around people was worse somehow than when I was all alone. When there were other people in my vicinity, my lungs burned like I was drowning right in front of them and no one cared. I had no one, and I was tired of it.

Forget friends—I wanted more. I wanted to grab hold of this short lease on life I had, and I might as well go for it, right? I wouldn't start small and work my way up; there was no time for that.

I'd go big, go so big that everything else would seem tiny by comparison.

So big it would erase that fear I had of never knowing what it's like to feel free.

I'd make it a first I wouldn't ever forget.

Maybe if I just did it, jumped in with both feet, I could finally get a taste of what I'd been looking for and things would change. It wouldn't feel so mind-meltingly scary.

Taking a deep breath, I sat back down in my chair.

By the end of this semester, I am not going to be a virgin.

I didn't have time to wait around to bump into someone at a coffee shop or follow the "normal" protocol for dating. It had been two months and I hadn't even made a friend yet; how was I supposed to find a boyfriend? No, that was out. The countdown clock was ticking. I didn't have time to find someone to fall in love with. I had seven months to live the life of a "normal" college student. It was now or never.

Staring at the screen, I typed it out. *Would you like to be my first?*

I made my post as clear as possible. Searching for a fellow student, preferably a junior or senior to assist me with losing my virginity. A complete questionnaire and background would be required. I set the time, date, and location for the interviews.

The moans from the next room sent me diving for my wireless headphones. I turned them on and stared back at the screen. Mozart helped drown out the porno going on feet from my bedroom. It wasn't even night time. Wasn't that when people had sex? At night, under the cover of darkness after a bottle of wine?

I paced and stared at the screen before pulling out a notepad to jot down my pros and cons list for doing this.

Pros: Lose virginity; Finally know what sex is like; Enjoy part of the college experience/adulthood; Go against what my parents would want; Do something on my own terms; Live.

Cons: Might not live up to expectations; Might catch a disease; Might get pregnant.

Slapping the notebook down on the desk, I stared at it. The cons were all things I could live with or that could be avoided by being smart and using protection, and the pros were too good to pass up. With my fingers above the enter key, I curled them back into a fist. Did I really want to do this? Did I want this to be the way I lost my virginity? Didn't this make me a total loser?

It wasn't like I had many options during my short time-frame other than randomly asking guys on the street. At least this way had a vetting process. Setting my finger on the enter key, I stared back at what I'd written. It probably came across as desperate and insane, and likely no one would answer it.

A hand landed on my shoulder and I jumped, inadvertently hitting the key. Panic shot straight up my throat like I'd swallowed a bug. The page reloaded and a big *Submitted* blinked back at me. *What have I done?* Ripping my headphones off, I spun around in my chair.

"Your phone has been going off non-stop for, like, ten minutes." A sweaty, slightly out of breath Dan stood in my room with a sheet wrapped around his waist. He shook my phone at me. My gaze was locked on his bare chest. "Earth to Seph." He waved the glowing screen in front of my face.

"Sorry." I grabbed it out of his hand, fumbling it and nearly dropping it on the floor.

"It's okay. Alexa just gets annoyed when anything distracts me." He left the room, closing the door behind him. A tiny bit of the sheet got caught in the gap under the door and zipped out from under it as he went back into Alexa's room.

As I leaned in my chair, it slid backward, hitting my desk. I slowly fell out of my daze, swinging around and staring at the post I'd just put up. It already had eighty views. If I could've thrown up, I would have. *Shit!* There was no going back now. The hyperventilating would have to wait until later.

I wanted sweaty, crazy, blow your socks off, curl your toes sex, dammit. I wanted intense feelings and to finally let go for once. This was a good thing; there was no reason for a freak-out. I flipped to a new page in my notebook. This wasn't going to be my only first. Before I left for a life of theorems, dusty old libraries, and crushing expectations that threatened to swallow me whole, I'd make this a year I'd never forget, one I'd look back on when the freight train of my life flew down the tracks and I had no say in its destination. This was going to be the year of perfect firsts.

3

SEPH

I wrapped my fingers around the light blue mug and held my phone between my ear and my shoulder. A steam trail rose from the top of the hot chocolate with mini marshmallows. I was being downright indulgent, and I was tempted to look over my shoulder for the disapproving glare of my father. It smelled like brownies and Christmas—well, how I imagined Christmas smelled from movies and display windows in stores, warm and cozy, just like this place.

Since I'd be in Uncommon Grounds, the coffee shop not too far from my apartment, for a while, I'd taken some time to read over the menu. Black coffee was my default. It was what I'd been trained to drink. My dad felt there was never time for frivolous things like sugar or milk. Not anymore. My first first.

I'd ordered a drink for each hour I'd be there and asked them to deliver them on the hour. I figured it would give me something to do with my hands while I met prospective... suitors? Dates? Bang buddies? I didn't think they'd invented a word for exactly what this was.

"Have you gone on any dates yet?" Aunt Sophie's melodic voice calmed some of my nerves.

"I've only been here a couple months." Though, I hoped to have more than a date in a few minutes. I thought perhaps I should have ordered a muffin or a slice of the coffee cake. This place smelled like a bakery and a coffee shop had gotten into a brawl. Sitting in the booth, I could have curled up and gone to sleep—that is, if I hadn't been about twenty minutes away from interviewing candidates for my de-virginization.

"And I'm sure your father has the timer counting down until he gets you back on the hamster wheel." I could picture her pinched face on the other end of the line, based on how short and clipped her words were. My mom's sister, my Aunt Sophie, was a terrible influence and a disgrace, according to my father. She was also my favorite person in the world.

"It's not a hamster wheel. There are a lot of things I can accomplish if I keep on the path they've set out for me."

"Like dying an old maid who's only ever been surrounded by men fifty years older than her."

"Hey, some of them are maybe only twenty years older." I pulled my phone away from my ear, closed my eyes, and then peeked at the screen out of one before quickly bringing it back up to hear.

"Listen, if you ever want to run away from that circus permanently, you know I've got a futon with your name on it."

"I think it would be more like running to the circus, at least that's what Mom says."

"Just because I juggle doesn't mean I'm a clown."

"Don't forget the trapeze."

"Trapeze is an excellent workout, young lady. Your

mom's actually the one who started me on all this silly stuff." Despite being nearly fifty, she was often confused for my mom's daughter, not her sister. I didn't know who that said more about, my mom or Aunt Sophie.

"She did? I can't imagine my mom ever letting loose like that."

"Yeah, she did. I used to call her Wild One. My crazy big sister..." Her voice sounded far away like she was somewhere else, maybe a long time ago. I wished I could have known Mom before she'd met my dad. If she had been anything like Aunt Sophie, I couldn't even imagine how she and my dad had ended up together.

Clearing her throat, my aunt quickly changed the subject. "How's your roommate?"

"Still the same. She's very nice."

"You can't lie to me, kid. She's a colossal bitch, isn't she?"

"We're still getting to know one another."

"You can't let people walk all over you. That only leads to you raging about stuff inside your head. Loosen up and take that stick out of your—"

"Aunt Soph!" I took stock of how I was sitting in the burgundy booth and let my spine relax. Glancing around at everyone else at the tables and booths around me, I loosened my shoulders, letting them round a bit. My legs made slight squeaking sounds against the vinyl as I moved. *Please don't let anyone think I'm over here ripping farts.*

People sat at high tables with their laptops, headphones on, power cords and stacks of notecards piled beside them as they pounded cups of coffee. No one even noticed I was there.

"Sorry, you're right. I've got a potty mouth. But one of these days you're going to snap, kid, and when you do, just know you're not alone, okay?"

"Okay."

"I'll try to come up for Christmas this year so I get to see you. I swear I'll be on my best behavior."

A chuckle escaped my lips. "Last time you said that Dad took nearly a week to calm down."

"Those brownies were delicious."

The bell over the door jingled. My head popped up, and I looked over the top of the booth. A group of people walked in. *Nope, not for me.* I still had almost twenty minutes before the time I'd listed in my post.

"Mom didn't stop giggling for almost 24 hours, not even in her sleep." That big vein in Dad's forehead had throbbed for a solid three days. It was the happiest I'd seen Mom in a long time.

"I'm glad. She needed a bit of a break, but I swear no baked goods of any kind this time."

"Or any other edibles."

"Scout's honor. Okay, I've got a painting class to get to. Love you loads. Miss you more and I'll talk to you later."

"Talk to you later. Love you."

She ended the call. I set my phone on the table and straightened the notecards in front of me. I also had my list of questions on the booth seat beside me. Wiping my hands on my navy wool pants, I bounced in place before catching myself. *Take a deep breath. It will be fine, and by this time tomorrow, you might no longer be a virgin.* I caught sight of my red knit hat peeking out of my bag. I'd ripped the tags off before I left the apartment. My pounding heartbeat slowed a little. My first purchase of something bold. This was the start of something new for me; I could feel it.

The jingle sounded again as the door to the coffee shop swung open. My head snapped up and my bouncing leg froze. The sun shone through the doorway and a figure stood there. He was tall, taller than anyone who'd come in before. His muscles were obvious even under his coat. He paused at the entrance, his head moving from side to side like he knew people would be looking back, like he was giving everyone a chance to soak in his presence. His jet black hair was tousled just right, like he'd been running his fingers through it on the walk over from wherever he'd come from. The jacket fit him perfectly, like it had been tailored just for his body.

I glanced around; I wasn't the only one who'd noticed him walk in. He seemed familiar, but I couldn't place him. He bent forward, and I thought he was going to tie his shoes, but instead he wiped a wet leaf off his pristine white sneaker. Heads turned as he crossed the floor toward me. Squeezing my fingers tighter around the notecards, I reminded myself to breathe.

He glanced around again and spotted me. The green in his eyes was clear even from across the coffee shop. Dark hair with eyes like that wasn't a usual combo. He froze and his lips squeezed together. With his hands shoved into his pockets, he stalked toward me with a *Let's get this over with* look. That didn't bode well. He stood beside the seat on the other side of the booth, staring at me expectantly.

My gaze ran over his face. Square jaw. Hint of stubble on his cheeks and chin. My skin flushed. He had beautiful lips. What would his feel like on my mouth? I ran my finger over my bottom lip. What would they feel like on other parts of me? My body responded and I thanked God I had on a bra, shirt, and blazer or I'd have been flashing him some serious high beams. This was a good sign.

He cleared his throat.

Jumping, I dropped my hand, and the heat in my cheeks turned into a flamethrower on my neck. "Sorry, have a seat."

I half stood from my spot in the booth and extended my hand toward the other side across from me. The table dug into my thighs and I fell back into the soft seat.

Sliding in opposite me, he unzipped his coat and put his arm over the back of the shiny booth.

"Hi, very nice to meet you. I'm Seph." I shot my hand out across the table between us. The cuff of my blazer tightened as it rode up my arm.

His eyebrows scrunched together. "Seth?" He leaned in, his forearms resting on the edge of the table. He was nothing like the guys from the math department. They were quiet, sometimes obnoxious, and none of them made my stomach ricochet around inside me like it was trying to win a gold medal in gymnastics at the Olympics.

I tamped down a giggle. I did *not* giggle. The sound came out like a sharp snort, and I resisted the urge to slam my eyes shut and crawl under the table. *Be cool, Seph. Be cool.* "No—Seph. It's short for Persephone."

He lifted one eyebrow.

"Greek goddess of spring. Daughter of Demeter and Zeus. You know what, never mind. I'm glad you agreed to meet with me today."

"Not like I had much choice." He leaned back and ran his knuckles along the table top, rapping out a haphazard rhythm.

I licked my lips and parted them. Not like he had much choice? Had someone put him up to this? Had something in my post made him feel obligated to come? I hadn't been able to bring myself to go back and look at it after posting it. Shaking my head, I stuck my hand out again. "Nice to meet you..."

He looked down at my hand and back up at me, letting out a bored breath. "Reece. Reece Michaels."

"Very nice to meet you, Reece. I'm Persephone Alexander. I have a few questions we can get started with, if you don't mind."

"The quicker we get started, the quicker we can finish." He looked around like he would have rather been anywhere but there.

Those giddy bubbles soured in my stomach. A server came by with the bottled waters I'd ordered. I arranged them in a neat pyramid at the end of the table.

"Would you like a water?" I held one out to him.

He eyed me like I was offering him an illicit substance, but then reached out. His fingers brushed against the backs of mine and shooting sparks of excitement rushed through me. Pulling the bottle out of my grasp, he cracked it open and took a gulp.

My cheeks heated and I glanced down at my cards, flipping the ones at the front to the back.

"I have a notecard with some information for you to fill out."

Sliding it across the table, I held out a pen for him. He took it from me, careful that our fingers didn't touch this time. I'd have been lying if I'd said I didn't want another touch, just to test whether or not that first one had been something more than static electricity. He filled out the biographical data on the card and handed it back to me.

I scanned it. He was twenty-one. Had a birthday coming up just after the New Year. Good height-to-weight ratio. Grabbing my pen, I scanned over the questions I'd prepared for my meetings.

"Let's get started." *Just rip the Band-Aid off.* Clearing my throat, I tapped the cards on the table. A few heads turned in our direction at the sharp, rapping sound. "When were you last tested for sexually transmitted diseases?"

Setting the bottle down on the table, he stared at me like I was an equation he was suddenly interested in figuring out. And then it was gone. "At the beginning of the season. Clean bill of health." He looked over his shoulder, the boredom back, leaking from every pore. *Wow.* I'd thought guys were all over this whole sex thing, but he looked like he was sitting in the waiting room of a dentist's office.

"When did you last have sexual intercourse?"

His head snapped back to me, eyes bugged out. "What?" I had his full attention now.

"Sex? When did you last have sex?" I tapped my pen against the notecard.

He sputtered and stared back at me. His eyes narrowed and he rested his elbows on the table.

I scooted my neatly lain out cards back toward me, away from him.

"No comment."

"Given the circumstances, it's an appropriate question."

The muscles in his neck tightened and his lips crumpled together. "Fine, at the beginning of the season."

"What season?" I looked up from my pen. That was an odd way to put it. "Like, the beginning of fall?"

"Like football season."

The pieces fit together—the body, the looks from other people around the coffee house. "You play football." That made sense, and he seemed like the perfect all-American person for the job.

"Yes, I play football."

"When did the season start?"

He shook his head like he was trying to clear away a fog and stared back at me like I'd started speaking a different language. "September."

"And..." I ran my hand along the back of my neck. "How long would you say it lasted?"

His eyebrows dipped. "It didn't last. It was a one-night thing. I don't do relationships."

Of course not. He was playing the field. Sowing his oats. Banging his way through as many co-eds as possible. Experienced. Excellent.

I cleared my throat. "No, I didn't mean how long did you date the woman. I meant, how long was the sex?"

The steady drumming on the table stopped. "Are you serious?"

I licked my Sahara-dry lips. "It's a reasonable question. How long did it last?"

"I didn't exactly set a timer, but let's just say we both got our reward."

"Interesting." I made another note on the card.

"These are the types of questions I'm going to be asked for the draft?" He took the lid off the bottled water.

The draft? Pushing ahead, I went to the next line one my card and cringed a bit. "Okay, this might seem a little invasive." I cleared my throat again. "But how big is your penis? Length is fine. I don't need to know the circumference, you know—the girth."

A fine spray of water from his mouth washed over me. "What the hell kind of question is that? I know you're trying to throw me off my game, but holy shit, lady."

4

REECE

I'd heard the expression 'swallowed my tongue' and thought it wasn't possible, but mine just about jumped out of my throat when the words "How big is your penis?" came out of her mouth. The water burned in my lungs as I coughed, slamming my hand against the table. Her bottles of water rattled and the spoon in her mug clinked against the edge. Her follow-up comment about not needing to know the girth sent me gasping for air.

"I'm sure this is not the usual way you go about having sex, but I thought given the ad, you'd want to give me some idea of what sex with you might be like."

The evil burn trying to suffocate my lungs evaporated in an instant as her words registered in my brain. "You think I'm here for some kind of sex ad? What sex ad? Who puts out an ad for sex?" Those were only the first three questions I could force out of my burning lungs from the mountain of inquiries piling up in my mind.

Seph looked like the head librarian at a library convention. The crown braid, button-down shirt, and blazer didn't exactly scream, *I'm looking to get so much strange I need to put out an ad.*

She slid a folded piece of paper across the table to me. I stared at it, slightly afraid of what I'd find. When I opened it up, my eyes raced along the page, devouring the words as my brain whirred and teetered on the edge of frying. I looked from the paper up to her and back to the paper.

"Are you out of your goddamn mind?" I looked back at her, really looked. She was young. The Heidi braid thing she had wrapped around her head aside, she couldn't have been more than twenty.

"Are you even legal?"

She pursed her lips then pulled them in, biting them. "I'll turn nineteen in three months."

Now that I knew she wasn't underage, I checked her out. She was cute. Light brown hair. Light brown eyes. They darted down at her cards and back up at me. Nice body. There was no reason she'd need to take out an ad for sex. "Are you trying to harvest guys' organs or something? You can walk into any party on campus and get laid if that's what you want."

She tugged on the buttons at the front of her shirt, which only drew my attention to that area. I added *great rack* to my mental list of her positive attributes. I couldn't tell how tall she was, but she looked like she was average from where I was sitting.

"I'm not very involved in the party scene. I felt this was the best way to find suitable candidates for this job."

"What job?"

Her fingers ran along the top of the stack of notecards in front of her and she said the words so quietly I barely heard them. "Losing my virginity."

Fuck me. A virgin. I didn't think those were still out in the wild once college started. "You want to lose your virginity to a guy who's willing to answer an ad like this?" I slapped the folded paper down on the table. "You're going to get hurt. Or killed. Only a psycho would answer this ad." Or someone so desperate they'd have no issues taking advantage of someone like her.

She peered up at me. "You answered it."

"No, I thought I was coming here to meet with a media specialist. There's no one else here who looks stuffy enough other than you, so I figured you were who I was meeting."

"Oh." Disappointment oozed from her voice. "Sorry, I didn't realize. I asked people to arrive at three. I thought you were exceptionally punctual. That earned you an extra point." She pointed to the little hash marks at the top of my card.

"You're completely serious about this." I couldn't piece together why someone like her would be doing this. It wasn't just stupid—it was dangerous. It wasn't that I was the upstanding picture of morality, but she was setting herself up for trouble beyond what someone who looked like her could handle.

"I wouldn't joke about something this serious. I have a lot to accomplish and only until May to do it."

The door to the coffee shop opened again and I glanced over my shoulder. A harried-looking woman wearing a suit came in with binders and folders tucked under her arm. Now, that made more sense. I'd thought Seph looked too young, but who else rocked a blazer on a college campus when they weren't headed to an interview? Everyone else in Uncommon Grounds had rolled out of bed either five minutes or twenty-two hours ago and parked themselves here. The forty-something woman at the door's gaze bounced from table to table.

I leaned in close to Seph, a terrible thought invading my mind. "Are you dying or something?" She was only eighteen, looked perfectly fine and healthy. *Shit!*

The woman who'd rushed in appeared at the end of the booth. "Reece?"

I nodded.

"Nice to meet you. I'm Rebecca." She held out her hand. "Your coach set up the meeting. My car broke down, sorry about that. Let's grab a table when you're finished here." Her wide smile dimmed a little when she glanced over at Seph with her notecards and business attire. "Were you in the middle of something?"

I shook her hand. "Just give me a minute."

Rebecca stood there, bouncing from foot to foot.

Seph still hadn't answered my question. "Are you dying?" I ducked my head and tried to catch her eye.

She nibbled on her lip, the plump fullness of it clenched between her teeth.

"Do you mean literally or metaphorically, like due to embarrassment?"

"The first one." I covered her hand with mine. A slight tremble went through her. She was scared shitless like a rookie running out of the tunnel for the first time. I wanted to pull her in close and whisper into her ear that it would be okay. *Whoa!* Talk about blindsided. This was what I got for not getting laid since the season began. It was turning me into a chick.

She peered up at me. "No more than any of us. I'm sorry for the mix-up. Go ahead to your meeting." She slid her hands out from under my grip and off of the table, and held them in her lap.

I wanted to get her out of there, wanted to grab her stuff and take her out of that booth where she was going to be interviewing guys to lose her virginity to. That was a sentence I'd never thought I'd say before. She sat still, trying to put on a brave face.

"Seph..." The words died in my throat. I didn't know her. Why did I feel like I needed to protect her from this massive mistake?

"I'll be fine."

I could only imagine what had gone around campus when she'd posted that ad. It would be equal parts people showing up to gawk, maybe make fun of her, and people who were interested. I shuddered at the thought of the guys who might actually try to take her up on the offer. My fingers tightened around the table's edge. My knuckles were white. Shaking my head, I loosened my grip and slid out of the booth.

"Are you sure you're okay? Just because you put up the ad doesn't mean you have to go through with this. You don't have to do it."

She straightened her shoulders and stared at me. This time her gaze didn't waver. Her entire body transformed from trying to fold in on itself to *I mean business*. "Yes, I do. I apologize again. Enjoy your meeting." That was some scary-ass determination, and she was in way over her head.

Rebecca had grabbed a table on the other side of the coffee shop, but I motioned toward the one directly behind Seph's. I sat facing the door, and Rebecca sat facing the direction I'd been facing before.

"Is everything all right?" She opened one of her many folders.

"It's fine. There was just a mix-up with who I was meeting."

A couple minutes after three, the first guy strolled into the shop. *Dude couldn't even show up on time?* Rebecca handed over a couple packets of information and I half listened to what she was saying about them. She dug around in her bag, looking for more papers.

I made eye contact with the guy who'd walked in. He spotted me and froze.

Maybe he was admiring my shiny white kicks.

Maybe it was the way my hands balled up the piece of paper in my grip.

Or maybe it was the face-melting glare I gave him.

We'll never be sure, but his gaze darted from me to Seph in the booth in front of me. I gave him one hard head shake and jabbed my finger toward the door. His eyes got wide and he took a stutter step closer.

I rose halfway out of my seat and his sneakers squeaked on the floor as he spun around and bolted for the front door. A parade of guys made their approach toward Seph, but I headed all of them off at the pass. At one point, I excused myself, got up, and went outside to the line of douchebags that had formed.

"Listen, under no circumstances are you to enter this shop looking for the girl from the ad, do you hear me? She's the sister of one of my teammates. She put it up to give him a hard time. If anyone touches her, you'll be answering to the whole football team. Do you understand?" I crossed my arms over my chest. My word was law.

The mouth-breathers who stood outside looked at me and back at the door. "Why would anyone even answer an ad like that? It sounded too good to be true and was probably a one-way ticket to ending up in a sting operation with your face plastered all over the news."

The frightened little bunnies nodded before running away. I went back inside.

Seph's hopeful look devolved into pink-cheeked disappointment when her gaze landed on me. Should I have been offended?

I stopped by her table. "No takers?"

"There's still time. I thought there might be a few, but most guys have come in, taken a look at me, and rushed right back out." She folded her hands in her lap, pursing her lips like a Sunday School teacher.

"Maybe it's for the best." I dropped my hand onto her shoulder. My fingers brushed along the exposed skin on her neck, and her pulse jumped under the tips.

She stared up at me, her pink lips glistening in the setting evening sun coming in through the windows.

"Reece." Rebecca's voice sliced through the connection. "We have a few more things to go over."

I went back to my table and glanced over the papers she gave me while also keeping an eye on the door. The bell jingled over and over. Every time, my blood pressure shot through the roof. A guy strolled in. He'd been in my freshman seminar my first semester. His name danced on the edges of my memory, but I'd never forget his face, mainly because of the smug-ass grin he'd given me when our first papers were handed back out, his with a nice, big, circled 98 and mine with a 75. We'd never hung in the same circles, and his feelings toward student athletes had been loud and clear back then. *Graham.*

He walked in and didn't even glance in my direction. His face lit up like a kid on Christmas when he spotted Seph. I slammed my hands on the table.

Rebecca jumped and stared at me, wide-eyed. "We're almost finished. I'll give a full report to your coach about how great you've been about all this."

I sat back in the seat while trying to x-ray vision my way

through her body and the seat across from her to see what exactly they were talking about.

"...and once you're able to give a good response to these basic questions, it will really help you with handling the press in the future." She stared back at me expectantly.

I nodded and plastered on a smile. "Thanks a lot for your help. I'll go over everything as soon as I get home."

"Perfect." She gathered up all her stuff and tucked the folders back into her bag. I flashed her a tight smile and got up from the seat. As I rounded the edge of the table, Graham got up and shook Seph's hand. She looked up at him like he'd just invented notecards. *Not that guy. He's a pompous asshole.* The door closed after him and that stupid jingling bell finally stopped.

"How'd it end up going?"

She jumped and her head snapped up when my shadow fell over her.

"It went okay. Not the reception I expected, but I'm new to all this."

"Do you think you found your person?"

Her eyebrows scrunched down a little and she nodded. "I think so, but I need final confirmation and my pro-con list."

She was going to sleep with Graham. Why did that piss me off? I barely knew the guy. I didn't know her, but she might have been covering for the fact that she was dying like in that movie my little sister had made me watch a few summers ago. She'd cried for about two days straight afterward.

Graham wasn't the kind of guy Seph's first time should be with. He'd probably pull out a protractor to make sure they got the angles right—though actually, from what I'd seen of her, maybe that was her thing.

Just drop it. It's not your business. I shoved my hands into my pockets. "Have a good one, then. And I hope you get exactly what you're looking for."

"I think I might." She smiled at me, the first real one I'd seen in the little bit of time I'd spent in her presence. It was the kind that came from way deep down, like Christmas morning or scoring your first touchdown.

Flicking my hand in her direction with a half-wave, I strolled out of the coffee shop. The Uncommon Grounds sign with two cups of coffee overflowing with beans shone overhead.

Standing outside, I waited to see if there were any stragglers lurking. None, but I still watched her leave. She tucked her gray scarf into the collar of her beige coat and pulled a red hat down over her ears.

What the hell was I doing? I'd tried to save her from herself, but she could always put up another ad, or maybe take my advice and just go to a party to get laid. *Not your business, Reece.* These were the types of entanglements that kept me far away from anything resembling a relationship. Getting wrapped up in someone else was a one-way ticket to killing your dreams, and that wasn't for me. Not by a long shot.

5

SEPH

Things had *not* gone as planned. For some reason I'd envisioned a line of guys down the block and had thought it would be a nightmare to sort through. Instead it had been worse. Two hours of me throwing back marshmallowy hot chocolates with one accidental interviewee and only one other candidate, the only *real* one.

Graham was nice. I'd seen him in the math building but never stopped to talk, just like I never stopped to talk to anyone. He had an easy smile, soft hands, and a gentle yet firm handshake. Light brown hair like my own and honey-colored eyes made him the best-looking guy in the department for sure. He'd probably be a great first partner, would take his time, wouldn't rush things, but I kept coming back to my accidental show-up.

Reece. He'd walked into the room and the whole place had lit up for him. He wasn't the type to sit back and let things come to him; he went after the things he wanted. His confidence radiated off him. When he put his hand on my shoulder, my insides went crazy. My dopamine levels must have been off the charts. Those weren't feelings you had every day—well, not me, anyway. The closest I'd come was when I'd gotten my acceptance letter to Fulton. It made it that much worse that he didn't seem at all interested in what I'd offered.

Graham was the safe choice. He'd answered the ad. He had kind eyes and a pleasant personality. He'd even said he'd be moving back to Boston after he graduated, so if anything did progress beyond a one-time thing, I could still see him when I moved. He was the logical choice.

But Reece...that was where my thoughts kept drifting as I stood outside the library after once again being sex-iled from my apartment. Being sex-iled with him would put a much different spin on things. *Don't get ahead of yourself. He's not interested. Focus on the issue at hand.* Why couldn't I just say something to Alexa? For the same reason I couldn't say something to my parents.

Baby steps. It hadn't been a total bust. Blowing into my hands, I looked for a place to get some food. My stomach had been a mess all day. Now that I'd ripped the Band-Aid off and survived, I was starving. The heavy scent of deliciously seasoned meat wafted past my nose. My mouth watered. Whatever that was, I needed it in my belly immediately.

There was a narrow stone staircase leading to the restaurant with a hanging sign decorated with oars overhead. The Vault. I'd heard students mention it before, but I'd never gone looking for it. I pushed the heavy wooden door open and stepped into the barely-off-campus bar-slash-restaurant Inside, a big guy in a tight thermal with his arms crossed over his chest stared me down. Refusing to shrink back, I met his gaze and smiled.

"Hi. I wanted to get something to eat."

"Let me see your ID." He flicked his fingers back and forth with his palm up.

I scrambled to get my wallet out of my bag and pulled out my driver's license. It had taken me until I was finally eighteen to convince my dad I should get it. I'd reasoned I might need to rent a car for any conferences I attended so it would come in handy.

"You've got to be out by nine. That's when we start serving alcohol." He stepped back to let me pass. The narrow brick-lined hallway led into the restaurant.

I checked my watch. It was only six. "Okay, I've got plenty of time." The shoulder of my coat scraped against the rough stone blocks as I pressed myself against the wall.

"And no hiding in the bathrooms." He turned around the second I passed him.

"I wouldn't do that."

He pursed his lips, looked me up and down, and nodded. "Yeah."

Tucking a stray hair behind my ear, I stepped into the restaurant and pushed through the second swinging door. Servers walked back and forth with trays. Most of the tables and booths were empty. This was the weird gap in between lunch and college dinner time, which seemed to start later than anywhere else. Someone walked past me as I stood, tugging my gloves off.

A woman with a half apron wrapped around her waist appeared. "Sit anywhere you want. Someone will be over in a second, and here's a menu." She handed over a plastic-covered menu and I looked for a spot.

I sat at a table and stared at the options. There were so many things I'd never even heard of. My stomach grumbled at many of the descriptions. *Bleu cheese on a burger? What are atomic fries? Can that many things even fit on a plate of French fries?*

"Do you know what you want to order?" I supposed this was my server. She pulled a pencil and notepad out of the pocket of her apron, her face vaguely familiar. Most of the people working there looked like college students.

My last time out without anyone looking over my shoulder at what I ordered had been with Aunt Sophie what felt like ages ago. I'd stuck to eating at home or packing snacks when I went to the library. "I'll have a Shirley Temple."

The woman nodded.

I raised my hand like a kid in class. She stared at me. "Can I have extra cherries?"

"Sure thing. And to eat?" She crouched down beside the table, resting her hand beside the menu.

"I really have no idea. Everything sounds really good. What would you order?"

"The Juicy Lucy with fries is pretty awesome. That's my favorite thing on the menu."

Cheese-stuffed burger with bacon and ranch. My mouth watered. "I'll take that."

"Perfect. I'll be right back with your drink." She took my menu and left. I drummed my fingers across my lap.

I looked around the restaurant. Some people studied. A lot of people sat with friends, talking and laughing. Even after moving away to college, I was still on the outside. The loneliness I'd attributed to my parents, being home-schooled, and only being surrounded by adults as a child hit even harder when I was surrounded by people my age, when I'd walk by them on campus or sit beside them in class and I remained invisible.

The server came back with my drink, extra cherries

included. Even here in the restaurant, friends laughed and joked. Couples flirted and smiled at each other. I plucked a cherry out of my drink.

I sat at the empty table by myself with my bag, my books, and a phone with no more than ten contacts on it. Sticking the stem of the cherry into my mouth, I tied it into a knot—one of many useless talents I'd entertained myself with as a kid. I'd needed some way to distract myself at all those boring computational math events.

"Hey, are you following me or something?" A shadow fell over my table.

Glancing up, I stared at Graham. A couple of guys walked past.

"I'll be right there," he called out to them.

"No, definitely not. It must have been the path from the coffee shop to here, maybe the wind direction or something. Generally, people are averse to walking into the wind, which is why when small children go missing, they always look for them with the wind at their backs. Feel free to stop me whenever this gets too awkward." I swallowed, hoping the floor would open up and swallow me whole. Maybe I'd get lucky and the campus was on top of an inactive volcano or a hell-mouth.

He laughed. "That's great information if I'm ever helping look for a lost kid. And I didn't actually think you followed me."

"Graham, you coming?" someone called out from the back of the restaurant.

"Here you go." The server was back with my plate of food.

"I'll let you get to your meal. It was nice meeting you today, Persephone."

I fought against the cringe. "It was nice meeting you too."

He backed away from the table and disappeared from view. My stomach, which had been in knots seconds ago, completely unfurled the second I stared down at my plate. It was a swirling pile of greasy food, and I couldn't wait to dive in.

More stuffed than I'd ever been in my life, I walked back to my apartment. It was like Mother Nature had arrived early for the season change from fall to winter and she was pissed. For some reason, I'd figured Philly wouldn't be this cold this time of year.

I opened the door to my apartment. Silence greeted me. I let out a deep breath. My fingers had itched for a moment alone like this. Rushing into my room, set my bag down and dragged my case out from under my bed. I flipped it open and lifted my bow and violin out of the velvet lining.

Being away from my parents, I'd anticipated having more time to play, but Alexa's aversion to string instruments was a lot like my dad's, which meant I hadn't played in almost a week. Resting the varnished wood on my shoulder, I lifted the bow and let my fingers dance across the strings. Like math, music was an outlet I'd embraced early on.

With math, there was always a correct answer, always a solution. It might take decades to find, but it was there. With music, it was the opposite. A note might be off, a key out of tune, but mistakes could create beautiful surprises.

Once my dad realized I had a better chance of breaking records in math than with the violin, my lessons were abruptly stopped. Funny how once it wasn't what they wanted—what he wanted—I could finally find the joy of my fingers on the strings, of the bow in my hand. On days when things just sucked or I couldn't figure out a problem, I'd play for a bit and the answer always came to me. I'd gently lay the instrument down on my bed and scribble down in my notebook everything my brain had pieced together while I lost myself in the notes.

But tonight, it wasn't math on my mind. It wasn't a complex theorem that would make most people cry. It was the guys who'd sat across from me that afternoon.

Graham was attractive, seemed nice, and was interested. He was the safe choice. Maybe that was why Reece kept coming back to me. He'd most likely say no; he hadn't even been there to respond to the ad anyway. Talk about embarrassing. Looking back on that conversation now, I did the full scarlet-cheeked scene replay in my head. I'd asked him how big his penis was. That should have been enough for me to never want to see his face again, but thoughts of his eyes and lips kept pushing their way back into my mind, shoving the sensible thoughts away.

And if he said no, what was lost? I could definitely ask Graham. The probability of the experience being acceptable was high—well, as high as anything could be when human nature was involved. The front door opened and closed. I wished Alexa was someone I could talk to about this, maybe pop some popcorn, make some drinks, and chat about it while painting our nails or watching a movie and getting her advice on what I should do.

I sat on the edge of my bed and took down my hair. The braids were an old habit. In the old black and white movies my dad watched, the women always had intricate braids, or maybe I'd just seen *Heidi* a few too many times. I'd spent hours in my room when I was tired of reading or didn't feel like turning in another equation and had taught myself how to do it so my mom didn't have to anymore.

Maybe that was why I embraced it so much. It was something I'd done for myself. Math, violin—everything else in my life had been foisted on me by someone else, but my dumb, way-too-intricate braids were all mine. Taking out the bobby pins, I dropped them into the little ceramic bowl on my desk, each *tink* a satisfying noise as my hair got heavier, falling down around my shoulders. Threading my fingers through it, I brushed it out and stared at myself in the mirror.

Alexa's heels clicked on the floor. I looked at my open door through the mirror behind me, and she appeared in the doorway. "I have friends coming over tonight." Without another word, she wrapped her fingers around the doorknob and closed it behind her. Her message was clear. Sometimes I felt like she was the evil stepsister and I was Cinderella. The braid thing probably didn't help.

After changing into my pajamas, I walked out toward the kitchen to grab some juice—my little act of defiance. The second my foot hit the floor in the living room, everything went silent. I could feel their eyes on me, boring into my back. Taking my time, I grabbed my glass, filled it from the carton in the fridge, and walked back down the hallway.

The second I was in the shadow of the hall, they came back to life again like someone had hit the unmute button. I had thought I would find a lot more kindness and warmth once I left my house, but that had been my own naivety. I was ready to shed that side of myself. Start making real choices. Taking real leaps. Which meant there was only one possible choice.

6

REECE

The driving pounding of death was being hammered into my head. We didn't have a game until the following week, so Berk and LJ had decided to celebrate our win one more time—with shots. I cracked my door open, and the creaks might as well have been nails straight into my brain. I braced my hands on the wall and walked down the steps.

Plastic cups littered the stairs and the place reeked of stale beer. *Nasty.* I stepped over one of the guys from the team who'd crashed on the stairs. Two people slept on the couches. Coach was going to kill us if we were late to practice at ten.

I made it to the kitchen and gingerly opened the cabinet where the oversized bottle of ibuprofen lived. Shaking out a few pills, I turned on the faucet and cupped my hand, filling it with water. Dropping the pills into my mouth, I gulped them down.

Resting my head on the cupboard, I groaned and wished for death. This was what happened when you didn't have a drink for a while. Since the season had started, I'd stuck to one or two, but the previous night I'd really gone for it.

Maybe it was trying to drown out the thoughts of what a possible virgin on campus might be doing trying to finally lose her V-Card. Why did I even care what she was up to? If I hadn't sat at that booth, I would have been none the wiser and would've avoided the whole thing. Instead, every time my thoughts had drifted to her, I'd done another shot. It was a hell of a lot of shots, and now my brain was kicking my ass for being so damn stupid.

Closing my eyes, I breathed through the pain when the shrill chirp of my phone went off. I peeled one eye open and dragged back the curtains above the sink. It was nearly the ass-crack of dawn. Who the hell would be calling this early?

I'd just made it to the bottom of the steps when my phone rocketed down the staircase and missed my face by an inch. My hand shot out and I caught it.

"Thanks, Nix."

He flipped me the double bird, yawned, and slammed his door.

The phone came alive in my hand. I jabbed at the screen. "Hello?"

There was a long pause. I pulled the phone away from my face to make sure I hadn't dropped the call.

"Reece Michaels?"

"Yes." Had I applied for a bank loan? The cool, professional tone on the other end of the line made me feel like I might be called in for an interview somewhere.

"I know you probably don't remember me. It was kind of a strange first interaction, and I completely understand." The rambling and tight way she spoke totally gave her away.

"Hi, Seph."

"You remember me?" Her voice shot up high.

"It's not very often you find out you're part of a sex tryout like something from the next season of *The Bachelorette*."

"The what?"

"It's a TV show. Forget about it. So, you've met your goal already?"

She cleared her throat. I could picture her tugging at the hem of her shirt. "No, and it's something I wanted to talk to you about, if you have some time today?"

The relief I felt at her response blindsided me. "I have practice at ten, but I can meet you at noon."

"You have practice on a Saturday?"

"We have practice or training every day we aren't playing."

"Wow, that's real dedication. Noon works for me. I found this awesome place—we could meet there." She rattled off the address of one of the campus staples everyone had been to at least once, like it was a hidden gem she'd slashed through overgrown vines with a machete to find.

"Yeah, I know The Vault. I'll see you there."

Berk rolled off the couch, hit the floor in the living room, and threw a pillow at my head. I ducked the cushion and regretted the quick movement.

"Shut up." It was a half zombie, half hungover groan.

"Am I talking too loudly for you?" I took the pain at raising my voice. It was worth it for his cringe. I threw the pillow back and it bounced off his head. He groaned again, grabbed it, and shoved it under his head on the floor. He would definitely be puking at practice.

I slowly went back upstairs and lay back in my bed with a giant bottle of water. I set an alarm to wake me up in a few hours. Hopefully by then I'd have slept most of this off, or Berk wouldn't be the only one barfing on the field.

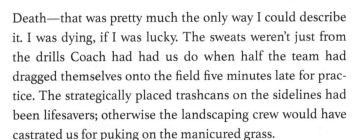

Death—that was pretty much the only way I could describe it. I was dying, if I was lucky. The sweats weren't just from the drills Coach had had us do when half the team had dragged themselves onto the field five minutes late for practice. The strategically placed trashcans on the sidelines had been lifesavers; otherwise the landscaping crew would have castrated us for puking on the manicured grass.

I grabbed the front of my pads and tugged them over my head.

"Remind me to never do that again." Berk's shade of green wasn't as bad as it'd been when he'd first stumbled onto the field, but it still wasn't great.

"I wasn't the one trying to celebrate our win with a shot for every point. I was perfectly fine with a few beers and some music—you're the one who pulled out the shots."

Nix plopped down beside me. He hadn't drank much, but he still looked like shit. His throwing had been less than stellar, though still miles ahead of anyone else on the team. He was a natural, but at that moment he might as well have been roadkill.

"How you feeling?" I squirted water into my mouth.

He dragged his hands down his face, stretching it out and massaging his cheeks with his fingers. "Did I miss the toll for the one-way trip into the underworld?"

"How much did you have last night?"

He shook his head. "It's not even that. My dad cornered me after the press conference after the game."

I sucked in a sharp breath between my teeth. "You should've told me. I'd have staged a kidnapping or something."

He shook his head. "It wouldn't have helped. He's an

unstoppable force. He's headed over to London at the end of the month for the game Philly and San Francisco are playing over there."

Nix's dad had retired from the NFL ten years ago and now did sports commentary.

I pushed open the locker room door. "At least he'll be off your back for a bit." The quiet shuffle of feet, distant spray of the showers, and groaning met us the second we stepped inside.

"He'll find a way to get on my case no matter what." He dropped his pads and grabbed a towel.

"Did you hear about that girl who put up the ad?" Berk ran a towel over his drenched head and dropped it into his locker.

My blood turned to ice, the sweat rolling down my back freezing in seconds. "What ad?"

"Some girl put up a prank ad trying to get laid." He grabbed his clothes from his locker.

"Seriously?" LJ dropped down onto the bench beside him.

"Yeah, apparently it was some psych student trying to do a case study or something. Some guys said they showed up and it was a chick with notecards and stuff. Probably trying to find out who the hell would be desperate enough to answer something like that." He headed into the shower.

If that was what everyone thought had happened, that was the best-case scenario. That meant if she tried again, guys would probably just ignore it. Why did I care about this so much? Why had trying to keep her from making this mistake been drumming at the back of my head since I slid out of that booth while she stared up at me with her big, caramel eyes?

I hopped into the shower, feeling less like I'd been run over when I got out.

With my gear stashed in my car, I walked the few blocks to meet Seph. I'd managed to keep my mind off her since our call. It wasn't too difficult when I had been fully focused on not puking for the last few hours.

My phone buzzed in my back pocket. I slipped it out and answered the call.

"Hey, Mom."

"Don't *hey mom* me. You were supposed to come over this weekend."

"The weekend is still young. It's only Saturday. That still leaves another weekend day where I could come visit."

"Yeah, you say that, but I bet it would have conveniently slipped your mind when I called tomorrow night."

"I just left practice and I'm heading to lunch."

"How was practice?"

"Good. Coach is working us hard to make sure the championship is ours this year."

"You've been playing well this season."

"Only well? Have you been watching the games?"

She laughed. "Fine, more than well. I might have to get your dad to work on the front door before you come, though."

My eyebrows dipped. "The front door?"

"I'm not sure your head will fit through with as big as it's gotten."

"I'm only speaking the truth." This was my best season ever, more touchdowns and yardage than any season before.

"Is Dad at the office?"

She sighed. "Of course. He'll be home soon. Who are you heading to lunch with?"

"Someone I met the other day."

"A girl?"

"She is, in fact, female."

"Are you dating her?"

"No, she's not really the dating kind."

There was a sharp sound from the back of her throat. "I know those kinds of girls. I remember them well from when your father and I were in college together."

"She's definitely not that kind of girl. There's something she needs help with and I'm going to see what I can do to help her. She's a little socially awkward."

"Aww, is she a nerd? I was a nerd."

"Was?"

I could feel her eyes narrowing through the phone.

"That's how your dad found me, sitting under a tree in the quad reading when he smashed his ball into my face."

"Boundaries, Mom. I don't want to hear about your extracurriculars with Dad."

"Hush. I know you have a game on Tuesday, but next weekend, we'd like you to come by."

"I'll see what I can do."

"And bring the young lady you're having lunch with since you've said she's not one of *those* girls."

"At this point, Mom, I'm not even sure she eats, but it's not that kind of meeting. I'll talk to you later. Love you, bye."

I ended the call before she broke out the giant overhead lights and slid a clanking metal chair up to the table to begin the interrogation. Most people would love to have parents as in love as mine were. Sometimes they were slightly embarrassing, but no one could miss how much they cared about each other. It scared the shit out of me.

That was the kind of thing you could lose yourself in completely, the kind of thing that could make you forget about all the plans and goals you had for yourself, where you were so blissfully happy nothing else mattered, until it did. Maybe not today or in ten years or even thirty, but how could you give up something you'd worked your whole life for and not eventually have that hit you in the face?

Dad worked hard for my grandfather. He put in crazy hours sometimes and missed a good chunk of family stuff because of work. Wouldn't it be better to make bank and then retire? Leave all that behind and then focus on family? At least that was how I saw it.

I jogged down the steps to The Vault. I wrapped my hand around the outstretched one of the bouncer then we smacked each other's backs and hit our shoulders together. He let go of my hand.

"Haven't seen you here in a while." He sat back on his stool at the entrance.

I'd hung out at The Vault a lot before. All I'd needed to do was sit back and the women came to me, but that wasn't my focus anymore.

"I'm meeting someone here. Maybe you've seen her, about yea high." I held my hand up to my shoulder. "Probably dressed in a suit or something. Light brown hair, maybe all braided up."

His eyebrows jumped up. "You're here to see her?"

"Yeah, you've seen her?"

"She got here like twenty minutes ago. She's not really your type." He smirked at me and crossed his arms over his chest, leaning back on the wooden stool pressed against the wall.

I shrugged. "I'll catch you later." What was I supposed to say? Stepping into the restaurant, I scanned the room. A few heads popped up and people waved. I nodded at them and walked around the bar, spotting Seph. She was studying the menu in front of her like it contained the cure for cancer.

"If you stare at it any harder, you'll burn a hole through it."

Her head snapped up and she smiled at me. "You came."

With the way she lit up when she saw me, I couldn't have stopped the smile from spreading across my face if you'd held a gun to my head. Stepping out onto the field with thousands of people cheering for me didn't come close to how she'd just made me feel—and that meant trouble, which was why sleeping with her was a one-way ticket to fucking up my future. You don't sleep with girls who look at you like that and get away unscathed. Just look at my dad.

"I said I would." I slid into the seat across from her. "What looks good?"

"Everything. I've already tried three of the menu items, but I'm going to need to take up running or something if I want to try the rest before Thanksgiving and still fit into my seat on the plane. I don't have much time left."

There were those words again. I leaned against the table, used my finger to tug down the top edge of the menu, and held her gaze. "Are you sure you're not dying?"

7

SEPH

I hated how my heart rate increased when Reece showed up at the end of my table. Hated the tingles in my fingertips. Hated the giddiness bubbling up and how much I'd looked forward to this meeting. I'd chosen the perfect table with a good view of the door, but I'd gotten so engrossed in the menu that I hadn't seen him come in. That was one way to keep my mind off him—delicious, greasy, flavorful food.

His smile turned my stomach into a baking soda and vinegar volcanic explosion. Was I smiling too wide? Was what I was wearing okay? I'd tried to go more casual and ditched the suit for a light blue button-down top and navy pants.

"No, I'm not dying, but I'll only be here for another year and a half, if I'm lucky. Seven months if I'm not, and Lady Luck is not usually on my side when it comes to my parents."

"Why would you have to leave Fulton early? You're only eighteen. You're transferring?"

"Graduating."

"At eighteen?"

I nodded. "Well, I'll be nineteen, but yes, unfortunately that's the case." That was what happened when you started on your first college course when kids your age were taking Algebra I.

"I should have known you were one of those geniuses."

My shoulders shot up and I hid my head behind the menu. "I'm not a genius. Einstein was a genius. I'm just really good at learning things quickly." I'd hated that label ever since I'd understood what it meant and what people expected out of one.

"I'm pretty sure that's a genius."

"A genius would've known what a bad idea it was to put an ad out to the whole campus to lose her virginity."

He leaned back and picked up his menu. "Finally seeing the error of your ways?"

"Perhaps, but I did get a possible taker out of it."

His brow creased. "Graham."

I dropped the menu. "You know him?" I stared at him intently. Inside information would make this a lot easier.

"We had a few classes together freshman year. He's fine."

"I think so too."

His lips tightened. "So he's your guy?" Why did his voice sound like that? Should I not pick Graham if Reece turned me down?

"Maybe." I mashed my lips together like I was ready to devour them. "Unless there's someone else who might be up for the task. I have a lot of things on my list, but I think this one would be a great way to kick things off." I put down the menu and rested my hands on top of it.

"Why are you in such a rush?" He leaned in closer, the smell of soap and aftershave wafting over from the other side of the table.

"Were you a virgin at eighteen?"

"What?" His face scrunched up like it was the most ridiculous question that had ever been asked and he made a *psh* sound. "No."

I raised my eyebrows.

The wheels started turning and the backtracking began. "Not that it's a bad thing to still be one. There are tons of people who are still virgins."

The server came up to the table with his notepad. "Are you two ready to order?"

"Not quite yet, but I have a question. How old are you?" I put my elbows on the table and rested my chin on my hands.

He let out a little laugh. "I'm twenty-two."

"And when did you lose your virginity?"

Both Reece's and the server's eyes went big and round. "You don't have to answer that." Reece tried to wave off the question. "Excuse her, she doesn't get out much."

"It's a perfectly normal getting-to-know-you type of question."

"What the hell do you consider an intimate question?" I opened my mouth but he shook his head and held up his finger. "I don't want to know." His head swung around to the waiter, who was staring at me like a stiff breeze would carry him away. "Just give us a second and then we'll order. Thanks."

The server nodded slowly and backed away from the table like it was covered in rattlesnakes.

Reece leaned forward. "What is wrong with you? You can't just go around asking people when they lost their virginity."

"It's not something to be ashamed about." Everyone else

seemed to have done it already. I was certainly treated to a non-stop soundtrack of it in my apartment.

"What if he was still a virgin?" he whisper-shouted through his teeth, pointing in the direction the server had retreated in.

I stared at the guy's glowing red cheeks. "I hadn't thought about that. Point taken."

"You must be a barrel of laughs when you go out with your friends." He dropped his gaze back to the menu, picking it up.

I ran my finger over my thumb and stared down at my hands. *Direct hit, Reece.* "I don't have any friends." That had been a crushing realization a few days earlier, and it sucked even more now. My college career was off to a seriously depressing start.

"I can see why."

I didn't realize I'd made a sound, but I must have. Reece glanced up from the menu and his eyes widened. He started shaking his head immediately.

"I didn't mean that, not like that—not like something's wrong with you." He ran his hand over his face. "Do you really not have any friends? Like none?"

Gathering up my bag, I slung the strap over my head. "This was a mistake. I'm sorry I made you come. I'm sure you have a lot of other things you could be doing right now." I fought to keep my voice from cracking. Why did it hurt so much, like a sawing in my chest? I'd never felt like this back home. Glimmers of light surrounded by the dull monotony was what I was used to. Not this.

Reece grabbed my hand, pinning it to the table. "Seph, wait. I didn't mean it like that. It was my attempt at a joke and it didn't work. I'd really like to have lunch with you. Please don't go."

His pulse pounded against the top of my hand. The shooting sparks I wanted to blame on static electricity shot up my arm. Whenever he touched me, it was the same thing. I dragged my gaze from the table top with my hand sandwiched under his.

He stared into my eyes. Sincerity shone in his, sincerity and concern. His thumb ran over the spot on my hand where my thumb met the rest of my fingers, a slow steady motion, like how you'd pet a scared puppy to soothe it.

I didn't want his pity. Dropping back down into the seat, I slowly lifted the strap of my bag back over my head.

"How can you not have any friends? Really?"

I shrugged.

"Friends from home? High school? Since you've gotten here?"

I stared down at the table, running my fingers over the dated wood. It had dents and nicks that had been lacquered over, giving the table an old yet still new feeling.

"Making friends is hard when you're homeschooled, and not the kind of homeschooled where your parents work with other parents to make sure you still have normal childhood experiences. I was homeschooled all by myself. Tutors were brought in. No extracurricular activities that were purely for socialization. Once I was beyond high school, I took college classes. My mom or dad would attend with me, sitting right beside me." I glanced up at him. "It's hard to make friends when you're four to five years younger than everyone else and your parents are right there. Four or five years doesn't matter much when you're in your 20s, but when you're fourteen and everyone else is nineteen, that's a big difference."

"That had to be tough." The pity train had pulled into the station.

I shrugged. "There are worse things."

"You didn't get to hang out with other kids your own age, ever?"

"Sometimes, my mom would take me to the park. She'd let me play there if my dad was traveling. If I finished my work quickly enough, I'd get to go to my room, and I had some dolls my aunt gave me. That was about it."

"Damn, that blows." He sat back in his seat, looking like I'd just told him I'd been locked in a basement for most of my life.

"Don't feel bad for me. I got to do a lot of amazing things. I've traveled the world with my parents. They want what's best for me."

"But you didn't get to have friends or hang out with kids your own age."

My latest sex-ile from my apartment came rushing back to me. "I'm learning that maybe I don't want to hang out with everyone my own age. My roommate is...." I searched my brain for something other than *a bitch*. "Difficult, but I'm determined to tackle everything on my list, and I'm not going to let anything stop me."

"Tell me more about this list."

The server came back and asked for our orders. I'd been waiting to try these for a while. "Chili cheese fries, bacon cheeseburger, and a milkshake."

Reece's mouth hung open, and he and the server exchanged glances.

"What?" I handed over the menu.

"Two grilled chicken breasts, broccoli and asparagus instead of the fries, and a water."

I raised an eyebrow at him as he handed the menu back.

"I've already beat my body up enough this weekend. I need to treat it right. Tell me what else is on your list."

Pulling my notepad out of my bag, I flipped to the page even though I'd memorized it already. "You already know number one on the list, but I've also got: eat dessert for dinner, stay up all night watching cartoons, go skinny-dipping, go to a college party, get drunk." I rattled off a few other things. "It's a lot to get done and not much time to do it."

"Why do you feel like you have to do all this in seven months? You have the rest of your life to do those things."

"Tomorrow's never guaranteed. We have no idea what the future will hold, so why not cram in as much life as possible while I can? At the end of the school year, my dad is probably going to pull some strings to get me into the PhD program at Harvard."

"You don't sound happy about that."

"I would be, if it were on my own terms. Math has always made sense to me. Way more than people, math clicks in my brain. But, going there is what he wants, and I have no doubt that when I'm living back at home or only a few minutes away, my life will revert back to how it was before." My stomach soured.

"It doesn't have to."

I pressed my lips together and a sharp exhalation shot out of my nose. "You've never met my dad."

"Fine, you've got seven months. That doesn't mean you need to cram everything in right now, this weekend. You can take your time." His gaze no longer held a hint of pity. There was a serious edge to his voice.

"What if I don't want to?" I'd been waiting my whole life for something, anything, to happen and I was tired of letting things pass me by.

His forearm muscles bunched and relaxed.

"This is about the sex, isn't it?" And then the crystal

clarity of his hesitation was dumped over my head like a bucket of ice water. The knot in my stomach turned to curdled milk. "It's not that you think I should wait—you just don't want it to be you."

"No!" He shouted and reached for me. His hand covered mine, though I'd tried to slip it off the table and onto my lap.

"Seph, it's not that at all. Of course I'd want to sleep with you, unravel those crazy braids and run my fingers through your hair while I—" He cleared his throat. "Let's just say I've thought about it." He pulled his hand back and sat back in his seat. "There are a lot of guys who'd like to sleep with you, probably enough that you'd be at least a little freaked out, but that doesn't mean you would want to sleep with them. Your first time should be special. You shouldn't rush it."

"Statistically, most women have horrible first experiences. It's a lot of pain, blood, and awkwardness. I want to rip that Band-Aid off."

"Maybe it's like that because people run into it headfirst. Just because it's that way for a lot of women, it doesn't mean you need to force it to be that for you. If you're with the right person, it will be amazing."

"And you don't think Graham is that person."

"You can find better."

"But you don't want to do it."

"You can definitely find better."

"So you're bad in bed?" I lifted an eyebrow. That was disappointing, but studies had shown that men who spend a lot of time in the gym aren't the most generous when it comes to sex.

"If there were a sex hall of fame, I'd be the first inductee, but I'm not a relationship guy. I'm not a cuddles after sex and curling up on the couch kind of guy. That's the kind of guy you need."

"So where do I find one of them? Should I put out an ad for that?"

"Would you stop it with the ads!" He threw his hands up.

The server came back with our plates and slid them in front of us. The bacon and cheese oozed out of the thick golden bun on mine. It was greasy, meaty, and messy, everything I'd never been able to indulge in before.

Pushing up my sleeves, I inhaled the salty, seasoned heat rising off the plate. I was ready to marry this burger.

"If I don't put out an ad, how am I supposed to find someone? Hand out flyers on the quad?" I picked up the sandwich and lifted it to my mouth. The juicy burger looked better than anything I'd ever had before. I sank my teeth into it and closed my eyes. My feet danced on the floor and I shook my head from side to side, savoring the flavor in my mouth. *So good.* There had never been a more delicious burger.

I opened my eyes and Reece was staring at me with a funny look on his face, a floret of broccoli suspended in air on the end of his fork, poised just in front of his lips. His teeth sank into his bottom lip.

"What? Do I have something on my face?" I covered my mouth with one hand.

His gaze darted up from my mouth to my eyes. He dropped his fork. "No—I mean yeah. You have something on your face." He pointed to a spot on the side of his mouth.

I picked up my napkin and wiped at the spot. Checking the fabric, I didn't see anything on it. "Did I get it?"

He cleared his throat and went back to his incredibly sensible meal. "You got it."

I demolished the burger along with polishing off half

the fries and milkshake. Sitting back in the booth, I rested my head against the back of the upholstery and held my stomach. I was bursting at the seams. "I think that was a mistake."

"See." He stole a chili cheese fry from my plate and pointed it at me. "What did I tell you? This is what happens when you rush things."

"It's not possible to gorge yourself on sex like you can on food."

"You'd be surprised," he mumbled.

"So you're a manwhore?"

"I'm not a manwhore. A manwhore would have pulled you into the broom closet of Uncommon Grounds and banged you without a second thought, but being an athlete on campus during a few winning seasons has given me many opportunities to entertain the opposite sex, yes."

"A baby manwhore, then?" I smirked at him and pushed my plate away.

"Maybe a little bit." He held up his thumb and pointer finger barely an inch apart.

"To make sure I don't end up exploding myself on indulgences, sex or otherwise, maybe I could use a guide, someone to help me navigate the world of excess without killing myself."

He ran a spear of asparagus through the melted cheese on my boat of fries and shoved it into his mouth. With his head tilted to the side, he stared into my eyes. The same charge that'd shot through me when he walked into the coffee shop sparked again. "I'll help you complete your list on one condition."

"Yes, whatever you want." I sat forward, barely wincing at the half a cow crammed into my stomach.

He popped the asparagus into his mouth. "No sex."

I sank back like a deflating balloon. That was like walking a kid into a candy story and only letting them buy spearmint gum. The hormones that had been running rampant around him would have to get shoved back into their box. Running through my options, I felt like none were great.

He'd show me around, maybe introduce me to some people outside of the math department. I could always run guys past him to get his take since my radar when it came to the opposite sex was all out of whack. He'd come here after practice when he didn't have to, and damn was he easy on the eyes. I could keep things platonic between us. I totally could.

Wiping my hands on the napkin in my lap, I held one out to him. "Deal."

We shook on it. He paid the bill. Did that make it a date? *Screw it, I'm counting it. First date!* So what if he wasn't in on it; I knew. My internal dance continued as we walked outside.

I buttoned my coat. Nervousness coiled in my stomach like a snake ready to strike. "When do we start?"

S aying yes to being Seph's life guru was a mistake. I'll admit that. Probably the biggest one since I'd bought that pair of Air Jordans that were one size too small because it was the only pair left and I nearly crippled myself, or the last time I even flirted with the whole relationship thing last year.

Seph walked like nothing could stand in her way. Literally, people jumped out of the way as she talked, her eyes focused on me. I grabbed her shoulders to stop her from running into a light pole. Knowing her, she'd probably knock it over and keep walking. Maybe it was the way she had no filter and blurted out things that could make Berk blush. Maybe it was how sad she'd looked telling me about being homeschooled and never having any friends. Or maybe it was the way she'd absolutely demolished that burger like she could go head to head with Nix in a speed-eating contest. I wasn't exactly sure why, but I'd said yes.

It had been two days since our meeting at The Vault. I'd checked over her list and tried to figure out which items I could help with and which I should probably stay far away

from. Skinny-dipping was a big-ass no. Naked Seph? Hell
no. Clothed Seph was cute enough; naked Seph might make
me forget my part of the deal. A bathing suit was bad
enough. When I'd told her to bring one, I'd hoped it would
be a one-piece like the grandmoms at our community pool
used to wear.

The freezing, not-quite-winter air sliced straight through
my coat. Damn, I'd have thought after spending my whole
life in the area, winters would be no sweat. Standing on the
sidelines with snow coating the ground in a short-sleeved
jersey and tight-ass pants, my focus was on the game, not on
the ice crystals forming on my eyelashes. Now though,
walking down the street, it was like someone was jamming
icicles down my back.

Seph fell in step beside me.

"Are you sure you want to start today? When you're
starting a new habit, studies have shown—"

I stopped and she banged into my arm. I turned to her.
"Why does everything start a line of interrogation with
you?"

Her lips parted and she lifted her index finger in the air
like that kid back in elementary school. You know the one—
the kid who just had to let the teacher know they'd forgotten
to assign the class any homework right before the bell.

"Zip it." I pinched my fingers together in front of her
face. "If you want my help, we're doing things my way."
Turning the corner, I started walking toward our
destination.

"You can't just tell me to bring my bathing suit and then
not tell me where we're going." Her steps clicked behind me
and she rushed to catch up.

"We're going to a bonfire. Where do you think we're
going?"

"Good point, but still. I'd like to know a bit more about what to expect so I can prepare myself."

"How well can you swim?"

"I've studied up on it." She bit her bottom lip and stared down at her feet.

"So, not very well, then."

"Correct." She ran to catch up with me. "But swimming wasn't on my list."

"Skinny-dipping was, and you can't swim."

"Who needs to learn how to swim when I'm just trying to get naked?" She let out an exasperated yell and a few people on the sidewalk turned to stare at us.

She ducked her head into her shoulder, and I barely held back my laughter.

"You do know how to make an impression."

"Shut up." She shoved against my shoulder.

Stopping in front of the door, I pulled it open. She stepped back and craned her neck, looking at the letters up above. "The gym?"

"Did you think we were going to a tropical island? They have a pool inside."

"They do?" She squinted her eyes like she wasn't one hundred percent sure I wasn't screwing with her.

"How much of the campus have you actually explored?"

She stared back at me, blinking repeatedly like her eyes were answering me in Morse code.

"Exactly. Let's go." I held open the door and she ducked under my arm with her hands wrapped around her bag, clenching it so tightly her knuckles were white.

I slid my campus ID through the scanner and walked through the turnstile. She patted her pockets, pulled her ID out, mimicking me, and ran straight into the metal bar across the entrance. Her whole body nearly folded in half at the waist. I did my best not to laugh.

"You have it to do it more slowly. Sometimes the turnstile glitches—wait for the red light to turn green."

Her head shot up and her cheeks burned a bright red. She looked at the card again, slid it through, and waited for the light. Pushing against the bar with her hand, she shoved it forward and followed me.

"Those things are tricky," she grumbled, sliding her ID back into her pocket.

"They sure can be." The corner of my mouth lifted when she glanced over at me.

Her eyes narrowed and she let out a small snort.

I pointed to the door on the other side of the hallway. "The changing room is that way."

I changed in the guys' locker room and walked out to the water. There weren't a ton of people there. Most students probably weren't looking for a swim on a wintery Tuesday afternoon.

The door to the pool swung open, and I'd have thought there was a poltergeist in the building if the light blue of her towel hadn't poked out into the doorway.

I cupped my hands over my mouth. "Swimming involves actually getting into the water." The door closed for a beat then swung open again.

Her towel was wrapped around her body as her flip-flops smacked and clapped against the tile in a steady rhythm and her gaze darted to the pool. She nibbled on her thumb, her eyes trained on the water. Standing from the bench, I grabbed the edge of her towel.

"You can't wear this in the water."

Her gaze snapped back to mine and she nodded. Like it

was her only lifeline, she slowly let the towel drop away from her body.

My previous appreciation of her body had been sorely inadequate. Her librarian look was hiding curves that could derail a train. The one-piece black garment was not the usual, look-at-me style, and maybe that was why it was harder to look away. Grandmom bathing suit be damned, it was still skin-tight and clung to her smooth skin.

Help her, not bone her. Clearing my throat, I took the towel from her and guided her toward the pool. We sat on the edge, our feet in the water.

"When you said you couldn't swim very well, what did you mean?"

"I've studied it a lot." She stared down at the water, nibbling on her bottom lip. Her feet kicked out in front of her, slicing through the water.

"So, this is more of a getting comfortable thing? Don't worry, I've got you." Pushing off the edge, I dropped into the water. Coming up beside her legs, I treaded water and wiped my eyes. "We can start slow and you'll be doing laps in no time."

Her death grip on the edge of the pool should have been enough to crack the tile. She turned and lowered herself into the water like it was acid. Her shoulders bobbed above the water. The braids came in handy as her hair was twisted and knotted on top of her head. A droplet of water ran down the long slope of her neck before disappearing into the water.

I swam next to her, shaking my head. "Take my hand and we'll take a tour."

She glanced over her shoulder and slowly turned, keeping her hands on the edge. Her eyes darted to every corner of the pool and she slipped her hand into mine. With a force I couldn't have imagined, she gripped me, and I swore my bones groaned.

"Ease up just a little, Seph. I need that hand to play and, you know, type and eat."

Her head snapped up and her eyes landed on mine. She didn't crack a smile, not even a lip lift, but she did loosen her grip. I pushed us off the wall. She wrapped her other hand around my arm.

"Hey, Reece, go wide," someone called out from the far end of the pool.

I spun around, letting go of her hand and kicking my feet, shooting out of the water and catching the football. The guy held out his arms and I threw it back. It landed solidly, hitting his chest with a thud. As I'd told Nix, I could've been QB.

The guy cocked his arm back to throw it again, then his throwing arm slowly lowered. "Is she okay?"

I flipped around. A Seph-shaped figure disappeared under the water. Her fingertips skimmed across the surface. Swimming as fast as I could to her flapping and flailing arms, I shoved my hands under them and pulled her head out of the water, holding her body against my chest as I towed her to the edge.

She coughed and sputtered. *Fuck.* I kicked myself for being so careless. *Hey, let me help you out Seph—help you with drowning, apparently.* Bracing her hands on the edge of the pool, she threw herself onto the blue and white tiles around the edge of the water. I boosted her up by her butt, and she slid onto the walkway. A few people came over, crouching down around her.

I jumped out of the pool and knelt beside her.

She was rolled over on her side, fingers splayed against the tiles. A tremble shot through her and she closed her eyes. This was totally my fault and I felt like a grade-A asshole. I'd never have let her go if I'd known she couldn't even tread water.

"Seph, are you okay?"

Nodding, she rolled onto her back and her eyes opened. Her gaze ping-ponged around at all the people crowded around her and she sat up straight.

"I'm fine. Thank you, everyone, for your concern, but I'm fine."

She coughed a few times and jumped up from the floor, scurrying into the locker room.

"Shit."

"Do you know her?" someone asked.

"Yeah, I was supposed to be helping her get comfortable in the water." I smacked my hand against the floor and a sharp spray of water hit me.

"Maybe just stick to the field, Reece." Someone laughed, and everyone backed away.

Rushing into the locker room, I grabbed my clothes. I changed like Clark Kent and parked myself outside the exit of the women's locker room. A few people came out, eyeing me as I tried to get a look in through the cracked door. I checked the time for what had to be the hundredth time. *Is there another exit? Did she go back to the water?* After what seemed like an hour, she finally came out.

She tugged the door open with her bag tucked under her arm and her hair in a couple of braids hanging down over her shoulders. The damp ends made small wet patches on the front of her coat.

Relief washed over me. "Seph!"

She jumped and nearly dropped her bag. Her gaze snapped to mine and she grasped a small strand of hair that had fallen in front of her eyes. She looked at that hair like a wayward student who'd stepped out of line.

"You waited." It didn't have a hopeful or excited tone. Her voice was flat and distant, nothing like the nervousness and eagerness from earlier.

"Of course. Listen, I'm really sorry about what happened back there. For some reason when you said you'd studied swimming, I didn't realize that meant your level of swimming was not swimming at all."

"It's a pretty comprehensive level of not swimming." She tucked that fallen piece of hair behind her ear.

"Now I know. We can stick to strictly shallow end swimming until you're more comfortable."

"That's probably not a good idea." Her gaze darted to the front door like she was ready to bolt at any second.

The locker room door opened behind her. A girl came out and stopped beside Seph. "Hey, I saw what happened out there. Are you okay?"

A scarlet flush crept up Seph's neck. She was becoming more of a human beet with each passing second.

I squeezed the back of my neck.

"Thank you for your concern. I'm fine." Her smile was so plastic I could practically smell it.

The girl left, and Seph stared down at the floor between us.

"We can give it another try."

"I'll let you know." She didn't look at me. Her eyes were firmly trained on my shoes. Good thing I kept them nice so she wasn't looking at an unholy abomination like the ones Berk wore. "I've got to go. I'll see you later. Bye."

It was all practically one word, and then she was gone.

As I got into my car, a sharp ping came from my phone.

Nix: Heard you almost killed someone at the pool today.

News traveled fast. Like I didn't feel shitty enough already.

Me: She's fine. No harm, no foul.

Nix: That's not what I heard.

Berk: We heard you tried to feel her up while giving her CPR!

Me: There isn't an emoji to tell you how stupid that is

LJ: You guys cool with Marisa coming over tonight?

LJ and his completely platonic but always around him best friend had been practically joined at the hip since they'd arrived at Fulton U.

Nix: No problem. I've got to have dinner with my dad tonight, so if anyone would like to run me over with my car, please feel free.

Me: You mean the brand new Mercedes S-Class your parents got you over the summer? That one? If I do, do I get to keep the car?

Nix's dad had played pro for a hell of a lot longer than my dad had and his family had reaped the rewards, not just in the money he made playing but in the endorsements and post-season contracts.

Nix: Everything comes with a price.

Me: I don't mind if Marisa comes over, but for the love of God don't let her cook anything in the kitchen. Not even popcorn.

We'd barely gotten the smell out from the last time she decided to pop a bag in the microwave.

LJ: She's not that bad.

Berk: I'm surprised we don't have ulcers from her Spaghetti Surprise.

Me: The surprise was rolling on the floor praying for death an hour after eating it.

LJ: She's trying!

Nix: To kill us.

Berk: And have sex with our corpses!

Me: What did we ever do to her?

LJ: ENOUGH! Leave her alone. Forget I asked, I'll go to her place. Her roommate makes better drinks anyway.

Nix: Touchy, touchy.

I got home, and it felt like I was trying to outrun my guilt.

Nix's music blared in his room behind his closed door. I had no idea how he studied with that pounding, but even with that, he still kicked my ass in the grades department.

Throwing my wet trunks and towel into the pile of clothes in the corner of my room, I pulled my phone back out.

Me: Seph, I'm really sorry about today. It's completely my fault and I take full responsibility.

Her little speech bubble popped up and disappeared for a solid three minutes.

Seph: It's okay. I appreciate your attempt, but I'll find a way to handle this myself.

Her doing it herself was a bad idea, not that I'd shown myself to be any better at keeping her out of trouble. *Why does this bother me so much?* I wondered. I tried to play it off as some kind of big brotherly protection, but big brothers don't think about their sisters like I'd thought about her when she walked out in that bathing suit and dropped that towel.

9

SEPH

The old math building sheltered me in its musty, wood-and-stone-constructed embrace. I'd sleep-walked through my classes since racing out of the gym like death himself was after me. Every trace of chlorine had been washed out of my hair days ago, but it would take a while for me to live down the embarrassment of having my life flash before my eyes minutes after dipping my toes into the warm, cloudy pool.

The collective gawking of everyone crowded around me poolside had nearly set my skin on fire. I was a complete moron, an idiot for thinking Reece would be there for hand-holding. He felt bad for me and I'd roped him into helping me, but I needed to do this on my own. The genius label stung a little sharper when my lack of life skills smashed me over the head and almost drowned me in seconds.

I'd like to say I didn't cry when I got back to the apart-ment, but the fat sloppy tears that soaked my pillow would call me a liar. Why did anything to do with other people outside of a classroom have to be so hard? Why hadn't my parents taught me how to swim? Why had I let myself be so giddy at the thought of Reece teaching me how to swim? Why hadn't I taken any precautions? Instead I'd jumped in headfirst and reaped the rewards for that act of exploration.

Never had I cursed my precise memory more. Each excruciating detail was vividly retained, from the moment I walked out of the changing room onto the blue and white tiled walkway around the pool to my gaze raking over Reece's muscled and tanned body sitting poolside.

His gaze had landed on me and goose bumps broke out all over my body. There had been a glint in his eyes and then it was gone. I wanted to think I saw something there, but it was just my mind playing tricks on me. I wanted him to want me and have that same breathless feeling when our eyes connected, but that was wishful thinking.

There was a vivid replay of the second my head dropped under the water, the looks on everyone's faces when I finally resurfaced, Reece's frantic look when he dragged me out of the pool.

Their gazes had singed the hair on the back of my neck as I'd scrambled into the locker room.

"Ms. Alexander?"

My head snapped up. "Professor Huntsman, sorry. Could you repeat that?"

"This is highly unusual, but given your talents, I've cleared it with the head of the undergraduate faculties. Would you be interested in teaching a course over the summer? There's a program we have for high school graduates starting in the fall. We could use someone like you." Professor Huntsman's kind eyes twinkled with the kind of caring you found in a mall Santa.

"Like me?" I jabbed my thumb into my sternum as my voice went up an octave.

The corner of his eyes crinkled even more, and his

bright white eyebrows dipped low. "I've seen you in the review sessions with your classmates. You do a wonderful job of helping them, even in the sessions you're not assigned to attend." He laughed.

I ran my hands over the page of neatly printed notes in front of me. The sessions he was referring to were ones I'd hidden out in when I'd been kicked out of my apartment. Sitting in math class was a second home for me, and listening to things I'd learned back when I was ten didn't bore me. It fascinated me to see how the professors explained the theories and to watch everyone around me as the pieces clicked into place. That spark in their eyes made it worthwhile, even more so if someone didn't get it and I had to challenge my own way of thinking to help them grasp the concepts.

"I'd love to, but I'm not sure I'll be here after the end of next semester." Dropping my hands into my lap, I picked at my thumbnail.

He made a noise that sounded halfway between a choke and a bark.

"What do you mean? You've only just gotten here." His face dropped like I'd just told him he'd missed the last flight to Aruba. I hated disappointing him. He'd bent over backward since I'd arrived to get me the exceptions I needed for some courses and to make sure I was settling in okay, and I wanted to stay.

"My father is speaking with Harvard now about them accepting me into their PhD program early."

His eye bulged and he dropped his hand onto the desktop. "Why didn't you tell me? We've kept things as they are for you because of how compelling your application was. You mentioned wanting to slow down and enjoy the college experience." He shuffled papers around on his desk.

I shot forward in my seat. "I do. I definitely do, but I'm not sure I have much choice in the matter." My chest tightened.

"My dear, you're an adult. You always have a choice." His kind eyes spoke volumes about how little he knew about my life. There were choices and then there were *choices*. I'd never been given too many of either, and it was a reflex to go along with what was asked—*ha, I wish*—what was *demanded* of me.

Our meeting ended with my promise that I'd think about completing my PhD there. Walking across campus, I checked the time. Why couldn't I be one of those ballsy people who didn't care what anyone thought? The kind of person who could stand in the middle of a crowded room and not want to run away? I just couldn't, though. That would draw more attention to me. Sometimes I felt like an animal out in the forest who made themselves bigger to scare off predators. Better that than trying to fit in and finding out no one actually liked me for who I really was.

My phone buzzed in my pocket, and a ball of dread curled in my stomach. My dad was the only one who called, and it seemed he had the ability to sense a hint of academic wavering from over five hundred miles away. I took a deep breath and tried to unfurl the growing knot in my gut. Doing a double take, I slid my finger across the screen.

"Hello?"

"Hi, Seph. It's Graham. From the coffee shop." His voice was higher, brighter, like he should work in a malt shop in the 50s.

"Yes, of course I remember." I held my finger to my ear and stepped off the brick path, cutting across the leaf-covered ground.

"How are you?"

"I'm good—great. Just left a meeting in the math department." I tucked my hand under my arm and pressed the phone into my ear. We'd exchanged numbers at the coffee shop. It was rude of me not to have called him back, especially after him being the only one to answer my ad. Reece swore only a psycho would, but Graham seemed far from a psycho. He was pretty straight-laced, much to my chagrin.

"So, you're free right now."

"Free for what?" The flicker of interest was there. *Maybe I should choose Graham.*

"There's an exhibit at the art museum I've been meaning to get to—would you like to go?"

And the flicker was doused with a gallon of water. The dream scenario of him inviting me to ride on the back of his motorcycle or sneak into an abandoned warehouse for a rave shriveled and died. Still, it was either the museum with Graham or going back to my apartment. "The museum would be great."

"Awesome, I'll come pick you up." He ended the call.

I pulled the phone back from my face and scared at the screen. Pick me up from where? Where did he think I was? A gentle tap on my shoulder stopped my confusion dead in its tracks. Turning around, I saw a grinning Graham staring back at me.

"I was leaving class." He pointed behind him at the English building. "And I saw you walking."

"You had me completely confused."

"I thought it would be a nice surprise." He smiled wide.

I waited for the butterflies to start their engines. It seemed they were shy, maybe still wrapped up in their cocoons. "Do you really want to go to the museum?"

"If you're up for it." He was sweet, nice—exactly the kind

of guy I should probably be looking for, someone my own speed.

"Sure, let's go." So why did I feel like I was headed to a class field trip, not the closest thing I'd ever had to an actual date in my whole life. This was more of the same, but I followed him nonetheless.

We walked across campus, our shoulders bumping as we passed by others on the walkways. I tugged my hat down lower. The red knitted addition to my wardrobe still felt like I was walking around with my hair on fire, but I figured I'd get used to it eventually.

"Do you know him?"

I followed Graham's gaze and my eyes locked with Reece's. Dropping mine back to the ground, I shoved my hands into my pockets and picked up my pace. "We've bumped into each other on campus before, but that's about it."

Graham caught up to me. "He's staring you down like you stole something of his."

"It must be the hat. It's getting me a lot of attention." Peering over my shoulder, I looked for Reece. He was at the center of a group of guys, probably his friends, or at least teammates. One of them threw their head back and laughed. The sound made its way all the way across the quad. Were they laughing about me?

"It's a nice hat." He peered over at me, his eyes soft and gentle. The perfect gentleman.

"Thanks." We went to the museum then grabbed some sandwiches from the coffee shop on the way back to campus, and all I could do the entire time I was with him was think about how this was exactly like everything I'd always done. He was exactly the kind of guy I was expected to be with. He said all the right things, knew all the right information, but somehow when it came to sliding that last puzzle piece into place, it didn't fit.

I was back to square one.

Friendless.

Dateless.

Sexless.

I opened the door to my apartment and was greeted by Alexa practically riding her boyfriend on the living room couch.

"You could knock." She flipped her hair and spat the words over her shoulder.

"It's only my apartment," I said under my breath.

"Hey, Seph." Dan waved over her shoulder as I trudged out of the room and down the hall into my room. How had a nice guy like him ended up with such an atomic bitch? I supposed that worked both ways—how had my mom ended up with my dad? Relationships changed people, it seemed. They could make people do crazy things they wouldn't normally do and put up with things anyone on the outside would think they were insane for tolerating.

Closing my door, I spotted my case in the corner. I flicked open the latch and lifted the smooth wooden body out of the case. Turning the lock on my door, I went back to my bed and picked up my bow. The wood warmed to my touch, and the cool metal strings pressed against my fingers. My anxiety from the day and worry about what lay ahead fell to the back of my mind as I started to play, running across the corded metal.

Maybe it was because playing relaxed me.

Maybe it was because I loved playing, and maybe it was also because of how much Alexa hated it. I ran my bow back and forth, trying something new—my own spin on a song I'd heard in the coffee shop with Graham. Hozier's "Take Me to Church" vibrated its way through my bones. I wanted someone to look at me the way he sang about, like there was no other place they could find peace but in my presence.

A sharp banging on the door brought a smile to my lips. Opening my eyes, I stared out the window of my room. Was it mean that I took pleasure in the volume of Alexa's voice coming in from the hallway? Or the way Dan told her it sounded nice and to chill out? I was tired of being nice and quiet and small. I was tired of being me, and the only way to change that was to stop being afraid of what I wanted.

10

REECE

I ran into the end zone with the ball tucked under my arm. Dropping it, I waited for the call from the ref and walked toward the bench. A pileup of teammates slammed into me. The celebration dance that usually followed just wasn't there for me. I jogged off the field and sat on the bench.

Home games were always deafening. Usually, it made every point that much sweeter, but tonight I had other things on my mind—the same thing that had been on my mind through the practices and weightlifting sessions. While I should have been focusing on studying and making sure my grades were where they needed to be, I was worried about a little fish who'd nearly drowned.

When I looked up, everyone was staring at me like I'd grown another head. "What?" I stared back at them. Grabbing my water bottle, I sprayed water into my mouth. I slammed my bottle down, and the ten pairs of eyes on me snapped back to the field.

The way Seph had grabbed hold of me as I'd helped her to the edge of the pool flashed through my mind. I could have killed her. When she'd said she'd studied it, I had thought she meant she couldn't swim well or hadn't swum in a while and wasn't comfortable, not that she flat-out couldn't keep herself above water. And, of course, she wouldn't want to admit to something like that, revealing something she couldn't do well.

Nearly a week later and I hadn't heard from her. Was she busy with classes? Had she and Graham hooked up already? Maybe she didn't even want to talk to me anymore, now that she'd gotten what she wanted from him. Maybe I couldn't get her out of my mind because she'd walked away from me, or maybe it was because I'd mentally made her off limits and said that under no circumstances was I going to sleep with her, forbidden fruit or something.

All her pent-up stuffiness made me want to peel every-thing off her, undo her ridiculous braids, and let her go absolutely wild. There was a wild streak under there. I could tell. It was a *smack you with a ruler and sit on your lap* kind of thing. *Just stop thinking about her.* The seconds ticked down on the field.

"What's up with you, man?" LJ sat beside me on the bench. He was riding the bench a lot these days.

"Stuff."

"Stuff that's got you distracted from the tenth win this season and pro scouts being in the stands."

I turned around and looked up. Most of the times scouts just watched tapes. Very seldom did they come to games, but they were always easy to spot. Steely gazes and road warrior fatigue were dead giveaways.

"So they are." My heart raced and my leg bounced up and down.

The clock hit zero and everyone was off the bench and onto the field, but I wasn't the last one off this time. I headed back to the locker room after high-fiving Nix for getting us another win with killer passes. His dad had to be so proud that his son was almost certainly going to be a first-round draft pick. He was pretty much a lock. Mine hadn't been to a game since I started playing in college.

Coach caught up to me in the tunnel. Tugging my pads off, I carried them off toward the locker room.

"I see the media consultant worked." He clapped me on the back. "Great job not showboating out there. The pro scouts love that kind of stuff."

Keeping my mouth shut, I nodded and rocked back on my heels.

"Let's get to the press conference." He clapped his hands on my shoulders and practically walked me into the room filled with camera flashes and a small pool of reporters. Their questions were the same that had been asked a million times. Usually that was a comfort—no one likes a curveball—but tonight I just wanted to get out of there.

Back at the house, things were in full swing. I barely made an appearance, heading straight up to my room. Keeping up appearances didn't matter to me anymore. Their opinions of me were worth less than nothing. It was almost worse having everyone show up at the parties when they thought the accusations were true. If I were that big of an asshole, why would anyone even want to be around me? Football was the drug, and I was the celebrity syringe. They were ready to use me up and toss me aside as soon as my usefulness was gone.

Opening the door, I jumped, spotting the figure lounging on the couch shoved into the corner of my room.

Even after a win, it seemed I wasn't the only one who didn't feel like partying.

"I knew we shouldn't have made you the key master." I flopped down onto the couch beside LJ.

"I come bearing beers." He held out a frosty bottle. Condensation streaked down the side of the glass. "What's up with you? You're all gloomy and moody."

"Am not." I grabbed the beer from him, sloshing some onto my lap.

"Right, definitely not acting like a moody chick."

"I'm not moody. I've just got a lot on my mind."

"Like nearly drowning that girl."

Dragging my fingers through my hair, I took a gulp of beer. "She's perfectly fine now. The game today was just more of the same. Nothing to get too excited about."

"At least you got to play. Coach has it out for me with a vengeance."

"What happened? You two were cool and you started nearly every game, but now he pulls you the second you sneeze wrong."

He stared out my window, picking at the label on his beer. "He's not a big fan of me right now."

"I know, that's why I said it. Did you run over his dog or something?"

"If only, but with him having it out for me, it looks like my chances at the pros are dwindling more and more with each game."

"You've got tape from other seasons. Anyone can see what kind of player you are."

He shrugged.

"Where's your shadow?"

He lifted his head and his forehead crinkled. "Marisa? She's hanging with her roommate tonight."

"Aww, that's sad. They didn't invite you along to girls' night? You'll have to paint your nails all by yourself."

"Har har har."

My door flew open. It was on the tip of my tongue to tell the partygoers to leave but then Nix stormed in like he was ready to set the floor on fire. Kicking the door closed behind him, he yanked his hands out of his pockets. He paced in front of my dresser like he was trying to wear a groove in the floor. He'd left straight after the game to go to his dad's place. His black shoes had a bright mirror polish, and the long black cashmere coat, black dress pants, and gloves he wore made him look like a guy in a magazine.

He unbuttoned the coat and chucked it straight at the floor.

"I take it dinner went well."

His head snapped up and he glared at us. "If by 'well' you mean a train wreck, then yes, it went perfectly."

"He's not satisfied with the six-and-oh season?" LJ rested his elbows on his thighs.

"Family expectations are a bitch," Nix grumbled. "And the pink-haired menace next door called the cops again."

We all groaned.

"At least it was the campus police this time, not the city." He squeezed his shoulder, massaging it.

"Her house is where fun goes to die." I peered out my window over at the house across the street. They'd pretty much been our nemesis from the day we moved in.

"You're in luck—I came prepared." LJ leaned over the arm of the couch and pulled out another beer.

I craned my neck. "How many beers do you have in there?"

"I'll never tell."

He slid the lid closed on the cooler he'd parked in my room.

"We've got to win the championship." Nix grabbed the beer from LJ's hand.

"What the hell do you think we've been trying to do?"

"You don't understand." He ran his hands through his hair and took a long gulp from the bottle. "Your dad's not like this? He's never been an unrelenting force pushing you to play no matter what?" He stared at me in disbelief.

"My dad wouldn't even let me try out for the team in high school."

"What?" LJ and Nix both yelled at the same time.

"I had to do it behind his back. It wasn't until my name showed up in the paper for a seventy-yard touchdown—the longest in my high school's history—that he even realized." Sneaking my gear in through my bedroom window day after day for practice hadn't been fun, but my dad had been strict about not playing. Part of me wondered if it was because he didn't think I'd measure up or if he was worried I'd show him up.

"He didn't want you to play? Why?" LJ leaned against the arm of the couch.

"We never really got beyond the whole 'no' part of that conversation. He quit when I was three, my brother was five, and my sister had just been born. Said he missed us too much and it was too hard on Mom to have to take care of the three of us all by herself."

"It's a hell of a lot easier when you can pay for a nanny. I should know, because that's what my dad did—when he wasn't making me run drills for hours every day in the offseason."

"Families are fucked up sometimes, man." LJ drummed

his knuckles against the side of the condensation-covered bottle.

"What about you? No family expectations now that the pros are right around the corner?"

Nix and I both turned to LJ. He shrugged. "Not really. My mom's happy if I'm happy. My dad still can't believe I've made it this far. You've seen them at the games. They look at me like there's got to be some mistake, not that this season is erasing any of their doubts." He ran his knuckle along the edge of the neck of the bottle.

"Coach is definitely gunning for you this season. Did you run over his dog?"

I grabbed a pillow from the couch and chucked it at Nix. "I asked the same exact thing."

LJ picked at the label on his beer. "You have to promise you won't tell anyone."

Nix and I both exchanged a look and leaned forward.

He took a deep breath and sank back into the couch. "I didn't run over his dog, but I did screw him over on a personal level."

Nix moved his hand in a circle, urging him to go on.

"You know how people get when family's involved."

Confusion swirled in my head. *Family...what the hell?*

"She's going to kill me if she finds out I told you." He stared down at his bottle.

"Would you just spill it?" Nix sat on the edge of my bed.

"It's about Coach and Marisa."

Nix shot me a look. "Coach is banging your best friend?"

LJ's head snapped up. "What? No! That's disgusting." His face scrunched up in a mask of horror. "She's his daughter."

"Whoa. What?! She's his daughter?" *The picture on his desk.* I'd known she looked familiar.

He nodded. "Estranged daughter. When she started here, they hadn't spoken in like five years."

"Why's he got it out for you?"

"She's my best friend."

"And?"

"And a condition of her being able to use his employment with the school for her tuition is weekly dinners at his house since the beginning of the semester. She didn't want to go. I didn't want her to have to leave school, so I offered to go with her. They have been uncomfortable, to say the least." His lips pinched together.

"You've been having weekly dinners with Coach."

"And Marisa."

"What the hell do you three talk about?"

"Nothing. It's literally like two hours of silence. I'd rather have bamboo shoots shoved under my nails."

"But why's Coach taking it out on you?"

LJ's shoulders lifted and dropped back even lower. "I've known her since we were six. She won't talk to him, but she talks to me. He gets two-hour silent treatment dinners once a week. I'm probably lucky he hasn't tried to kill me during practice. He's just determined to torpedo my career, is all."

Talk about being blindsided.

"Damn, this growing up shit is no joke." Nix leaned back against the wall, resting his head on his interlocked hands.

"Even when you try to keep things simple and easy, shit always finds a way. It's like Jurassic Park but with way worse special effects." LJ chuckled at his own joke and tipped back his beer.

"It's only a few more months and all that goes away for you. Ready to get drafted?" Nix rolled the bottle between his hands, his eyes focusing on the top of the beer like he was a thousand miles away.

"I've been ready since freshman year. What about you? Golden boy, finally following in your dad's footsteps?" I lobbed a sock at his head. Him entering the draft was a foregone conclusion for pretty much the entire population of the Eastern Seaboard.

His mouth twisted and he stared up at the ceiling. "Of course." Shoving against the arms of the chair, he stood and picked up his empty bottle. "I've got a term paper to work on, might as well get started on that. What about you? How are classes going?"

I picked up my bottle and tossed it between my hands, the empty, hollow sound shooting out the top with each toss. "They're fine. Not like I'll need them once I get drafted."

"It's always good to have a backup plan."

"Like skipping straight to commentating instead of playing pro? We don't all have the connections you have."

Nix chucked a balled-up piece of paper straight at my head. "Get to work, ass hat." He opened my door and disappeared into the sea of people milling around in the hallway.

I dumped my bottle into my trashcan. LJ stood by my window with his phone pressed against his ear.

"Ris, if you don't want to go, don't go. He can't force you to spend the break with him. You know I'll back you up no matter what." He ran his fingers through his hair, his reflection showing all the concern running through his face.

If that was about her dad, LJ was signing his own no-draft agreement, but people did stupid things when it came to people they loved. That was why I was staying so far away from anything that might distract me, I might as well have been in a different solar system.

He left my room. I locked the door and grabbed my noise-canceling headphones to block out Berk's loud-ass voice carrying over the music and all the commotion downstairs.

Staring at one of my papers, I re-read the same sentence three times. I closed my laptop and drummed my fingers on the warm metal. I picked up my phone and put it down. Hopping up out of my chair, I ran my hands through my hair and paced my room. *She said she's fine. She said she doesn't want my help. She's going to have to figure things out on her own anyway. Just let it go.*

She'd probably already slept with Graham. Sure, I thought he was a dick, but he didn't seem like a bad guy. She was smarter than him, and he'd probably be in awe of her massive brain.

But I needed to make sure she was okay. If he'd hurt her, I'd break his nose. I snatched the phone up off my desk and tapped on her name, next to the picture I'd covertly snapped the last time I'd seen her. She'd had on a bright red hat, which somehow clashed with everything else she wore. Two herringbone braids stuck out from under the hat and lay over her shoulders.

My finger hovered over the green button on my screen.

11

SEPH

"If this attitude is what I get for allowing you to go to Philadelphia, why don't I see if the committee would accept you after this semester is over rather than in the spring?"

Bile rose in my throat. "No, you're right, Dad. I'm sorry."

His sound of displeasure brought back memories of the thumbprints bruised into the base of my neck. I rubbed my hand across my skin. They were gone now, hadn't been there for years, but sometimes those old memories washed back over me and made it hard to breathe.

"I'll decide when you're back here over Thanksgiving."

Tears welled in my eyes. Arguing would only cement the idea in his head. I let out a breath to keep the shakiness from my voice. "I'll see you then." Ending the call, I sat on my bed, staring down at my phone.

There was a gentle knock on my door. Before I could say anything, it swung open.

"Persephone, Dan is coming over and we're going to watch a movie." Her plastic smile was so big I was surprised her cheeks didn't crack. Maybe this was her way of making amends. After my violin concerto to beat all performances, she'd been less pushy. Maybe standing up for myself in my own roundabout way had shifted things.

"Sounds great. I'm sick of looking at these proofs anyway." I closed my books. As I stretched my arms overhead, my spine cracked. I pressed my fingers into the small of my back, giving it a good stretch. All work and no play made Seph even more boring than she already was.

Her smile dropped. "That's not what I meant."

"Why else would you mention watching a movie?" I stood from my chair and walked closer to her at the door.

"Because I want you to leave."

I glanced up at the door frame for the bucket of pig's blood. Of course that was what she wanted. Why would anyone want to be around me? Hell, Reece had almost let me drown at the pool. People either pretended I wasn't there or wanted me gone. Unless I was *Good Will Hunting* it in a dusty old classroom, no one wanted me around. Maybe it made sense to just go along with my dad's plan. It's not like I was going to have a thriving social life anyways. That hard lump in my stomach grew and I needed some fresh air. *So much for turning over a new leaf.*

Slamming my lips together, I nodded. "Right, I'll go for a walk." I grabbed my coat off the back of my door.

"Make it a long one." She waved and closed her door behind her.

I put on my coat and stuck my hand into the pocket. My fingers wrapped around the folded piece of paper inside. *Should I call Graham?* He had seemed like he'd be up for my offer.

Walking out of the apartment and outside, I opened it up and stared at the neatly printed list. Not a single one checked off. No closer to my goal.

Holding it in my hand, I stared at it again, really looked at it. It was a list of things I'd made...why? So I could feel like I had a little control over my life. A list of things that would piss off my parents, maybe make me a bit more like my Aunt Sophie. It was stupid to even try.

I couldn't even rebel properly. How do you rebel when the person you're rebelling against doesn't even know you're doing it? And who the hell made a list to rebel anyway? It was like penciling in a revolution. Rebellion was supposed to be messy, and somehow I'd managed to not only not tackle anything other than buying a stupid red hat, but also to have the most boring end to a rebellion ever. I balled it up and threw the paper into a trashcan outside the building.

I made it two steps before a hand wrapped around my arm, tightening around my elbow. Yelping, I whipped around and slammed my hand into the grabber's head as hard as I could. His hand dropped off my arm and he cradled his face.

I spotted the bright blue sneakers with white stripes and the unmistakable head of black hair, and my hands shot up to my mouth. "Reece? Oh god, I'm so sorry. I thought you were a mugger or something."

"Yeah, I got that." He rubbed his hand over his cheek, the street lights catching the deep tones of his eyes as he moved his jaw from side to side. "That's a good swing you've got there."

"What are you doing here?" I looked up at the building. Was he visiting someone?

"I came looking for you."

"Me?" I pointed my gloved fingers into the center of my chest.

"You say that like it's a total shock."

"After how we left things at the pool, I think it's a

warranted shock." *Don't go back through a play-by-play again, standing in the middle of the sidewalk like a deer about to get hit by a Mac truck.*

"I'm sorry. I was an asshole. It's a habit I sometimes fall into. And you dropped this." He held up the crumpled piece of paper—my list.

"No, I didn't. I threw it away."

A pained look flashed across his face. "Don't do that because I messed up."

"It's not because you messed up. It was a stupid list to begin with." I ran my fingers down the list. "Dessert for dinner? What am I, five?" I went to throw it toward the trashcan, but he caught my hand. His fingers skimmed along the separation between my coat and gloves, landing right on the pulse point on my wrist. My blood pounded in my veins, rushing to the surface and heating up my skin.

He plucked the paper from my hand and stuck it in his pocket. "Don't do that. Where are you going?"

"I've been banished from my apartment again, so I was going to see a movie."

"I like movies."

"You won't like this one."

"Try me." He smiled back at me like a guy who'd never lost a bet in his life.

I took my phone out and looked at the showtimes for nearby theaters. That was the best way to kill some time. There was a new French indie film playing at the multiplex, a limited run for only a few days. *This should be good.* I smiled right back at him and selected two seats.

～

"This doesn't make any sense," he leaned over and whispered in my ear, the air from his lips brushing across my neck.

Focus, Seph. I took a breath and brought out the bug zapper for the butterflies. "It's about the existential crisis of knowing you're going to die."

"But everyone knows they're going to die." He held the giant tub of popcorn toward me.

"There's a difference between knowing it and *knowing* it." I stuck my hand into the bucket Reece had bought at the concession stand and shoved the buttery, salty goodness into my mouth. I'd long since abandoned taking a single kernel at a time.

A rumble from the theater next door rattled our seats.

His head snapped up, longingly looking toward the wall.

I stared at the other people in the theater: all couples. Pairs of occupied seats dotted the rows. There were less than ten people. As the film dragged on, the distance between their heads evaporated. I craned my neck and glanced back. The three couples in the five rows behind us were all in various stages of exploring each other's tonsils.

Settling back into my seat, I stared over at Reece. His face was a mask of confusion, but he was sticking with the movie, sticking it out because I'd chosen it.

There was a big cheer from the audience in the theater beside us. I stared at the wall. It was probably one of the new superhero movies. I'd never seen any of them. At least with these movies, you were expected to be a little lost. Over there, I'd probably be the only one with no idea what was going on. Another place where inside jokes would go straight over my head.

Leaning back in my seat, I reached into the bucket. Time slowed as our hands brushed against each other. His completely enveloped mine. The coarse rub of his fingertips on the back of my hand sent sparks shooting through my arm. I needed a bigger bug zapper.

I pulled my hand back at the same time he snatched his away. He handed over the entire tub and I was ready to be ditched at the movies. Blinking quickly, I shoveled a handful of popcorn into my mouth, not tasting a single piece. I couldn't even go to a movie with someone without freaking them out.

The low light from his phone filled up his lap. He tapped the button on the side and put it back in his pocket. No one around us seemed to notice.

He stuck his arms into his coat and my stomach plummeted. He was definitely ditching me. My heart sped up and the old feelings of watching the other kids riding off on their bikes and leaving me in their dust rose to the surface.

Covering our shared arm rest with his arm, he whispered into my ear. "Let's go."

Jerking back, I stared at him, wide-eyed. "The movie's not finished yet."

"So? Let's go." He lifted his chin, tilting his head back toward the exit. His eyes blazed with the challenge.

Buckle up, buttercup. I grabbed the bucket of popcorn and followed him out. The dim lighting from the theater hallway made me feel like I was a vampire who had stepped out at noon. "Where are we going?" I whisper-shouted, trying to keep up with him.

"You'll see." He grabbed my hand. "Hurry up." Popcorn flew out of the bucket as he pulled me along.

I glanced at the different names lit up in red LEDs above each theater. He walked up to the concession stand at the far end of the hallway. Taking the bucket from my hands, he handed it over to the concessions guy. "Can we get a refill?

My girlfriend dropped it just as we were heading into our movie."

The guy nodded and turned to refill the bucket.

My eyes widened and I stared at him. Reece winked and put his finger under my chin, closing my wide-open mouth.

With a newly refilled bucket, Reece guided me back down the hallway. More people flowed in from the other end, coming from the lobby. His hand guided me at the small of my back. Any time I slowed down, he added a little pressure to keep me walking.

"But the exit is that way." I craned my neck toward the steel double doors behind us.

"I know," he said out of the side of his mouth.

He grabbed the popcorn and pressed his other hand harder into my back. As he tugged me against his side, my shoulder rubbed against his chest. I peered up at him. His green eyes darted back and forth before steering me into the flow of traffic, turning into the theater everyone else walked into.

"This isn't our theater." My eyes widened. Someone was going to see. Someone was going to figure out we were going into the wrong theater.

"Shh. No one will know. I've been dying to see this movie and it looked like you were about to die of boredom in that other one, so I improvised one of the things on your list."

We rounded the end of the narrow walkway that led into the theater. "Which one?"

His shoulder brushed against my chest and he spoke out of the side of his mouth again. "Breaking the law." His lips curled into a smile.

I stared straight ahead as he led me to a half-empty row of seats.

"What if someone finds out?" I swung around, nearly shouting into his chest the second my butt hit the seat.

"Then we leave."

"What if they call security on us?"

"Then we leave." He sat back in the seat and took over popcorn-holding duties.

My leg bounced up and down and I perched on the edge of my seat, ready for an usher to come up at any second and haul us out of the theater. Maybe make us walk through the lobby shouting that we were thieves. Adrenaline pumped through my veins and I was ready for someone to show up with a flashlight shining in our eyes and the police trailing close behind. The lights dimmed, signaling the start of the previews.

Reece reached around my shoulder and tugged me fully back into my seat. "Relax, no one is coming after us."

I sat back, the tight muscles of my body slowly relaxing, and my eyes no longer trained on the entrance to the theater, now focused on the screen. The previews played. Movie franchises I'd never heard of flashed by with their fifth or sixth installment.

The lights went down even lower and the screen was filled with more action and color than I'd seen since that one time I tried my hand at chemistry. Every explosion, quip, volley of banter, and spectacular CGI had me glued to the screen.

Every so often, I'd lean over and ask Reece a question. He was wrapped up in the movie too, but he never shushed me or shot me one of those looks, the 'if you ask me another question I'm forcing you to write the Pythagorean theorem one thousand times' look. Or maybe that was just my dad.

I squeezed my hand around Reece's arm during the last battle where the reformed bad guy sacrificed himself for the hero. Wiping the moisture from my eye with the back of my hand, I looked over at Reece. He stared back at me with an odd expression on his face.

Everyone around us erupted into applause and there were even a few whistles as the credits rolled up the screen. We got up from our seats and filed out along with everyone else.

"That was better than I'd have thought." The place radiated with a fun energy. Everyone around us talked about what the final bonus scene meant, throwing out character names I'd never heard before.

"And you got to check something off your list." His smile made me forget my name. I wanted to feel those laugh lines against my skin, wanted to lift my head from his chest when we were both covered in sweat and have him press a kiss to my forehead.

"What do you say we mark it off one more time?" Mischief leaked into his smile, and I couldn't hold mine back.

"Where to next, my corrupter?"

12

REECE

The music from the club shook the sidewalk. People filed in through the doors. A bouncer stood out front, checking IDs and handing out wristbands.

"I'm not twenty-one." She dug her heels into the pavement.

Grabbing her hand, I dragged her closer. "I know. Just follow my lead."

"He's going to know I'm not old enough." She spoke through clenched teeth and tried to shake my hand loose.

"He's not." I tugged her along.

I walked up to the front of the line. When the bouncer spotted me, his hand shot out. I clasped it and we bumped shoulders as he said, "Hey man, haven't seen you out in a while."

As he clapped his hand on my shoulder, my head dipped. *Yeah, the partying loses its shine when you end up with two black eyes in the morning.* "Been busy killing it this season."

"Nice kicks." He nodded toward my blue and white striped Adidas.

"Thanks, got them a few weeks ago. Listen, I've got a sports reporter here with me, but she forgot her ID back in her hotel. She's doing a story about me for *Sports Illustrated*. Do you think you can let her in? If not, we can go back to get it, it's just a pain in the ass. I just figured you might be able to help me out."

I glanced over my shoulder and prayed Seph hadn't backed herself into traffic trying to escape. He looked her up and down. Black cashmere coat, scarf expertly tucked into the collar. Dark pants and sensible footwear. Hair in intricate braids wrapped around her head hidden under that red hat. Her stuffy meticulousness was working in our favor.

I squeezed her hand to keep her from squirming and let go before he saw.

His lips tightened and he nodded, lifting the rope. "No problem, man. Head inside."

I held out my arm, letting Seph go first. She nodded to the bouncer, but she was practically vibrating out of her skin.

The door closed behind us and she grabbed hold of my arm. "I can't believe that worked!" She jumped up and down with nervousness radiating off her.

"You've got to sell it, that's all."

"You're a bullshit artist to the extreme." Her compliment hit me square on the chin like an accidental elbow that wasn't meant to hurt but stung.

We walked inside, and she unbuttoned her coat.

I should have known there would be tweed under there.

She pulled it off and draped it over her arm like she'd just walked into a restaurant looking for the coat check.

Berk hopped up and waved his arms from the far end. Being over six foot three had its advantages.

"You made it." He punched my shoulder. "And this must be the elusive Seph. Reece has told us a lot about you."

Seph's gaze bounced from his to mine.

"All good things, of course. I ordered a few beers, and there's a round of shots coming."

"Didn't you learn your lesson after last weekend?"

"Do I ever?" He grinned and handed out the drinks when the bartender slid them onto the bar beside him.

Seph held the glass between two fingers like it was a dirty diaper. She leaned against my shoulder. "It smells terrible."

"It's booze—most of it doesn't taste too good either." I lifted the shot glass. "Have you never had any alcohol before?"

She licked her full, pink lips. "I've had some wine at a couple of math department mixers. The bartenders just assume everyone there is a graduate student."

"I can assure you this is nothing like that wine."

Berk spun around with two shots in his hand then handed one over to LJ. "Bottoms up." We clinked glasses and everyone downed their drink in one gulp. The strong sting of the alcohol shot straight down my throat. One was more than enough for me tonight. We'd be traveling the next day for our next game, and I wasn't sitting on a bus for five hours with my head in a plastic bag.

Seph stared at her empty glass, inspecting it. Not a bark or a cough from her.

"You okay?" I said into her ear.

She stared back at me and licked her lips like she was still trying to make up her mind, testing the punch of it in her stomach and the flavor on her lips. "Can we do another one? Or maybe something with cherries?"

"Hell yeah." Berk dropped another shot into her hand and turned to order a drink from the bartender.

LJ and I hung back and watched the two of them go drink for drink. "What's her deal? She's not still pissed after you almost let her drown?"

I shoved my elbow into his stomach. "She's here, isn't she?"

After she had two more shots and half of a bright red drink, I took the next one out of her hand and put it back on the bar.

"Wait," she called out, grabbing the cherry floating in her glass and popping it into her mouth.

Berkley spun around with a pink and red drink in his hand, holding it out to her. "Don't spoil her fun!"

"Pretty." She grabbed at the frosty, sweet concoction with the stem from the cherry sticking out between her lips.

I plucked it out of her reach and slammed it into his chest. The frozen blended mixture sloshed out onto his shirt.

"Come on, man," he grumbled, wiping at the mess.

"Let's not send her to the hospital on the first night she starts drinking."

She laughed at our back and forth and plucked the now knotted stem out from between her teeth.

Berk, LJ, and I exchanged a look.

LJs mouth hung open. "Did you just do that with your tongue?"

Seph's eyes got wide and she nodded. "It took me a little longer than usual because the stem was so short. Why?"

Berk wrapped his arms around her shoulders. "You're a freaking legend, Seph."

My brain sputtered and sparks were probably flying within my skull. Grabbing a mental blanket, I smothered the growing flames generated by me picturing what else she could do with her tongue.

The music kicked up a level, and she spun around toward the people on the dance floor. "I've heard this song before." Happiness radiated off her as she mouthed some of the words.

"Do you want to dance?" I pointed at the sea of bodies beyond the bar area.

"Dance." She said the word like she was testing it out, something in a foreign language she hadn't heard before. Staring up at me, she nodded. "Let me take this off though."

Her fingers dropped to the buttons of her blazer, which had to be insanely hot in the packed club. Leather elbow patches and all, she shrugged the thing off and held it out to LJ. She smiled and thanked him when he took it. LJ dropped it onto the bar stool at his side.

Glancing over her shoulder, her fingers went straight to the buttons of her blouse. Berk and LJ's eyes bugged out and my hand flew to hers.

"What are you doing?"

She stared at me and back down at my hand. "Taking my shirt off." She said it like it was totally obvious that someone like her would be stripping down in the middle of a bar. When she opened it completely, there was a collective whoosh of relief that she was wearing one more layer and hadn't lost her mind. She probably had on another tweed blazer underneath her shirt at the rate we were going.

"Let's go." She grabbed my hand, propelled by liquid courage, and pulled me out behind her. She popped up on her toes, trying to peer over the crowd. She looked like a curious meerkat until she actually jumped a couple times;

then she just looked adorable. She searched for the perfect spot. There wasn't much room, but she eventually found something she was happy with. Recognition lit up people's eyes as I walked past. More than a few hands brushed against my back. *Is this a meat market or a club? One and the same, I guess.*

It wasn't until we stopped that I realized what she had on. Under that thick wool and tweed, Seph wore a white camisole, the kind with super skinny straps going up and over her shoulders. It clung to her torso, which only made me want to take a closer look.

Her hands went up over her head just like any good woo girl. Shaking her hips and moving her body, she kept up with the beat of the music. I definitely wouldn't have thought someone like her would have moves.

The gap we'd created closed as more people filled the dance floor. Someone pushed against my back and I grabbed hold of Seph to keep us both from toppling over. My fingers ran along her waist, hitting that gap between her top and the waistband of her pants when she raised her hands in the air again. Her skin was silky smooth.

"This is an amazing song." Her grin was infectious. She danced like someone who'd been out at clubs before.

"You're a pretty good dancer."

"I've watched a few tutorials to make sure if I ever got the chance, I wouldn't make a fool of myself."

"You're a fast learner."

"At everything but swimming." She rested her hands on my chest and her tongue darted out, running along her lips. The lights from the club streamed over us. They were strong enough to shine right through that camisole top, and I got a full-on view of her pale pink bra underneath. It was a tease that made it hard to look away, which meant there were probably other guys who were also having a hard time averting their eyes. I craned my neck at the other people dancing around us.

"Are you sure you don't want to get your coat? You're not cold?"

"Cold? It's freaking hot in here." She lifted her arms and ran her fingers through her hair. The intricate braid that seemed to be a go-to for her slowly unraveled with each drop of the beat. She wasn't just beautiful—she was stunning.

When she finished, flowing waves of hair cascaded down over her shoulders, way longer than I'd have thought from the style. Berk popped up beside us.

"I've got another drink for you." He handed it off to Seph before I could stop him. She danced away from me while she wrapped her lips around the tiny black straw, and Berk blocked my path. "Let her have her fun." He stood in front of me.

"Yeah, let me have my fun." She popped up over his shoulder, balancing on her toes.

"She'll be fine. I'll look after her," Berk called out.

"That's exactly what I'm worried about." Trying not to let myself get too wrapped up in what she might be doing and knowing Berk would never let anything bad happen to her, I gave her some space to let the music take her wherever she wanted to go. Craning my neck, I kept her in my view. Heads turned and people watched her; how could they not?

The music got louder and louder until I could barely hear my own thoughts. Berk and Seph drifted back to me, and we met in the middle. She rocked her head from side to side, sending her hair flying with each turn and shake.

Sweat made her skin glow and her top stick to her body, making it even harder not to stare.

"Let's get you some water." I slid my arm around her shoulders and guided her back toward the bar.

"This is awesome. I'm having so much fun." She was practically bouncing up and down with the happiness that only comes from being super drunk. Ordering two bottles of water, I handed one over to her. She cracked open the top and downed the whole thing in what seemed like one gulp.

Rivulets of water streamed down the sides of her face. She wiped her mouth with the back of her hand.

"How drunk are you right now?" I yelled beside her face into her ear.

"I'm not drunk at all," she yelled back.

Pulling back, I stared at her. Flushed skin. Droopy eyes. She'd been going drink for drink with Berk, who'd slung his arms around the shoulders of two women at the bar.

"If you're not feeling it now, it'll hit you like a Mac truck later."

"I'm serious. I feel good, maybe buzzed—that's what people call it, right? But I'm not drunk." She stood proudly with her hands on her hips like she was a superhero for the booze not hitting her already.

Spinning her around, I ran my hands over her back, lifting her shirt by the hem.

She wriggled out of my grip. Whipping around with her eyes wide, she ran her hands along where I'd touched her. "What are you doing?" She smacked my hands away.

"Looking for your control panel. No one has ever drank Berkley under the table, so I'm going to go with you being an incredibly lifelike android. It would explain so much." I pinched my chin between my thumb and pointer finger, eyeing her up and down.

She stretched her arms out to her sides, nearly clotheslining a girl walking by in wobbly heels. "Sorry!" she yelped, which turned into a laugh. Slowly, she touched one pointer finger to her nose and then the other. Each gesture pushed the corners of my mouth up a little, and I bit the inside of my cheek so I wouldn't laugh as I crossed my arms over my chest.

"Say the alphabet backward." Her eyes darted up to the ceiling and she chewed her lips. "See?" I picked up my drink.

"ZYXWVUTS..." People at the bar turned around and gawked as she rattled off every letter. "And A."

My eyes narrowed. "Fine. It will hit you in the morning." I took a gulp from my beer.

She squeezed her water bottle, spraying me with a thin stream of water. The cold was a welcome reprieve from the stifling heat inside the club even though it was nearly freezing outside.

"Hey!" I grabbed it from her and shot some back. It sprayed all over her with a lot more force than I'd intended, covering her face.

She gasped, covering herself with her arm. The water dripped off her skin.

I clenched my teeth together and sucked in a breath. *Shit.* I was probably going to get a kick to the nuts.

She dropped her arm and faced me with her mouth hanging open. "You jerk!" Her shocked face quickly changed into a smile and I could breathe again. Most girls would have freaked out about water on their face messing up their makeup or hair, but she didn't care. Now she was out for revenge. We wrestled with the bottle, each getting the other a little bit wetter before I let her wrench it away from me.

She held it out in front of her menacingly. "You'd better be glad I'm thirsty." She squeezed the remains of the bottle into her mouth, spilling even more water on herself.

Without thinking, I reached out and wiped away the liquid dripping off her chin, rubbing it away with my thumb. The tip of my finger grazed her bottom lip. My heart collided with my ribs. The world froze. The people on the dance floor disappeared. Nothing existed except for my thumb and her smooth, full lip. Her tongue darted out, nearly grazing my thumb, and I swore my dick jumped like a drill sergeant had called him. I wanted her to wrap those lips around my thumb. I wanted to taste those lips and even more of her. A hunger I'd never felt before pounded in my gut. I wanted to taste all of her.

She looked at me and tilted her head to the side like she was trying to figure out what the hell I was doing. *Get in line, Seph.*

"We need more shots." LJ stumbled into her and I dropped my hand.

She laughed and took the glass from his hands. The depths of the trouble I was getting myself into hadn't even been calculated yet.

13

SEPH

Lifting my arms over my head, I yawned and sat up in bed. Other than my mouth feeling like a dirty dish, I'd have thought the morning after a night out would be rougher. In movies and TV shows, people were always like the walking dead in the morning after drinking, but maybe that was just an exaggeration. I swung my legs over the side of the bed and hit a lump—a grumbling lump.

Jerking my feet back, I peeked down with my knees up against my chest. On my floor, the lump peeled back the blanket covering his face. Reece dropped his head back down onto one of my pillows and pulled the blanket down a bit.

Biting my lip, I looked down at myself. I was completely clothed and in my bed. Why was I still wearing the clothes I'd gone out in? I never went to bed without changing into my pajamas.

He rolled over and opened one of his eyes. "How are you feeling?" He shoved his hands behind his head. The muscles in his arms bunched, showing off the definition from his dedication to the gym. I wondered what they would feel like wrapped around me... *Stop setting yourself up for another disappointment. He's a friend.*

"Morning." I pushed my blanket the rest of the way off and stared down at myself. "I'm still in my clothes from yesterday." My top gaped open at the bottom where Berkley had unbuttoned the bottom four buttons and knotted it when I'd asked for a club makeover. It was the best he could do. My camisole was bunched up under my bra.

"I know. That's why I'm here."

"You're here because I'm still in my clothes?" I scrunched my eyebrows.

"No, the fact you didn't change your clothes before falling asleep made me believe you were in for a world of hurt in the morning, and no one was home when I dropped you off. I didn't want to abandon you here for your first hangover."

My memories of the previous night were crystal clear. Reece had made me get into a cab after LJ and Berkley tried to get me to go up onto the stage with the DJ to dance. That was the type of thing people were supposed to do when they went out drinking, right? Embarrassing things their friends would tell them about in the morning?

"Why didn't you want me to dance on the stage?" I put my hands on my hips.

Reece's gaze dropped to my stomach. A slight chill ran through me, not because of my now exposed stomach but because of the sizzle on my skin as his gaze raked across my body. I wanted to grab him, wrap my legs around his hips, and shove those boxers down over his ass then convince him he was more than up for the job. Maybe I *was* drunk. Alcohol made people drop their inhibitions like undies around ankles.

"I remember getting home and then...nothing." I ran my fingers—well, attempted to run my fingers through my hair. My braid had turned into a tangled mess on the crown of my head.

"You were talking and normal the entire time we were on the way here in the cab. You re-braided your hair, going on and on about your hand-eye coordination. You kept telling me you weren't drunk and not to worry, but I figured I'd escort you home like a gentleman, especially since I'm working as your guide.

"We got in the elevator. You unlocked your front door and told me it was fine to leave and then curled up in a ball on the floor right inside the open door. I'm talking out cold. I tried to wake you up for a good ten minutes before bringing you in here." He sat up, his broad, muscled body slowly revealing itself from under my white, quilted afghan. "It wasn't hard figuring out what room was yours, so I put you in bed."

My shoes were thrown by the side of the door. I'd never have done that.

"I must have been super sleepy."

"More like super drunk."

Scooting to the bottom of my bed, I put my feet on the floor. The cold, hard wood sent a shiver through my body.

"How many times do I have to tell you? I wasn't drunk, and I'm fine now." I took stock of my condition. Other than a little dry mouth, there wasn't anything going on in my body that didn't feel normal.

He eyed me like I was the biggest liar he'd ever met.

When I stood up straight, the whole room swayed. My stomach rolled and I slammed my mouth shut. The feeling passed and I swallowed against the thickness in my throat. "See, I'm totally fine."

"I'm glad. I didn't want your first night out drinking to end with you waking up caked in your own puke. Trust me, been there—not fun." He stood up, letting the blanket fall away from his body. In nothing but boxers, he stood in my bedroom.

My mouth watered, but it wasn't because Reece was standing there half-naked with that V thing I thought only existed in movie posters, dipping dangerously low toward a part of him I'd thought about way too much. Slapping my hand over my mouth, I ran into the bathroom and puked up everything I'd ever eaten or thought about eating. My head and the toilet became one in a communion of violent regret and prayers for death.

Sitting on the floor beside the toilet, I rested my head on the porcelain edge of the sink. A glass of water appeared in front of my face, held by the harbinger of my undoing.

"Sounded like you could use this, Iron Stomach."

Glaring at him, I took his offering and sipped it, trying to clear the taste from my mouth. He held out his hand. I slipped mine into his and stood.

"Do you need to puke some more?"

I held my hand against my stomach. The churning cauldron was gone, replaced by an eerie emptiness and silence. "There's nothing left."

"Good, then we can get some breakfast."

The thought of food sent me back to the toilet.

A shadow from the doorway loomed over me from my crouched spot on the floor. Thank God I'd cleaned it over the weekend. If my cold war with Alexa had continued, I'd have been tangled in her mile-long hairball right now.

"I don't want to say I told you so."

I whipped my hand out behind me, holding up one

finger. "If you say it, I swear, I'll spend the rest of my time here destroying every pair of shoes you own."

"That's just mean. Why would you say something like that?" His voice hitched up an octave like I'd just threatened a pet or a child.

"A girl's gotta do what a girl's gotta do." Standing, I looked at myself in the mirror. Death. I looked like the Grim Reaper's new girlfriend.

"I'll get you some coffee." He disappeared from the doorway and walked back to the kitchen. The definition of every muscle reflected back to me in the mirror. He'd slept on my floor all night to make sure I was okay. If he hadn't already turned down my whole proposition, I might have thought he *liked* me liked me, but that would only complicate matters. He'd go wherever football people went, and I'd be going back to Boston.

The door opposite mine opened and the tangled mess that was Alexa stepped out of her room. My hands tightened around the rim of the sink as she stumbled her way toward me. Bending down, I washed my face and grabbed my mouthwash to rinse again.

"Do you have to take forever?" She stood in the doorway, actually tapping her foot. With her arms crossed over her chest, she stared at me like I was a cleaning lady who'd run late.

"I'll be ready in a second." I grabbed the towel off the rack and ran it over my face.

She let out a huff. "Why can't you just do all this when I'm finished?"

"I'm almost finished."

"Honestly, the things I put up with."

"I do live here too."

Her eyes widened. "What?"

"She said, she lives here too." Reece appeared behind her and Alexa spun around and yelped. Her eyes darted from Reece's bare chest and boxers to me and back to him. Her mouth opened and closed.

Lifting his chin back toward the hallway, he held out the mug for me. "I made it with cream and sugar. Finish this and I'll take you out to breakfast as a treat after our awesome night last night." He threw on a smile that could have melted the panties off a nun.

I let out a noise that sounded like a giggle. Had I ever giggled before? Then his words registered. My face scrunched up. His eyes widened and he nodded toward Alexa while moving his eyebrows up and down.

"Oh, yeah, totally—a night you won't soon forget." I cringed inside at how not sexy that sounded.

A sharp noise shot out of his mouth and he handed me the coffee.

Sliding past her, I followed him back down the hallway. I could feel her staring at us the whole way. Her door opened again and Dan stepped out. "Hey, Seph." He walked past and did a double take. "Hey, Reece."

"Hi." Reece waved, pulled me backward into my room, and closed the door.

"Do you know Dan?"

"Nope."

Reece was just someone people knew of... "Did you see her face?" I whispered, wrapping my hands around the hot mug. My look of shock had mirrored Dan's as the crack in the door got smaller and smaller. I still stood there staring at the white paint, wanting to see the look on their faces as they tried to figure out why Reece was there. The number of heads that had turned the night before when people saw him confirmed what I already knew: he was a big man on campus and there was no reason at all he had to be with me.

"Why did you let her talk to you like that?"

I turned and Reece was way closer than I expected. My mug bumped against his chest. I backed up, but there was nowhere to go, my butt hitting the door and making it rattle in the frame.

"Like what?"

He got even closer. The backs of my fingers pressed against his chest. His heartbeat drummed against them.

"Like a total bitch." His eyes bored into mine.

"She's..." I shrugged. "Alexa."

"She's an asshole and I don't like her talking to you like that." Anger radiated off him and he stared at the door over my shoulder like he had laser vision.

Lifting one hand, I cupped his cheek. "Calm down, it's okay." I ran my thumb across his cheek. "Yes, she's a bitch, and yes, I should stand up for myself more, but sometimes it's just easier to give in." My shoulders dropped and I lowered my hand.

He caught it before I could pull it away and held it there, his hand holding on to the back of mine. "You can't let people run all over you, Seph. You think it's easier that way, but it's not. Don't ever let someone treat you worse than you deserve to be treated." His gaze locked with mine like this was something he didn't just want me to hear, but to really know.

I nodded and he stepped in closer, bumping my hand. The coffee spilled over the edge of my mug and he hissed, backing up.

"Sorry." I darted to the side and put the cup down on my dresser. Opening the top drawer, I grabbed the first thing I saw and used it to wipe at his chest.

"It's okay. It's my fault. Not like I didn't know you were holding it." He covered his hand with mine and pulled the fabric out of my grip. All the blood drained out of my face as he held it up in the air.

Please not the underwear I just bought. Please not the blue cotton lace. It was my first foray into exciting and bright colors beyond my hat. I lunged for them, but he held them up above his head.

"Give them back." I grabbed for them, jumping up onto my tiptoes to reach.

"My, my, my, Persephone, look at you taking a walk on the wild side." He stared up at the underwear dangling from his fingers in the air.

I jumped as high as I could and caught the edge of the fabric between my fingers. Reece's arm came around me and wrapped around my waist. His hand skimmed under my top and landed on the bare skin at the small of my back. My stomach, exposed from my top rising up, landed flat against his. Our struggles stopped. Had the acoustics in the room changed or was that my heart pounding like a drum in a marching band? We stared into each other's eyes.

An undercurrent pulsed between us. His other arm dropped and the electric blue underwear were forgotten. He lifted his hand and ran it along the exposed nape of my neck. My fingers sank into the softness of his skin, pressing into his firm, muscled chest.

My tongue darted out and ran along my lips. There were too many points of contact between us for me to think straight and not enough to satisfy the new craving I'd developed over the past couple of weeks. It would only be satiated by the one thing he'd told me I couldn't have. *Him.*

14

REECE

Normally, after a girl had just puked her guts out, I wanted to be nowhere near her, let alone her mouth, but Seph had never been just a girl. Plus, she smelled minty fresh right now. My fingers were splayed across her back and her body pressed against mine.

I hoped the half boner I was sporting could be chalked up to morning wood and didn't scare her off. But damn, how do you put your lacy electric blue panties in a guy's hand and not expect that reaction? On anyone else, I'd have thought it was a seduction technique, but with her I had no doubt she hadn't even realized what she was doing—what she was always doing whenever she was around me: innocently tempting me in the worst ways, the ways that made me want to say, *Screw it, I don't care that your first time should be with someone slow and gentle with rose petals and shit.*

Someone knocked sharply on her door and threw it open, like it was their place to barge into. Seph jumped back, breaking the connection between us.

"Hey, Reece." Her bitch of a roommate stood in the doorway with her arm running up the wooden frame, leaning against it like it was a stripper pole. "Hey, Seph." She barely looked in her direction. "Dan and I were going to grab some breakfast and thought maybe you two would like to tag along." Her eyes roamed all over my body like I was a steak and she was slobbering dog.

"You're inviting me to breakfast?" Seph eyed her like she'd barged in with an oversized Publishers Clearing House check and told her she'd won something.

"I thought it would be good for us to spend some time together. We almost never do." Insincerity dripped from her every word.

I grabbed my jeans off Seph's chair and tugged them on. Buttoning them, I turned around. That didn't change the hungry look in Alexa's eyes. I'd been ogled before—hell, I'd been straight-up groped—but this made me uncomfortable, especially in front of Seph. I picked up my shirt off the desk and threw it on.

"She'll have to take a rain check. I'm taking her out and want her all to myself." I grabbed Seph's shoes and threw them at her. She caught them and slipped them back on.

Pushing Alexa out of the doorway with my body, I shoved my feet into my sneakers, half in, half out, crushing the backs and not even lacing them up. The laces dragged on the floor, but I didn't care; I needed to get Seph out of there. I grabbed her hand and walked out into the living room.

Her roommate kept trying to find out where we were going. I handed Seph her coat and grabbed mine then we were downstairs and out of the building.

"I'm still in my clothes from last night," she said the second we hit the cold November air.

"I figured you'd prefer day-old clothes to sitting through

breakfast with her." I jerked my thumb in the direction of her apartment.

"You were correct." Seph shoved her hat on. A bit of static cling from the fabric had her hair levitating around her shoulders.

I laughed and turned her toward me. "You look like you stuck your finger in an electrical socket." Running my hands along her hair and down to her neck, I tried to get it under control.

"That's what happens when you rush me outside in last night's clothes." She glared, but her lips told a different story. Then her eyes brightened. "Wait, I'm back out super early in the morning and I'm wearing my clothes from last night—is this a walk of shame? Am I doing my first walk of shame?" She looked up and down the sidewalk like she expected a banner to unfurl in congratulations.

"It doesn't usually work that way. Usually, you're walking home by yourself, and it's not after just sleeping." I stuck my hands into my pockets.

She shoved her hands into hers. Her lips thinned and the mental calculation Olympics were going on in her head.

"Then we're doing a double walk of shame." She looped her arm through mine and tugged me playfully toward her.

When she put it like that, who could disagree? "Sure, I'll give you that one. Another thing marked off the list then?"

She nodded. "Something new gets added every day. Things I didn't even know existed get added every time I turn around. That's a lot to get done in six months."

I'd thought it was seven months, not that it mattered. She'd be gone. I'd be gone. *Don't get too attached. Don't get too involved.*

We made it two blocks away before my name was shouted from behind us. Looking over my shoulder, I saw her roommate barreling down the sidewalk with her boyfriend behind her.

"Do you usually have this effect on people?" Seph glanced behind us.

"Unfortunately. Some people are always looking for what they can squeeze out of me. I know where we can go." Guiding her around the block, I ordered a taxi on my phone and we hid out until it pulled up to the curb. Jumping inside like we were on an escape mission, I told the driver where to go.

The faint smell of beer mixed with copious cleaning supplies hit me when I opened the door. Home sweet home. Like a homing pigeon returning to the coop, I stepped inside the Brothel.

Berk stumbled down the steps when I closed the door. He shielded his eyes from the early morning light and hissed at me like a vampire.

"Morning, Berkley." Seph's chipper voice sliced through the air, and Berk held on to the sides of his head.

"How the hell are you standing up right now?" He groaned and banged his shoulder into the wall on the way to the kitchen.

"Last night hit you a little hard." She walked over to him and wrapped her arm around his waist, taking one of his arms and looping it over her shoulder, helping him the rest of the way. His head lifted and he stared at her like she was an alien who'd crash-landed in our living room.

A little flare had sparked in my chest when she put her hands on him. Shaking my head, I shoved it down and took off my coat. *This is Berk we're talking about. Yeah, but it's also Seph.*

A bang came from upstairs. LJ hit the top of the steps like he'd been launched from a cannon.

"What the hell?" He sat on the top step and rode his way down flat on his ass.

"I told you two to go easy."

He tilted his head and glared at me, slowly standing once he got to the last step. "Risa's going to straight-up murder me."

"Is she baking for you again?" I leaned against the banister.

"She isn't that bad." His stomach made a noise like a cross between a gurgling swamp pit and a werewolf transforming. He jumped up from the bottom step and rushed into the downstairs bathroom, slamming the door behind him.

Seph got Berk into the kitchen, where he braced himself on the counter.

"At least I'm not the only one who puked." Seph's fresh-faced voice drew out a groan from Berk, as well as one from LJ through the closed door.

"Make it stop. Make her stop." Berk bent over at the waist and rocked his forehead back and forth on the counter.

"Chill out, I'm making breakfast. It'll help you recover." I pushed off the banister and crossed the living room.

The toilet flushed and LJ popped out of the bathroom. "Did someone say breakfast?"

"Didn't you just finish puking?"

"Exactly, so now my stomach is empty." He stared back at me, shaking his head like everyone knew how ravenous people got after a solid three-minute puke.

"You helping?" I looked to Seph.

Her smile brightened and she nodded. "Can you do me a favor? As much as I enjoyed our walk of shame..."

LJ's eyes bulged like a cartoon character behind her.

"Do you have something I can change into?" She pulled at the hem of her now wrinkled and rumpled button-down.

"Sure, I can find something for you. Let's go upstairs." I guided her toward the steps.

LJ mouthed, *What the hell?* and I waved him off, snapping my head back to face her when she looked over at me.

Our steps creaked up the uneven wooden stairs. LJ's head dipped so low as he watched us climb the steps that he tripped and nearly face-planted. That was what he got for being an ass.

"It's this one." I opened the door to my room and let her step in. The pile of clothes on my bed was still there, the messy desk still covered in books and papers. I cringed at how different this was from her pristine place. My Nerf gun arsenal clattered to the floor as the door hit the wall.

"What are those?"

"Nothing." I kicked them under a stack of dirty clothes. The couch in the corner held my gear and even more clothes.

She was probably afraid she'd catch something from being in there.

"Wow." Slowly turning in a circle, her gaze swept over everything.

"Sorry, I wasn't expecting anyone." I grabbed an armful of laundry and kicked open my closet, dumping it on top of my sneakers.

"Don't clean up because of me. I was just thinking how much this looks like a real college room. You've even got the naked girl calendar thing."

I darted across the room and batted it off the wall. It slid straight under my bed. "Berk got it for me as a joke."

"Don't be embarrassed. She was very pretty."

She's got nothing on you.

Seph sat on my bed, bouncing a couple of times with her arms behind her, propping herself up. The warning ringing in my head might as well have been a bullhorn. I should've handed her some shorts and a t-shirt in the hall and pointed her toward the bathroom. Having her in my room, on my bed—that was a step too far, a temptation much too hard to resist.

"Let me get you something to change into." I spun around and tugged open my middle drawer. "There aren't many things that will fit." I lifted the big ball of clothes and shoved them to the side.

"Do you have a brush?"

"No, but I have a comb. It should be somewhere on my bed, maybe." As soon as she left, I was cleaning this place up.

Underneath the tangle of sweatshirts, t-shirts, and pants was a folded shirt. It sat at the bottom with a pair of my old high school sweats that had gotten mixed up with my clothes when the semester started.

"It's not going to look the best, but here's what I have." I spun around and the clothes slipped out of my fingers. Recovering, I caught them midair and stood there frozen.

Seph's hair fell in waves around her face, longer than I'd have expected, like back in the club, but now I could see every deep and light brown tone. She ran her fingers through the strands.

I dropped the clothes to the front of my jeans, hoping I didn't punch a hole straight through them.

She looked up at me with the sun shining through my

window and lighting her hair up like a halo. "They look perfect." She made grabby hands motions with her fingers.

Stumbling like my legs had fallen asleep, I got closer until I stood beside her.

"What's up? Is the booze just hitting you now?" She picked up the comb from beside her and ran it through her hair. Tilting her head to one side, she tackled the ends, getting out the tangles.

I cleared my throat. "No, I'm good." Setting the clothes on the bed beside her, I watched her fingers work, releasing the last of her hair. "Did you want some help?"

Her eyes lit up and she smiled. "Sure. I don't know why I still do these. As a time killer, I guess." Turning her back to me, she combed at the front of her hair.

My fingers shook. Flexing them, I took a deep breath. I followed along with her work, unraveling the last braid down the back of her head. Her soft, silky strands brushed across my hands. I ran my fingertips along her scalp, raking them across her skin.

Her head fell back and she let out a moan. "Oh, that feels good." Her low moan might as well have been her wrapping her fingers around my cock and tugging me forward.

I did it again, letting my fingers explore her hair, massaging her scalp. Her small sounds of appreciation had the blood pounding in my veins.

"Reece, hurry up! My stomach is eating itself," Berk called from downstairs.

Her head snapped up straight and she looked over her shoulder at me with wide eyes. Our moment was over, and I was kicking my own ass for saying no to being her first. In my head, that was the right choice, the honorable one—not that I'd been particularly honorable throughout my life, but damned if I didn't want to be that guy for her.

"Then start the food yourself," I shouted back to him. Getting off the bed, I put the clothes on her lap. "I'll meet you downstairs." I looked back at her from the doorway as she combed out the rest of her hair. "Bacon and eggs good for you? We might have some bagels down there too."

"Whatever you make, I'm sure it'll be perfect."

Nodding, I closed the door behind me and stood outside. My head leaned against the door. I wanted nothing more than to rush back inside, rip her clothes off, and bury myself inside her until the only name she remembered was mine. And that was exactly why I needed to get my ass downstairs and stop thinking about the fact that Seph was going to be naked in my room in the next few minutes, about how soft her hair had felt in my hands. I could imagine wrapping my finger around it before trailing it down her exposed neck, still sweaty after giving her the most explosive orgasm of her life.

I jogged down the steps. *Stop thinking about it.* I'd give her the other firsts, as many as I could, because if I gave her too much, I wouldn't be able to stop myself from never wanting to stop.

15

SEPH

Reece's restraint was killing me. If he was any more of a gentleman, I might stand in the middle of his room naked until he did something about it. He kept saying my first time should be special. There wasn't a doubt in my mind he could be the one to make it more than special—the one to make it perfect.

His room was the typical guy stereotype: movie posters, piles of clothes everywhere, and way more sneakers than I'd have imagined, all neatly lined up in rows inside his open closet door.

Taking off my clothes, I shivered as the cool air swept over my skin. I picked up the outfit he'd grabbed for me. They were probably the only clothes in his whole room that were folded. And no, I didn't hold them up to my nose like a stalker might—okay, maybe I did, but only a little bit. They smelled like freshly mown grass, like someone who'd spent most of their time outside in nature, sweating, working at something they loved.

I folded my old clothes and stacked them on the bed. Putting the shirt on, I looked at myself in the mirror on his desk and imagined for just a second I was his girlfriend rolling out of bed and wearing his clothes.

The sweatpants took a little bit of maneuvering to get the drawstring tight enough and the cuffs rolled up, but I made it work. With my clothes under my arm, I scooped up my shoes off the floor. They dangled from my fingers as I walked back down the stairs. The voices from the kitchen filtered over the creaking of the steps.

"In her bedroom on the floor?" Berk's voice froze me dead in my tracks.

"Why's that so hard to believe?"

I leaned against the banister, making sure they couldn't see me.

"Have you ever had a platonic sleepover before?"

"Sure, plenty of times."

"Let me rephrase that. Since the age of twelve, have you ever had a platonic sleepover?"

There was silence then more pans clanking and the kitchen sink being turned on.

"That's what I thought. So what's the deal? She's hot, can hold her liquor like a boss—how have you not already banged her seven ways till Sunday?"

Right, Berk?! At least there was someone on team Reece Should Bang Seph. *Wait, Berk thinks I'm hot?*

"I'm not talking about this with you." Reece's voice was tight and clipped. Pots and pans banged together.

"Why the hell not? I tell you all about when I get some." Berk talked like he was chewing something, muffled with a grin behind it.

I peered through the wooden dowels of the banister and craned my neck.

"Even when we beg you not to." LJ shoved at Berk's shoulders.

"Just because Marisa has your balls in a vise."

"You wouldn't know what caring about someone looked like if it smacked you across the face."

"Right, LJ, that's why you're running around after her and putting your career in jeopardy *caring*. You're playing the long game."

"Does everything have to be about sex? She's my friend, has been my friend since long before I knew you."

"Then you won't mind if I ask her out. Her ass is stellar and her rack is even better."

LJ bolted from his seat so quickly he was barely a blur. He slammed Berk against the fridge. The whole thing rattled and a box of cereal toppled over, hitting him on the head. Berk held up his hands in surrender.

"Don't go near her." LJ shoved his hands, which were still fisted in Berk's shirt, against his chest.

"Just friends, huh?" Berk took another bite of the piece of bread in his hand.

"Can I listen too?" The sharp whisper tickled the hairs on the side of my neck.

I jumped and yelped. Clutching my hand against my chest, I whipped around. Nix sat on the step beside me, rubbing his hands over his eyes and rotating his shoulder. My cheeks were ready to spontaneously combust. *So busted.* My mouth opened and closed like a fish on land. "I didn't mean to eavesdrop. I just didn't want to interrupt."

"Don't worry about it." He yawned and stretched his arms over his head.

Reece popped up beside my spot on the steps with a pan in his hands. "You coming to help or are you freeloading like the rest of them?" He gestured to the guys with the pan, butter sizzling appetizingly in it.

"I'll help." Seizing my chance to escape, I hopped up

from the steps. The eyes of everyone else were on me and I hoped the flames didn't burn them too much when my face set on fire. Setting my clothes down on the couch, I followed him into the kitchen.

"Do you want to do the eggs? I'll do the bacon."

"Eggs—on it." I saluted and opened the twenty-four pack.

Nix came in behind me and turned on the coffee machine. He grabbed a mug from the cabinet and shoved it under the outflow.

"Where'd you disappear to last night?" Berk took another bite of his bread.

"I met up with a friend."

"A friend who needed help with a dick delivery."

A laugh shot out of my mouth before I could stop it. Everyone else around me froze, and the only sound was the sizzling bacon in the pan in front of Reece.

I shrugged. "What? It was funny." Cracking an egg into a bowl, I kept my head down.

"As if I needed another reason to like you, Seph." Berk laughed behind me. "She likes dirty jokes too. Tell me, Seph, why hasn't some lucky guy snapped you up yet?"

"Probably because they know they could never match up to the ridiculous amount of research she's done into every possibility and eventuality in life. She's a walking encyclopedia of human knowledge."

Was that what I'd done? Had I freaked everyone out, freaked Reece out because he was afraid to not measure up?

I cracked all the eggs and stirred them with a fork. Turning on the burner, I added more butter into the pan and waited for it to melt.

The guys banged and bumped around the kitchen in their hangover stupors. Mixing the eggs gently, I took them on and off the heat to make sure they didn't cook too quickly and burn. I was shoulder to shoulder with Reece, but he felt miles away. I once again felt like an observer from space trying to fit in.

"You're quiet. What's up?" He ducked his head, trying to catch my eye.

"My stomach isn't feeling too great. I think scrambled eggs was a bad choice." The once lumpy mix had turned fluffy and wasn't actually turning my stomach, but it was a better excuse than 'I'm worried I might have freaked you out too much to ever try anything with me.'

He looked from me to the pot. "Let me take over. You grab the bacon. The salt will be good for you."

Nodding, I moved over to the pan filled with popping, sizzling strips. I stole a piece from the paper towel-covered plate and closed my eyes the second it hit my taste buds. It was like music playing in my mouth.

"No fair, Seph's stealing bacon." Berk's chair skidded on the kitchen floor.

"Are you five?" Nix leaned against the counter with his mug in one hand, reading a folded newspaper.

"What are you, fifty? Who reads the paper anymore?"

Nix's head shot up. "There's a lot of good information in here, the financial section and sports too. Better than zoning out in front of a screen."

LJ's head popped up from scrolling through his phone. "I feel personally attacked."

Berk and Reece laughed. Reece stepped back from the stove and reached around me. His chest pressed against my back as he flipped open the cabinet beside me and pulled out some plates. My heart sped up and I held myself still so I didn't attempt to rub up against him like a cat in heat. He smelled so good. Even after a night out and sleeping on my floor, he smelled like the outdoors and his own special aroma.

Two weeks of firsts later, we'd checked off dessert for dinner with cupcakes from a bakery near campus, Bread & Butter. I needed to find that place, like, yesterday. Chocolate, vanilla, red velvet. I'd taken a bite out of each one. *So delicious.* Breakfast for dinner was French toast at an all-night diner, and—best of all—dinner for breakfast, which was cold pepperoni pizza. Who knew it tasted so good? Our time together got more frequent. I didn't think twice about calling or texting him.

He was my friend and so were the rest of the guys, and that scared me because all those feelings I'd tried to bury when it came to him kept bubbling up. What would happen when it ended? I'd lose not only him but the only other friends I had so far.

Reece grabbed hold of the back of my coat as I tugged open the door to the bar. The flickering neon light overhead looked like one straight out of the movies. He pulled me back and I slipped, slamming into his chest.

"What are you doing?"

"I want to go in here."

"Does this look like a bar you want to hang out in?"

I craned my neck and looked at the sign. "Yeah."

He smacked his hand against his forehead. "You're not going in there. Why don't we go back to The Vault?"

"We've already been there. How much of the city have you actually explored?"

His lips tightened as I dropped the words he'd laid on me before our disaster of a swim lesson back on him.

Letting out the sigh of a thousand-year-old man, he shook his head. "Fine, but if I say we need to leave, we need to leave."

"Yes, boss." I saluted him and opened the door. The beer-and-booze mixture wafted out over us. I stepped inside. There were booths and tables, and the bar on the right had lots of bottles behind it. Unlike at The Vault, they weren't lit up on glass shelves, and the music playing was older.

Reece kept a hand on the elbow of my coat like he might have to rush me out at any second, like he was my Secret Service detail.

There were pool tables along the back with dim lighting hanging over each green felt-covered surface. The bartender behind the bar turned to us with his hand inside a tall glass, running a towel over it.

I spun to walk toward him and Reece pulled tighter, steering me away toward the booths.

"What do you think you're doing?" he asked.

"I was going to get a menu."

His hand slipped down to the small of my back, fingers inches away from my ass. I'd never cursed the thick wool of my coat more. "Why don't you just ask him to boot us?"

"I made it into the club we went to."

"With my friend who eyed you like he was inspecting a bag of bread for mold and let that one questionable piece go."

Reece guided me toward the pool tables. I ran my hand along the felt. "Want to play?" I scanned the walls for the sticks.

"Maybe we should find another place for you to show your wild side, Wild Child." His gaze darted around the place.

I sucked in a breath. *Wild Child.* Aunt Sophie had called Mom Wild One back in the day. Seemed fitting.

"It's fine here. Have we run into any problems so far?" I bent over, looking under the table for the pool sticks.

"Way to jinx it," he mumbled under his breath.

"If you want the table, you can always play us for it. I'll even lend you my lucky cue." A guy with a dragon tattoo on his neck held out a pool cue.

Reece shook his head so sharply it looked like he might sprain his neck.

My fingers were an inch from the long thin wood when he tugged me back.

"What are you doing?" he hissed into my ear.

"I'm going to play them for the table." This was exactly like a movie. They were pool sharks. We weren't playing for money, though, so what did it matter?

His eyebrows dipped and he leaned in closer. Why'd he have to smell so good? I wanted to rub against him like a cat, purring my appreciation for his concern, but I also wanted to impress him.

"Have you ever played pool before?"

"I've studied it a lot. It's all angles and inertia. I've got this." *How hard could it be?* I ran the chalk over the tip of the pool cue as the other guys arranged the balls into a triangle.

Reece stood behind me, perched on the edge of a stool, looking ready for action at the first sign of trouble.

"What do you say we make this interesting?" Crooked Nose smiled at his friend and turned back to me.

My eyebrows scrunched together and I bit my bottom lip. Glancing over my shoulder, I saw Reece shake his head the slightest bit with his eyes wide.

I turned back to the guys in front of me. "What did you have in mind?"

16

REECE

S tanding in the middle of the bar with my hands cupped over my junk, wearing nothing but my boots, socks, and boxers, I stared a hole into the back of Seph's head.

Her striped balls were dotted all around the pool table like abandoned children. The volume in the bar had picked up as more people came inside, and our game drew even more attention than a normal one might because of, you know, the nearly naked guy standing beside the table, namely me. Her opponent sank the eight ball into the side pocket.

Gently toeing off my shoes, I pulled my socks off and dropped them into the pile of my clothes on a bar stool. Thank fuck I'd worn a t-shirt under my sweatshirt or I'd have had to choose between leaving my shoes or my boxers behind.

Seph looked back at me with a pained expression.

I pinched my lips together and watched her come around from the other side of the table like a puppy with its tail between its legs.

The guy she'd played against picked up my pile of clothes. "Thanks for these. Nice game. Come back any time." He and his friend laughed and carried them off to who knows where. Probably the dumpster around back.

"Angles and inertia, huh?" I crossed my arms over my chest. Nippling in front of a bar full of people wasn't exactly my idea of fun.

"That was a little harder than I expected."

"You don't say, Wild Child."

"At least you still have your coat?" She held it up with a winning smile.

I grabbed it out of her grasp and threw my arms into it. "Now I just have my boxers flapping in the wind."

"They're cute. Are those Pikachu?"

"Everything else was dirty," I grumbled under my breath. The bodies filling up the bar took away from the cold breeze rushing past my legs. A few people lifted their heads and stared at my yellow and blue boxers. I was tempted to stand on the pool table and let everyone get a good look. I was sure our coach's media specialist would burst a blood vessel if that ended up in the papers.

I looked to my right and shook my head at Seph's pained look. I'd have almost felt bad for her if I couldn't see her internal struggle with the little laugh lines on her face tensing up every other second.

"I'm sorry, okay. Let me buy you a drink." She looped her arm through mine and tugged me over to the bar. Throwing elbows like she was on the field with me, she made a small hole. People turned and looked at her then spotted me—all of me—and moved out of the way. Seemed all you had to do to get a spot at a crowded bar was show up in your underwear and jacket. Or maybe they just knew I really needed a drink with the way I looked.

"This is going to take a hell of a lot more than a drink to make up for. Those were my favorite jeans." I pointed back to the pile of clothes on top of the table between the two pool sharks.

"Oh no." Her eyes widened, worry etched deep in her face. "Do you want me to try to get them back?"

I grabbed her arm when she spun around, searching for the guys. "So you want to try for double or nothing? No thanks—I'd like at least one of us to leave here with our dignity intact."

"No one's even looking at you."

"I was talking about you. You got spanked out there."

She leaned over, waving her finger to get the bartender's attention. I covered her extended digit with my hand and pushed it down against the bar.

When she glanced over her shoulder, her eyebrows dipped. "I'm ordering us some drinks."

"What are you going to do when he asks to see ID?" I whispered in her ear.

"I'll tell him I left it in the car." She bit her bottom lip.

"Your skills of deception need a bit more honing. Stand aside and let the grownup handle this."

"The grownup in Pikachu underwear," she muttered, but she moved aside to let me get us something to drink.

I ordered, making sure to get her one with a cherry in it. Turning, I leaned against the bar, resting my back against the rail.

"If it had been a chess competition, I'd have kicked ass." Her brain was likely to explode under the strain of not winning at something.

"Why am I not surprised?" The *thunk* behind me signaled the arrival of our drinks. She handed over a twenty and I put it down on the bar. The bartender eyed her suspiciously and slowly slid the beer and Tequila Sunrise—with extra cherries, of course—toward me. Balancing both in one hand, I took her by the elbow and guided her far away from the bar. We spotted a couple of people leaving and slid into their empty booth.

"I don't usually suck that much at anything."

"Such harsh language, Seph. And no shit. The way that vein bulged throughout the game would have almost been endearing if I weren't the one losing my clothes with every missed ball."

Her hand shot up to her forehead. "I don't have a bulging vein."

I took a gulp of my beer. "Never said it was on your forehead."

She scowled at me and took a sip of her drink. Her face screwed up then shifted to something more contemplative. "This isn't bad."

"That's not what your face said a second ago."

"It's a new taste. Surprised me, I guess." She took another sip. It was like her mental calculations of the flavors and feelings packed into the little glass were being categorized by the millisecond.

"There are lots of new things out there for you to experience." *Like me.*

She plucked a cherry out of her drink, and my gaze was riveted to her every move. Completely oblivious to me, she stuck the stem in her mouth and her chin moved back and forth. Her lips pursed and she bopped to the music.

Lifting her fingers, she pulled out the double-knotted stem. *Fuck me. I mean, not fuck me, but damn.*

The night wore on with a few more drinks, dark bar lighting, and music in the background. It had all the makings of a night I'd had so many times before, but this time it was different.

Seph's eyes widened and she let the small black straw fall free from her lips. They glistened in the low light. I wanted to run my thumb across the bottom one, taste it. Shaking my head, I tried to push those thoughts aside.

"I love this song. Can we dance?" She was out of the booth and on her feet, tugging me out of my seat before she'd said the last word.

We went out there. She moved like she couldn't get enough of each note, like a person who'd been locked away and only recently discovered the raw energy of a driving beat and an infectious melody. She held my hands, lifting them up in the air as she danced around, uninhibited like she seldom was anywhere else. She didn't care that she was dancing with a guy in his underwear, didn't even seem to notice the odd looks we both attracted; she was alive and happy. I couldn't help but feel like I was being included in something special, like I was with someone special.

Maybe it was the drinks that gave her an excuse to be a little braver or maybe the fact that no one there knew us, but she danced like no one was looking. The flare of jealousy burned brightly and I pulled her close.

The music shifted, the dance tune replaced with something slower.

Her hands looped around my neck. "I had fun tonight."

"Of course you did. I'm standing here in my underwear and my coat like some chick showing up to surprise her boyfriend."

She threw her head back and laughed, exposing more of her neck, the long smooth lines of it and the way her flushed skin glowed. The lack of pants was totally apparent to me with her in my arms. That also meant there was nothing to keep the sneaky freaking boner that was trying to form and embarrass me in check. Wiping tears from her eyes, she put her hand back along my neck.

"You're going to hold this against me forever, aren't you?"

I clenched all my muscles to keep my dick from answering that question with a knock against her body.

"You're so tense." She ran her fingers along the back of my neck.

That was not helping. It was so far from helping she might as well have set me on fire.

"I'm sorry I've made you stay out after you lost all your clothes." Her fingers toyed with the hair at the back of my neck.

My arms tightened around her, running small circles along her back with my thumbs, the same skin I'd felt under the pads of my fingers that morning in my room.

"No biggie. It's like being out in my swim trunks."

"Thanks for coming out with me." She stared into my eyes like I'd hung the moon and stars by getting a drink with her.

"You never have to thank me." Her lips glistened under the lights shining from behind the bar. More people moved onto the dance floor, and I used that as an excuse to hold her tighter.

"Even when I lose your clothes."

"Especially then. Think of the epic stories I'll be able to tell about that time Seph went up against pool sharks and I got hustled out of my clothes." I smiled and swallowed. My Adam's apple bobbed up and down. I'd never wanted to kiss someone more than I did right then, standing in the middle of a crowded dance floor in nothing but my Pikachu boxers, dancing with a woman who was unlike anyone I'd ever met. She'd gotten so fully and completely under my skin, I didn't know how I'd existed before I met her.

Her lips parted. My heart slammed into my chest like fists on a punching bag, every thud bridging the gap between us.

"Reece?"

"Yeah."

In a flash, her lips were on mine. I tightened my hands around her waist and ran one up her back, pressing her harder against my chest. She tasted like her Tequila Sunrise and a sweetness that made my head swim. Her mouth opened, lips parted, and I was never one to leave an opportunity unexplored.

Every part of me wanted to wrap around her, wanted to make this a special kiss, make every touch one she'd crave, because I was slowly becoming an addict and I didn't want to be the only one. A few weeks earlier, I would have been able to resist her. Stepping back hadn't been a herculean effort, but now I couldn't do it. Not this time. I wasn't that strong.

Her hands were in my hair, pulling me even closer, exploring my mouth with her tongue as I lifted her off her feet. The music changed again and more people crowded the small dance floor.

I set her down, and we broke apart. Panting with my pulse pounding in my veins, I looked into her eyes. She looked back into mine, shell-shocked like I'd just dropped a bomb in the center of the dance floor.

"I think I should go."

∾

"Usually you want to come out early in the morning, but it's too damn cold for that." I let out my line and there was a gentle plunk when the fishing lure hit the water. The kiss had been all I could think about since that night. She'd avoided me for the past week, or had I been avoiding her? Not talking to each other for so long felt weird and awkward after getting into an easy rhythm of seeing or talking to each other every day.

I'd missed her off-the-wall questions that often had the guys doubled over with laughter, and how she lit up whenever she tried something new. I'd missed seeing her. I'd missed her. Making the call under the guise of another first had been my in to test the waters, to see if I'd fucked things up permanently or if they could be repaired.

Her feet kicked back and forth on the small bridge not too far from my parents' house, and she fiddled with the reel before letting it loose it out like I'd shown her. She'd watched every move I made and had me repeat it about fifteen times to make sure she'd get it right.

With her line cast, she rubbed her chin against her shoulder. "I didn't think you'd call me after our pool hall adventure."

The kiss. The kiss that had somehow blown away every other kiss I'd ever had and made me forget every pair of lips other than hers? Was that the adventure she was talking about?

Gravel crunched as a car rumbled down the road. Saved by the car—or so I thought. My face dropped when the tell-tale plate crested over the edge of the little hill before the bridge. Glancing to the creek bank about ten feet below us and my car ten feet away, I knew there was no hiding. I threw the hood up on my sweatshirt and prayed for a miracle, like maybe the driver having temporary blindness.

"Is someone coming? Are we going to get arrested?" Seph's voice shot up so high there were probably dogs howling in the distance. Dropping the rod, she braced herself on the edge of the bridge ledge.

"Worse."

I grabbed Seph's hands, which tightened against the railing like she was about to go all *Fugitive* on me and make the leap into the creek, then run through the water like there were dogs after her.

The truck stopped right in the middle of the bridge. "Did you really think that hood was going to keep me from knowing it was you?" That voice I knew oh so well came through the open passenger side window.

"I hoped." Pushing my hood back, I swung my legs over the other side of the railing. The tiny ball of dread in my stomach grew. I was in deep shit. Looking at Seph, I jerked my head toward the truck.

Her face dropped like I was walking her to the gallows.

"You're lucky it was me driving by and not your dad. How'd you get the rods out of the shed without anyone seeing you?"

"I have my ways." I held my arm out and pressed it against the small of Seph's back to steady her as she stepped up to the side of the truck.

My mom put the vehicle in park and leaned over the passenger seat, sticking her hand out the window. "I'm Mary, Reece's mom. And you are?"

"Seph." Her voice came out as a cross between a squeak and an exhalation of relief.

"Reece brought you all the way out here to fish?"

"He—I've always wanted to fish, so he was nice enough to take me."

"You hate fishing." The laughter in Mom's voice matched

the deep frown on my face. "Wait until your dad hears about this."

"I've fished before."

Seph looked at me, and she figured out my angle.

"Don't think you're running away without coming to the house for dinner, and you need to clean those hooks before your dad sees them."

Dammit, clean getaway hampered by Mom. *This should be fun.*

17

SEPH

We pulled up to Reece's parents' house, and there were three cars in the driveway of the two-story red brick home. There were blue slatted shutters on either side of the windows facing the street, and a bright red door that made it look like something off of a Hallmark card.

There were colorful Christmas lights strung up along the gutters and all over the roof even though it wasn't even Thanksgiving yet. Inflatable cartoon characters in Santa hats waved back and forth in the gentle winter breeze.

Reece shut off the car. His hands tightened around the steering wheel. "Be prepared. My mom is going to bombard you with questions. You don't have to answer them. My sister will probably want you to teach her how to braid her hair like yours."

"And your dad?" My stomach knotted. If he was anything like mine, it would probably be best if I just waited in the car.

"He'll like you since you know nothing about football."

His mom came to the front door and waved at us.

He let go of the steering wheel and climbed out of the car. I grabbed my bag off the floor and he jogged around the front of the vehicle, opening the door for me. "If she asks if you're my girlfriend, just tell her—" He glanced over his shoulder. Turning back to me, he licked his lips, his breath coming out in small puffs. "Just tell her things are new and we're not putting a label on it." He stared up at the house.

"Sorry I made you bring me out here."

"I invited you, remember? We'll eat some food, my sister will make fun of me, Mom and Dad will try to hide their mini make-out sessions from everyone, and they will fail. That's the basic rundown of how things will go. Be prepared."

I nodded. Somehow this was scarier than all the other firsts: first family dinner. I'd been to math department mixers, even some small dinners at the professors' houses, and I'd of course had dinner with my own parents, but that might as well have been with strangers for how much talking was done. Usually, it was my dad talking at me and telling me what I'd messed up that day.

This was something wholly different.

"Let's go." Reece held out his arm with the fishing rods in it and let me go first. His other hand settled on the small of my back, and the warm feelings that shot through my body seemed to deposit themselves right there in my cheeks. Our kiss on the dance floor had been better than I could have imagined.

It wasn't my first. My first kiss was actually something I'd already done. No need to include that on my list. It had been at a museum overnight with other teens. I'd begged Mom to take me and she'd persuaded my dad to let us go.

Pretending I was going to check out the T-Rex skeleton, I'd snuck off with a boy who'd smiled at me every time I looked at him throughout the visit. I'd gone back to my sleeping bag wiping his slobber off my face.

Maybe I shouldn't have counted that one.

"Seph, I'm so happy to meet you." His mom wrapped her arms around me like we were friends reuniting. She rocked me back and forth before letting go and stepping back so we could enter the house.

The warmth inside wasn't just from the heat. There were pictures lining the walls, and each child had a frame with eleven little oval cutouts surrounding one larger one. The small ovals were filled with their pictures at different ages, and the largest oval was from their high school graduation. Pictures covered every available space on the walls, laughter and happiness filling every corner.

"Take those to the utility room," his mom said without even looking at him. She held my hands in hers. They were warm and soft and reminded me of my mom, but her gestures weren't stifled and held back.

"You're the first girl I've been able to convince Reece to bring home."

"I don't think he's a *bring girls home to Mom* kind of guy." I cringed. This was his mom—what was I saying? "I mean..." My mouth opened and closed, trying and failing to grasp at the words, any words to shove what I'd said back into my mouth.

"Oh yes, my son the ladies' man. They can be like that until they find the right person." She looked at me like I was that person.

"Honey, why is Reece in the garage with my rods?"

The deep baritone from behind me made the hairs on the back of my neck stand up. He was going to be pissed. I braced myself.

He walked around me and put his hand around to the

back of Reece's mom's neck. I cringed, my neck aching. Instead of tightening his grip, though, he gently brought her close and pressed his lips against the side of her head.

"You know Reece, always getting into trouble." She smiled at him like there wasn't anyone else in the world.

"And who is this?" His gaze turned to me. Instead of narrowing, his eyes were open and welcoming, just like Mary's.

"I'm Persephone—Seph." I stuck my hand out.

His enveloped mine and he covered it with his other one. "Nice to meet you, Seph. I'm John." His hands were warm but rough, the calluses on his fingers and palms rubbing against my skin. He looked a lot like Reece with the same green eyes and dark hair.

"She's Reece's friend, who he took fishing." Mary gave him a knowing look.

John let out a whistle. "Fishing, huh?"

She nodded.

"Well, that says a lot." He looked from her to me. "What do you know about football, Seph?"

I crinkled my nose and ducked my head. "Not much. Sorry. Reece mentioned you played, but I can't even pretend to know much about anything he says when it comes to football."

"Don't worry about it. Mary was the exact same way when I met her." He wrapped his arm around her shoulder and held her closer.

"You'll pick it up through osmosis, whether you want to or not." She laughed. "You'd better get into the kitchen. That pie isn't going to bake itself." She smacked John's butt, not even the least bit covertly, and pushed him toward the kitchen. "He makes the most delicious fudge pie I've ever had in my life." Her face beamed with pride and love as she said it.

I swallowed back the emotions squeezing my throat tight. Was this what families were supposed to be like? For some reason, it was easier to think that was only the case in TV shows and movies.

"Rods are done. What did I miss?" Reece came up from behind me. He glanced from his parents to me and his eyebrows crinkled. "What's wrong?" He wrapped his arm around my shoulder like his dad had done to his mom. His thumb ran along my arm, a comforting move that only made it worse. This was for six months at most. He was going off to the pros and had no interest in a girlfriend.

"Nothing, I'm fine. Your mom was just telling me about your dad's fudge pie." It felt like I was pushing the words out through a cocktail straw. I widened my smile and held my arm out in his parents' direction.

"No one told me fudge pie was on the table."

"If I'd known that was all it took to get you home, I'd have had your dad making them every week." Mary and John disappeared into the kitchen.

Reece turned to me. "Are you sure you're okay?"

I waved him off. The front door opened and a figure the same height as Reece strode inside.

"Mom said to get my ass over here. I thought it was just because of the pie." He pulled Reece into a big hug.

"Should have known she'd circle the wagons and call you in. Seph, this is my brother Ethan. Ethan, Seph." He looped his arm around his brother's shoulder and shook him.

Ethan held out his hand to me, but the gesture didn't cover the surprise in his eyes. Beneath the hat he wore, his eyes glanced from me to Reece and back. "Nice to meet you, Seph."

We hung out in the living room. I tried to offer my help in the kitchen, but that was quickly shut down by Reece's parents. His sister did ask me about the braids, and I tried to show her as best as I could. It felt weird doing it for someone else, kind of how I'd imagined it would be doing it for a little sister.

We all sat down to eat and the meal was the best home-cooked food I'd had in a long time.

Reaching over to hand the pie dish to his sister, my hand knocked against a glass of wine. The fall was in slow motion, at least in my mind. The red liquid sloshed out, spreading all over the white tablecloth.

My stomach dropped and I jumped up, knocking my chair over. Grabbing my napkin, I dabbed at the spill. "I'm so sorry. I'm so sorry." I repeated the words over and over again as dread clawed at my gut.

The time I'd knocked over a glass of wine and it had shattered on the floor at my parents' house, I'd been berated for a solid hour with my dad nearly pushing my face into the spill like a disobedient animal and made to feel like I'd never be able to do anything right.

Even though I picked up the glass and rubbed at the spill, the spot kept growing, and the prickles of tears itched my eyes. "If you have some club soda, I can get it out. I'll get it out, I swear."

No one had moved. Everyone sat still, staring at me.

I flinched when Reece covered my hand with his. It slid up to my arm and he forced me to stop my frantic attempt at cleaning. "Seph, it's okay. Stop."

I looked over my shoulder at him. Concern settled deep in his eyes. I glanced around the table at everyone else.

"Honey, it's okay. Nothing to worry about. This thing has been bleached to hell and back—I'm surprised it hasn't fallen apart by now. Really, don't worry about it." His mom's kind smile nearly broke me.

Swallowing past the lump in my throat, I tried to shove the humiliation down. Reece righted my chair.

"If you'll excuse me, I need to use the restroom." I bolted from the table and out into the bathroom in the hallway, though what I really wanted to do was dash out the front door.

Staring at myself in the mirror, I dropped my head, resting my hands on the side of the sink. There was a gentle knock on the door.

"Seph, it's me." Reece's voice filtered through the wood.

I cracked the door open. "I'm so sorry. Tell your parents I'll get the tablecloth cleaned or replace it, and that I'm so sorry for ruining dinner." The edge of hysteria I'd beaten back by running cold water over my wrists was back with a vengeance and might have brought along a few friends. "Are they really upset?"

He pushed the door open and slipped inside, closing it behind him. Wrapping his hands around my arms, he held me close. "I'm telling you, don't freak out. No one cares at all."

I rested my head against his chest. He smelled like nutmeg and chocolate, like Christmas, like the kind of holiday I'd always hoped to have. Laughter came from the other side of the door. My muscles tensed. I'd nearly lost it —hell, I could safely say I had lost it. His family must have thought I was insane.

"They aren't laughing at you. They're probably laughing at Ethan's new haircut. He's been wearing that hat for a reason."

Letting go of him, I chewed on my bottom lip.

"Take as long as you need in here. Come out when you're ready, but just know they'll all be talking about you while you're in here and wondering just what kind of bowel issues you have that have you stuck in here for this long." He grinned and darted out the door.

Staring at myself in the mirror, I gave myself the best pep talk I could under the circumstances. "Maybe a stray meteor will take you out on the way back out there." Taking a deep breath, I opened the door and walked back out to the kitchen, slowly enough that an unforeseen astrological event could put me out of my misery. Sadly, I made it to the dining room fully intact.

When I got there, everyone was finishing up their pie. Reece helped his brother gather plates and walked them into the kitchen. I hung back in the doorway.

"Seph, we saved you a piece of pie." Mary waved me over and patted the seat beside her.

"You didn't have to do that." I rounded the table.

"Of course I did. John's pie is something no one should miss out on." She leaned in close like this was a secret between us, a secret between friends. "How do you think he got me to go out with him?"

I sat beside her and took my first bite of the pie. The deep rich chocolate flavor made me feel like I was doing laps in a giant mug of hot chocolate.

"Now can you see why I married him?"

"Right? Who could turn down a pie like that?"

Reece came out with a glass of milk. "It makes it even better." Our fingers brushed against each other when he passed me the glass, and he didn't pull back this time. He didn't jerk his hand away and put that distance between us. All the looks and touches I'd tried to keep myself from thinking too deeply about all came rushing forward at once.

I'd fallen into something I couldn't describe. The thing I thought could be explained away by science and biochemistry had blindsided me. It was a chemical reaction. My body was taking all these new experiences and attaching crazy levels of hormones to them, making me feel like this. Chemical reactions or not, I couldn't get Reece Michaels out of my head.

The roar of the crowd was a distant memory by the time I walked down the tunnel toward the jam-packed locker room. My hands still stung from that last catch of the game. Nix had a hell of an arm. He'd bombed it from nearly sixty yards away, and the heat on it had made my hands itch.

Everyone laughed and cheered at another kickass win in our column, their voices bouncing off the cinderblock and concrete tunnel. Fans snuck into the area and stopped guys for pictures. Flashes went off as twenty people held up their phones. I hung back. The big smiles, excitement radiating from every person around me—I was usually right in the center of it, but today I stepped back.

We were closer than any team had been to the national championship in almost ten seasons, but that wasn't the stat that had made it hard to sleep for the past few nights.

Seph had to be at her apartment by now. She'd said she'd watch the game, but that didn't mean she was above saying it just to make me feel better or had any idea what had gone on. There were only two games left in the season. I wanted her up in the stands watching me on the field.

I wanted her to see me out at the fifty-yard line with thousands of fans' eyes on me, killing it and running through defenders like they were cardboard cutouts. A small part of me wanted her to be proud. Anyone who spoke to her could tell within about a minute she wasn't like anyone else. Her mind worked in mysterious and brilliant ways, although she was shit at playing pool. I didn't want her to think I was just another dumb jock.

It was a stupid thing to worry about. Us seeing each other was about her list. Things I took for granted, she relished and stared at with wide-eyed excitement. Watching her conquer her fears, taking that deep breath before she went for it made me look at it all in a different way.

At this point, I was probably looking forward to some of her firsts because I couldn't wait to see how she'd react. It wasn't *been there, done that* with her, because she hadn't. These were more than checkmarks on a list and going through the motions.

She would always be someone with a special place in my heart—that is, in my *memories*. The ticking countdown hanging over our heads made each first even more special. It made me want to make them special so she wouldn't forget about me.

Tonight, another line on her list was getting checked off, one I wasn't sure I was prepared for. I bounced up and down on the balls of my feet, shaking my hands, trying to will the nerves away.

"Where are you going?" Coach called out from behind me.

"To change?" My hand wrapped around the door handle.

"We've got a press conference to get to."

The plans I'd put in motion were finally ready. My stomach tightened and I wanted to fast-forward the next hour between now and when I'd knocked on her door. Tonight would change everything, but this was what I needed to do. I'd been fighting what was building between us for so long, and I couldn't do it anymore.

I could do this for her, mainly because the thought of someone else being her first made me want to break something, but what happened after that? I shook my head; I'd worry about that later.

"Can you do this one without me?" My gaze darted toward the closing locker room door.

Coach looked at me like I'd asked if he'd punch me in the dick.

"After that catch? You're out of your mind. Every opportunity in front of the press is another chance to help you get drafted and to help build up Fulton's name. Get your ass in there." He placed his hand firmly in the center of my back and gave me a small shove. *Pushy old bastard.* He was right, though. Taking my spot in front of the cameras to show that I wasn't the fuckup everyone had tried to paint me as at the end of last season, to show that I could be a team player was an increase in my draft pick number.

Sitting in front of the reporters, my leg bounced up and down under the table. It was standing room only in the press conference. That was what happened when you were only a few games away from the national championship. Cameras lined the back wall. Reporters with press passes hanging around their necks held notepads or tablets in their hands. All eyes were focused on us up behind the table at the front dotted with microphones.

Nix looked over at me with his eyebrows drawn down.

His gaze dropped to my hands on my thighs, squeezing them to give me patience to get through this thing. Nix had thrown the ball. I'd caught it. The end.

The last question was answered and I jumped up from my chair, nearly knocking it over. I stuck it back under the table and headed into the locker room, pulling off my shirt before I even got all the way inside. Grabbing a towel, I didn't stop until I stepped under the warm spray of the shower, setting a new speed record for the quickest one known to man.

Back out at my locker, I tied up my sneakers and sat on the bench, waiting for Nix. Checking the time, I packed up everything else in my bag. Nix strolled out of the shower a couple minutes later.

"Why are you so happy?" Berk stared at Nix, his face a mask of suspicion.

The sharp snap of the towel flew in front of my face.

"We just won a game—isn't that enough?"

"You always look the same, win or lose, like you're paying off a debt or something being out there, but you're all smiley lately."

I didn't have time for this; I'd figure out whatever the hell was going on with Nix later.

"What's the big rush?" Berk stared at me with big mocking eyes.

I looked to Nix. "Is everything good to go?"

"Everything's ready. Don't worry about anything, and call me if you run into any issues."

"What's ready?" Berk's gaze darted from me to Nix.

"Nothing for you to worry about." I picked up my bag.

"Since when do we keep secrets?"

"Yeah, Reece. We saw the press conference—looks like

someone's eager to get out of here today. I wonder why." LJ tapped his finger against his chin.

"Shut up."

When I finally got to her building, I hoped the world's slowest elevator would get me to her floor before it was time for me to collect Social Security. I shoved my hands in my pockets and rocked back and forth on my heels. The doors finally opened and I rushed out.

Wiping my hands on my jeans, I took a deep breath. Lifting my hand to knock on her door, I came up short when it opened before I touched it.

A sour-faced Alexa walked out, nearly running into me. "She's been playing for the past half-hour and it's driving me crazy."

Playing what? Was Seph a secret gamer? I could imagine her huddled up in her room with the controller trying to finish each round as perfectly as possible.

Alexa huffed, clearly wanting attention or sympathy. Like I'd care about anything that pissed her off. Before I could say a word, she spun around, flinging her hair into my face, and stormed for the elevator.

I stared after her. How in the hell had Seph put up with being her roommate this long? Stepping into the apartment, I closed the door behind me. The sounds I'd chalked up to someone playing classical music out in the hall weren't coming from speakers after all. They were coming from Seph's room.

Every time I thought I had a bead on her, she changed things up. Apparently she was a musician too. I swore she had more talent in her pinky than most people had in their whole body. How had I not known this about her? How had she not brought it up before?

The classical melody was equal parts familiar and

totally new. The notes were beautiful, winding into a crescendo that gave me goose bumps. As I listened longer, I recognized it, the lyrics floating through my head. She took it and made it into something different. She owned it.

Pushing open her cracked bedroom door, I stepped inside. She was facing the window, but her eyes were closed. Her fingers flew across the strings. The sway of her body to the rhythm of the music was mesmerizing.

Seeing her like this added another thing to the growing mountain that made her unlike anyone I'd ever met before. Her hair was up in a different intricately braided style. It was her very own crown; she was like something royal plunked down in the middle of so much normal.

Her fingers flew faster over the strings as the song reached its crescendo, and the hairs on the back of my neck stood up. *I could spend the next fifty years with this girl and I'd still be learning more about her.* That thought sent a jolt through my body. She finished the piece and I stared at her, entranced. That was the kind of thing I shouldn't have been thinking. I wanted to say it made me rethink my plans for the night, but like roots had sprouted from my feet, I couldn't take my eyes off her. I could have watched her forever, could have let her show me more of who she was and peeled back the layers she wore like a shield.

She dragged the bow across the strings, wiggling her fingers and creating a vibrato on the final note.

"That was unbelievable." I clapped after my private performance.

She jumped at my words and spun around. Her hand clutched to her chest, but she slowly relaxed and a smile spread across her face, the same kind that kept thoughts of her eclipsing all others.

"How did you get in here?" She put her violin on the bed beside me, flipping open the case.

"Your roommate was walking out and she let me in."

"More like storming out."

"Kind of."

"She asked me to stop and I told her I'd be finished in thirty minutes." Her mischievous smile made my chest swell with pride. "I feel bad for subjecting her to that though."

"To the most beautiful music I've ever heard?" I could have listened to it all day every day.

She ducked her head and slid the bow into the case. "You don't have to say that to make me feel better."

"Who's doing that? That was amazing, and I don't even like classical music."

"To the untrained ear, maybe, but my fingering was sloppy."

I let that one slide. "You weren't subjecting anyone to anything. People should be paying you to play for them."

She gave me the kind of patronizing smile you give a small kid before patting them on the head and telling them to run along.

Reaching over, I covered her hand with mine as she closed the case. "Seriously, I'm not blowing smoke." My thumb ran along the back of her hand, her skin so smooth under my callused touch. A tingle spread across my skin, the kind that only happened when I was around her, the kind that kept me up at night reliving the kiss in the bar and the brush of her against me on the dance floor.

Her lips parted and she stared into my eyes. Her pupils dilated and her entire body stilled. She cleared her throat and tugged her hand out from under mine. "You played a great game." She sat on the bed with the violin case between us.

"You watched?" I peered over at her.

"I told you I would. I don't break promises." She stared back at me like the question stung. "I tried to read up on as much as I could about the rules and everything, but I think you're going to have to explain things to me."

"That I can definitely do, but not now. I've got a surprise for you."

Her eyes twinkled with excitement. "What kind of surprise?" I could practically see her rubbing her hands together. A part of me wondered if I was a temporary amusement to her. She played the violin. She was graduating from college at nineteen. She was a math genius and headed for her PhD. I ran across a field and caught a ball—faster than most, yes, but one wrong move and my career was over.

Once the excitement of her firsts list was over, did she even have a use for me? I was getting in over my head with her in the worst way, in the kind of way that twisted me up in knots and made it hard to sleep or concentrate on anything other than when I'd get to see her next.

"A list surprise."

She grabbed her coat. I held it up and she slipped her arms inside, smiling at me over her shoulder. Her lips were so close to mine. The taste and feel of them had been etched on my soul.

Sliding my hand down to hers, I led her out of her apartment. I opened my passenger side door for her then jogged around to my side. The engine purred and I pulled out into traffic, headed toward our destination.

"What's up with you? You did win the game, right? I don't know much about football, but I can read the scores."

My hands tightened on the steering wheel. "You're right. We won."

"Then why are you so quiet?" She peered over at me, trying to catch my eye.

Because I want to kiss you again. I want to do more than kiss you again, and I want tonight to be special. I don't want to fuck up and make you regret it. "No reason."

She put her hand on my arm. Her fingers tightened and massaged the spot. "You don't have to keep indulging me with list stuff. We can watch a movie or grab something to eat instead."

"You're going to love it. How do you know I'm not doing this to entertain myself?" I gave her a strained smiled and snapped my eyes back to the road. If I wasn't careful, I'd get distracted and wreck the car. My body hummed in anticipation of getting to where we were going just like it did before a game.

She dropped her hand into her lap.

"We're almost there. How do you feel about trying out a pool again?"

Her eyebrows scrunched along with her nose in her telltale confusion face. "I didn't bring my suit."

My smile was real now, and I couldn't have held it back if I'd wanted to. "Oh, I know."

19

SEPH

We pulled up around the corner from a house and as Reece flicked the headlights off, I glanced over at him. He put on that devil-may-care smile and climbed out.

Taking my hand in his, he walked down the sidewalk toward a white three-story colonial house. Instead of walking up to the front door, he walked down the driveway to the side gate. When he hopped the fence, my heart jumped into my throat.

"Hop over." He held out his arms to help me.

"What if we get caught?" I glanced over my shoulder.

"Isn't that the whole point?"

I swallowed against the boulder in my throat. Taking a deep breath, I grabbed hold of the top of the fence. My feet slipped on the wood, but I found a groove to jam my foot into and, between that and his arms, I made it over. We stumbled forward, and I clutched his coat as my cheek slammed into his shoulder. When I stared up at him, our lips were inches apart.

I licked mine and he straightened himself up, taking me with him.

"Let's go." He took my hand and tugged me around the side of the house. Peering over my shoulder, I stared back at the safety of the car, wondering about the minimum jail sentence for breaking and entering.

At the back of the house there was a beautiful, shimmering blue pool. Steam rose off the surface of the water; it was heated. Blue lights dotted around the sides and bottom gave it a summer oasis look in the dead of winter.

"What are we doing here?"

"Skinny-dipping's on your list, remember?" He sat on one of the loungers and tugged off his boots.

"You can't be serious," I whisper-shouted.

"Deadly." He unzipped his coat and tugged his shirt up over his head. The muscles in his stomach tightened as the freezing air hit them. He turned his back to me, the wide expanse making me want to run my hands over it.

His jeans went down right along with his boxers. I spun on my heels, trying not to think about his toned ass. And, oh, what an ass it was. A warm water droplet hit my face, which quickly turned into a cold splash as the freezing air cooled it. The sharp sound of him hitting the water was the only thing I heard over the thundering jackhammering of my heart.

"I'll turn my back. Get naked, Wild Child. Where I am is only four and a half feet deep. Stick to this end and you'll be fine."

Our last time in a pool flashed back to me, but this time was different. He was different, and there was no doubt in my mind I'd be safe this time.

Staring at him, I sucked in a shuddering breath. I glanced around at the high white wooden fence around the sides of the pool. Beyond that there were tall trees lining the edge of the property as far as I could see. A lot of the houses on the drive over had had their lights out. There hadn't been any sounds other than us for a while.

"I'm turning around and covering my eyes." He spun in the water and made a big show of bringing his hands up over his face.

My trembling fingers slid off the buttons of my coat three times before I finally undid the first one. From there, things went quicker. I shrugged off my coat. Unbuttoned my shirt. Unzipped my pants and hesitated before leaving my underwear on. Kicking off my shoes, I hopped across the cold concrete surrounding the pool and lowered myself into the water. The chilly wind forced me in quicker, frostbite battling against nerves. A tingling spread throughout my body as the heated water lapped against my chest.

He spun around, and droplets of water clung to his eyelashes.

He swam closer to me. The lyrical jingle of his body cutting through the water sent my stomach flipping. His gaze dipped down to the purple cups of my bra. "That's cheating, but I'll allow it." His finger trailed along my collarbone, running it under my bra strap. Goose bumps rose along my arms and I bit my bottom lip. "You do know you're going to have to get dressed without a bra now." His lips turned up into a Cheshire Cat smile. He moved us until my back hit the wall of the pool.

My face dropped. "Crap."

"I can't say I'm complaining about it." Pushing away from the wall, he swam away toward the center of the pool. I lifted my hand, reaching out for him. I wanted him back in front of me, so close I could smell his freshly showered scent even over the chlorine of the pool.

My heart settled back into a normal rhythm after twenty minutes in the water. Nothing was going to grab me from the deep end. We played a whisper version of Marco Polo. We had a running race to the edge of the pool, keeping to the shallow end. Our laughter bounced off the walls surrounding us and every trace of fear related to drowning was gone, but the whole being-naked-in-a-stranger's-pool part was still very present.

"Shouldn't we go soon? What if they come home?" I stared up at the darkened windows of the three-story house steps away. There was a one-story pool house close to where we'd undressed. It was probably bigger than a lot of people's homes.

"What if they do?" He swam closer. The water crested over his back and shoulders. He caged me between his arms and the steps.

The backs of my knees hit the concrete and my butt hit the flat of the step. "You're going to have a lot of explaining to do about why you're in here naked."

He moved closer, his hips making contact with my legs. I relaxed, letting the gentle ebb and flow of the water part my thighs—or maybe that was all me. I'd been really good about not peeking beneath the water at what exactly Reece was packing, but that didn't mean I hadn't caught a glimpse or two.

I leaned back on the steps, propping my elbows up on the next highest one.

He grinned wide and moved in closer. His hands were just above my shoulders, brushing against my skin, and it wasn't just his hands that were making themselves known.

Against the wet fabric of my underwear, there was the insistent nudge of a dangerous instrument. Unable to stop myself, my gaze darted down. His muscled thighs rubbed against the sensitive skin between my legs. I caught my lip between my teeth. The pressure and sharp nip on my lip were enough to keep me from wrapping my legs around him and tugging him forward.

The one thing I'd wanted since the beginning was so close. He shifted his body against mine. The nudge of his head against my blazing, hot core nearly made me moan. Why was he torturing me? I could feel how much he wanted this; couldn't he? My clit throbbed with every brush of his cock against me. I bit back a moan that threatened to escape my mouth.

"There's something I need to tell you." The gentle movement of the water was agony as we gave our bodies over to it.

"What?"

His lips were inches from mine, full and soft. He was equal parts raw masculinity and caring that made me almost come out of my skin. My body was on fire for him and I wanted him to devour me. I knew he'd make my first time one I'd never want to forget.

"I think I heard a car pull up in the driveway."

My head shot up and I snapped forward, nearly head-butting him. "Oh my god!" I slapped my hands over my mouth. *What if they heard me?*

Scrambling out of the pool, I raced toward my clothes. He'd been right—how the hell was I going to put all of it on with my wet underwear? Puffs of frozen breath floated in front of my face.

Reece scooped everything up in his arms. The water on the ground instantly turned to ice and we skated along the concrete surrounding the pool. Instead of turning to rush back to the driveway, he swung a right, straight up to the door of the pool house.

I grabbed his wrist and tried to yank him back. "We can't go in there."

"Where else are we supposed to go?" He tugged me toward the door. His hand was on the knob and it turned. The click of the latch opening sent my heart rate spiking. No alarm. No sirens. I rushed inside and he closed the door behind us.

"I can't believe we did this." I shoved against his shoulder as he peered out the door.

He spun around and faced me. Water dripped off him and the splatters on the floor were the only sounds over our breathing.

"We're going to get arrested." My dad would bail me out and have me on a plane back to Boston before I could blink.

"We're not going to get arrested." He dropped our clothes onto the chair beside the door. "We'll be fine. No one's even turned on the lights in the house."

Walking past me, he walked farther into the pool house. I grabbed my clothes from the pile. There was a small door at the end of the hallway, maybe a linen closet. I'd find a towel so I could dry myself off and then get out of there. Opening it, I sighed with relief at the sight of the neatly stacked light blue towels. I snagged one, planning to fold it up when I was finished so no one would know.

I jumped at the sharp sound of a cork being pulled. "You're drinking their wine?" My mouth hung open.

Reece stood behind the counter and put the corkscrew down.

"It's here." He shrugged and poured two glasses.

He'd actually lost his mind. I'd heard of people in high-stress situations acting oddly, but this was another level of insanity. Not wanting to drip even more water on everything and the deathly fear of getting caught for trespassing, burglary, and theft sent me racing back to my clothes.

"I can't believe you're doing this. You're going to get us caught. What if something happens and you get arrested? What about playing this season? They could kick you off the team."

Trying to minimize my water drippage, I turned my back to Reece and reached behind me to unclip my bra. Normally, undressing in front of him would have sent me into an anxiety spiral, but I was already there with the whole B&E thing. Shaking out the towel, I dried myself off. "Of all the irresponsible, insane things," I grumbled under my breath.

A pair of lips pressed against my shoulder, and goose bumps that had nothing to do with the cold spread throughout my whole body. The chill from outside was replaced by a heated flush that crept all over my skin. His bare chest pressed against my back, the definition of his muscles imprinting itself on me, and the tap of his dick brushing against my ass made my head swim.

"We're not going to get caught because we're guests."

I glanced at him over my shoulder. "Guests?"

He planted another kiss on my exposed skin, crossing that unwritten line he'd drawn between us and I'd redrawn after our kiss, the same one that had gotten so faint it might as well have been painted in invisible ink. "This is Nix's house. His dad's away and he gave me a key."

I whirled around, my nakedness completely forgotten. "Are you kidding me? You nearly gave me a heart attack." I shoved him with both my hands, but he didn't move. He was a solid wall of delicious muscle.

His gaze dropped to my chest, to my breasts, and the temporary insanity was wiped away. I lifted my hands to cover myself but he caught my arm. "Don't do that, Wild Child."

A thrill ran through me whenever he called me that. It had started as a joke, but the more he said it, the more if felt like anything could be possible, like I had it in me to be a little wild and crazy sometimes. His fingers ran along the inside of my wrist. Blood pounded in my veins like a jet engine ready to take off.

"Don't hide from me."

"I'm not."

Like there was a magnet attached to my eyeballs, my gaze dropped to the part of him I'd only seen through a foot of water and felt against me. I wasn't the only one naked. This time, his cock was ready for its close-up. My pulse raced under his gentle hold on my wrist.

The air whooshed out of my lungs and I stared at him, slack-jawed like I'd just been introduced to a new wonder of the modern world. Despite all the five-dollar words I knew, there was only one word I could muster. "Wow."

"Damn, you know how to make a man feel appreciated." He smirked as his other hand skimmed along my arm, every cell in my body aware of what was happening, what I'd wanted to happen since he slid into that booth and sat across from me.

My cheeks heated, but I didn't try to cover myself. He bent over and picked up something from the coffee table a step away.

The glass of white wine in his hand caught the little bit of light streaming in through the gauzy curtains in front of the pool house windows. "Nix recommended a few bottles from his dad's wine cellar. Do you want some?" He held out the glass. The clear liquid swirled against the sides at his movement.

I nodded. My voice would have been a quaking mess if I'd even managed to get a word out. I could use some liquid courage—a whole vineyard full, but a glass would do.

"Good." He smiled and stepped in closer. Dipping two fingers into the glass, he pulled them out, dripping with wine, and ran them over my chest. Down between the valley of my breasts, he painted a line with his fingers before cleaning it up with his tongue.

My shoulders shook. I let out a shuddering breath as the wine formed into small droplets streaking their way across my skin.

"I've never had this kind of wine before, but I want a whole lot more. Do you want more?" His voice deepened, his struggle for control all too real. My nipples tightened almost painfully. I needed his mouth on me.

Biting my lip, I nodded. Tendrils of my wet hair flicked forward, trailing water down my body.

He dipped his fingers into the glass again and painted the top of my not quite D cup. His lips attacked the spot then he ran his tongue along my skin. His patience was only matched by his ability to tease.

It seemed like the glass was nearly halfway empty when his lips finally made contact with my straining nipples. Every nerve in my body was centered on those peaks, and the way his tongue and teeth worked in unison nudged me toward an edge I'd never experienced before.

"Do you forgive me?"

I blinked twice, my earlier anger evaporating like the wine left on my skin.

"Forgive you for what?" My words were shaky at best as he set down the glass and ran his hands over my nipples, rolling them between his fingers and sending shocks straight through my body to my pussy. I squeezed my thighs together, trying to ease the building pressure.

"Lying to you." His words were strained like this was taking as much of a toll on him as it was on me.

"On one condition." My words were a breathy whisper.

"Name it." His lips were inches away. All this and we hadn't even had a proper kiss yet, not that there was anything proper about kind of breaking into someone's pool house to get naked together.

"Take me to bed." I looped my arms around his neck and pulled him close. My body was one match strike away from being engulfed in flames, and he was holding the matchbox. I braced myself for him to pull back or change his mind, to tell me this was a mistake or say I deserved better.

Instead, he bridged the gap in an instant, and I consumed his lips like an inmate presented with a last meal. He tasted like wine and chlorine.

Momentarily breaking the kiss, he bent his knees and scooped me up in his arms. "I thought you'd never ask."

20

REECE

She was the most beautiful thing I'd ever seen. More than any win on the field, any pair of limited-edition Adidas, she was so many things, and I couldn't even believe she was there with me. *Take me to bed* had to be the sweetest words ever spoken. The emotional charge of them was almost more than I could handle, so I focused on the mechanics of it: lifting her into my arms and kissing her while she squirmed, squeezing her thighs together in my hold.

Nix had given me full access to the pool house. I'd prepared ahead of time, making sure we'd have everything we needed. Nudging the bedroom door open, I stepped inside with Seph in my arms. Her lips peppered my neck and shoulder with kisses, sweet kisses like a touch from the gods.

Standing in front of the bed, I set her down on her feet. She glanced up at me, the confusion bright in her eyes even in the low light.

"I wouldn't want you to get into bed with these wet things on." I stepped back and stared down at the purple triangle of fabric covering her pussy. The heat of her had made it hard to think straight back in the pool, had made it difficult to keep from peeling it off her and taking her in the clear, blue water.

Her throat jumped and she swallowed. I could practically hear the cartoon gulp. Kneeling down, I ran my hands over the smooth curves of her hips. My fingers dipped below the waistband and I squeezed her ass.

She went up on her tiptoes. I looked up at her through the valley of her breasts. Her eyes were filled with the kind of humbling trust that would have brought me to my knees if I weren't already there.

Moving my hands lower, I pushed at the waistband of her underwear, rolling it down over my hands. Like I was my own torturer, I pulled them down her legs one inch at a time, my eyes getting well acquainted with the shape of her body, the smell of her. They fell free from the curve of her ass and down her thighs, pooling at her feet.

She ran her fingers through my hair, her nails skimming along my scalp. I groaned at the pulsing pleasure coursing through my body. My dick smacked against my stomach between my spread legs. Resting my hands along the backs of her thighs, I nudged her back until her knees hit the bed.

Sitting down with a bounce, she reached out to me. I came to her like a moth to a flame, the fire within me burning with desire. "We can go slow." I tried to keep the strain out of my voice. My need to make this special and go slow warred with my cresting need to be inside her.

"I've been going slow my whole life. Restrained, calculating, methodical. I want to feel you, and this feels more right than anything I've done in my life." She leaned back, her arms behind my neck bringing me with her.

Our bodies were flush against each other on top of the

cool bedspread. My cock nestled at the apex of her thighs, and the wetness coating the head of my dick wasn't from the pool. My mouth watered to taste her. I wanted it second to only one thing, but I could exercise some patience.

Shifting my hips back, I sank lower on the bed. I pressed a kiss against her stomach, circling her belly button. She shuddered beneath me.

"Grab the pillows and put them under your head." I kept going toward the part of her I needed to get properly introduced to first.

With a question in her eyes, she grabbed the pillows from the top of the bed and stuck two under her head, propping herself up so I could see her, so she could see me.

I dropped a kiss on the small patch of hair right above her clit and she sucked in a sharp breath.

"This wasn't on your list, but I thought I'd improvise." Settling my chest on the bed, I spread her open. Pink and glistening, she was ready for my mouth. "Are you ready?"

She sucked in a shaky breath and nodded her head.

Worry shot through me. *Am I going to fast?* "Do you want me to stop?"

If she shook her head any quicker, she'd get whiplash. I couldn't hold back my smile. Opening her wider, I lathed her clit with the flat of my tongue.

Her hands shot to my head, tightening her grip on my hair. I glanced up and her gaze was riveted to mine, not wanting to miss a moment. That made two of us.

I feasted on her sweetness, driven to draw out as many of her cries and moans as possible. I watched her watching me. I didn't need to be told this was a first; I felt it and saw it in her eyes. The dazed and dreamy look surpassed every other I'd seen before. My cock strained against the comforter, each movement torture because it wasn't where I wanted to be, needed to be. As I sucked her clit into my mouth, her thighs trembled, and her hold on my hair was going to make me bald.

Her back arched off the bed and her eyes snapped shut as she threw her head back. Her hold tightened even more.

I gently kissed the inside of her thigh and wrapped my hand around her wrist. "You're going to give me a bald spot."

"Come here," she said, panting. Her chest rose and fell, and she didn't let go of my hair.

Crawling up the bed, I did as my lady asked. Her arms settled around my neck with her hands running along my shoulders.

"How about an encore?" I rested my forehead against hers.

"Maybe later." The corner of her mouth lifted.

She lifted her legs and hooked them around my hip. My cock slipped between the lips of her pussy, running along them, gathering more of her essence and nudging at her opening. Her fingers raked down my back and she moaned as my head tapped against her clit.

A moment of clarity shot through my head and I shifted us to one side, reaching for the pack of condoms I'd stashed on the nightstand earlier. Ripping it open in what had to be record time, I shifted my hips and rolled on the condom.

Dropping my forehead against hers, I stared into her eyes. "Are you sure about this?"

Her hands came up to the sides of my face, their warmth settling deep into my skin. The light brown of her eyes was like melted caramel. Running her thumb across my bottom lip, she closed her eyes and parted her lips.

I closed the hairsbreadth gap between us. Our tongues

mimicked the gentle rock of our hips, and her heels dug in deeper against my ass. This wasn't like the kiss out in the pool. It wasn't playful and teasing. This was raw and carnal with a helpless lust that threatened to consume her, and I was the only cure.

21

SEPH

My body was on fire. The heft of his cock resting against my clit made my thighs tremble around his body.

I wanted all of him.

I needed all of him.

The stories and studies about first times didn't matter. This would be different because it was us. Reaching down between us, I wrapped my fingers around the head of his cock. The thick mushroom tip would be a challenge, but I was up for it. A shudder wracked his body and I smiled against his lips.

I wasn't the only one ready to come out of my skin. Lining him up against me, I lifted my hips and squeezed my thighs around him all at once. His body lurched forward, not expecting my assault.

He plunged deep into me so quickly, my back arched off the bed and a vise tightened around my chest, squeezing my lungs, the sharp burn stealing my breath away. I kept my arm wrapped around his back, the other pinned between us.

He froze and tried to pull back. "Seph, what are you

doing?" He planted his hands on the bed, but I held on, moving with him. Tugging my arm free, I wrapped it tighter around him.

I clenched my lips between my teeth. The metallic taste of blood invaded my mouth. I'd bitten my own lip trying to hold back the yelp, knowing he'd probably call the whole thing off. Relaxing my mouth, I breathed through the stretching, raw ache in my pussy.

"It's okay." I buried my head in his shoulder.

"It's not okay—I hurt you." His voice was filled with accusation, not at me, but at himself.

I held on to the back of his neck and ran my fingers through his hair, shushing him. "Give me a second. It'll be okay." I breathed through my mouth and some of the burn ebbed away. Shifting, my clit rubbed against him. A flicker of the pleasure from before came sparking back, small little shocks with each shift that canceled out the pain. I moved again and that flame grew.

"We were supposed to go slow." He ran his hand along my back, the rough pads of his fingers caressing and comforting me. It brought tears to my eyes. Why hadn't they mentioned this in the papers I'd read? How you could want something so much with another person? How they could hold you close and help you discover a whole different side of yourself?

"You know me, always rushing into things without thinking them through." I hitched my legs higher on his hips and he sank in deeper. I moaned into his shoulder again, my teeth scraping across his skin.

"Yeah, sounds exactly like you." His words were clipped and strained. His muscles tightened like he was hanging by the thinnest of threads.

Lifting my butt, I rolled my hips, and more of his cock

slid into me. This time my breath was stolen away by a pleasure that pulsed from the top of my head to the tips of my toes. "You can move now." I ground my hips on him, the pleasure blooming and growing with each passing second.

His head jerked back. He stared into my eyes for a hint of deception. "Are you sure?"

Lifting myself, I slammed my hips against him in a thrust that lit me up like a Christmas tree. We both groaned and his arms locked around me so tightly I could barely breathe. Leaning back, I took him with me, back on top of me on the bed.

"I'm sure." The words came out like a choked whisper.

Bracing his arms on either side of my head, he stared into my eyes, searching.

My hips lifting seemed to be the answer he was looking for. Brushing my hair back from my face, he thrust his hips forward, burying himself deeper in me. My back arched off the bed and I moaned out his name. Apparently, that was the magic word.

His slow, measured thrusts transformed with each hitched breath and moan ripped from my lips. I met every movement and clung to the razor-sharp edge of the climax hurtling toward me. He canted his hips and my body shot forward. This wasn't a leisurely stroll of an orgasm; this was careening over the side of a cliff into free fall.

My nails bit into his back and I screamed louder than I'd ever thought possible. His thrusts got more erratic and his cock thickened inside me, stretching me to my limit. Slamming his hand against the bed beside me, he braced himself on his arms, driving into me one last time. His cock pulsed inside me, triggering another orgasm. This one was a wave cresting in slow motion, spreading warmth throughout my body. I collapsed back onto the bed.

Resting his forehead against mine, he stared at me. The sharp pants of his breathing matched my own. My smile was so wide my cheeks ached, along with a few other parts of me.

"That was unexpected."

Uncertainty clouded his eyes and, if anything, made him even sexier. He was worried. "Was it okay?" He lifted his hips, pulling himself free from me. The cool air of the room replaced the warmth of his possession of my body.

"That's supposed to be my line." I brushed the hair back from over his ears and ran my hand along his cheek. "It was more than I ever could have hoped for."

His relief was absolute. Rolling off the bed, he got rid of the condom and ducked into the bathroom. He came back with a towel and washcloth.

I pushed up onto my elbows. His knee sank into the bed and he dragged the warm cloth over my skin. My heart fluttered at his gentle touch.

He wiped away the marker of my first time from between my legs and gently dried me. I blinked back tears at his tender care. *Now that would freak him the hell out.* He put everything back in the bathroom and climbed back into the bed with me, dragging down the sheets on one side.

We got under the covers and he held me in his arms. "You sure you're okay?"

I ran my fingers along his muscled chest. "I'm more than okay, Reece. Are you sure it's okay with Nix that we're here?"

"He's the one who suggested it when I was trying to come up with a place for a late-night swim under the stars. He's totally fine with it."

I slapped my hands over my face, the flush from earlier returning, only this time it wasn't from sexual release. "That means he knows." How was I going to face him again? *Hey, Nix, your guest room bed is the perfect banging spot.*

Reece peeled my hands away from my face. The tips of my ears had to be on fire.

"I didn't say anything about the naked part. Don't worry." His Adam's apple bobbed up and down. "You'd tell me if you weren't okay, right?"

"Stop worrying. I'm fine—better than fine. Sore"—his muscles tensed—"but that's to be expected. There had to be a first, and I'm glad it was you."

A cloud flashed across his eyes and he pulled me closer, hugged me tighter, and held on to me like I was a buoy in a hurricane.

"What's wrong?" I asked softly.

His lips tickled my shoulder. "Nothing. Let's get some sleep." He pulled the blankets up higher.

Glancing up at him, I swallowed. Putting on the bravest face I had, I reached down between us and palmed his semi-hard dick. "Do we have to?"

His neck tightened and he sucked in a sharp breath between his teeth. "You're sore."

"I am, but that doesn't mean I don't still want you. I think I know exactly what can help me feel a lot better." Tightening my grip, I pumped my hand up and down his length.

He tugged me forward and captured my lips in a demanding kiss, covering my hand with his own and tightening the grip around it.

"You're playing with fire, Wild Child."

I licked my lips. "I'm playing with you."

"I am your jungle gym. Play to your heart's content." He released my hand and rolled over, opening the drawer on the nightstand. The silver foil package caught the low light filtering in from outside and my clit throbbed as he ripped it open with his teeth.

"Are you ready for this?" I shoved the blankets back, showing myself to him completely.

He rolled on the condom. "I thought that was my line." He grinned and fell down, covering me with his body. Rolling me over so I straddled his hips, he grabbed my ass and pulled me forward. His dick stuck up straight, resting between my thighs.

Pushing forward, I lifted off my knees and held on to him, slowly lowering myself. I stared down at where we were joined, watching more of his length disappear inside of me while relishing the feeling of him thickening within me and rubbing against every pleasure spot I had.

My ass finally hit his thighs, and I rocked back and forth.

"I swear you're going to kill me," he murmured.

"Glad to know I'm a quick study."

"Any quicker and you might be a lethal weapon."

"But what a way to go." Using all my studying to my advantage, I moved my hips in a figure eight. His hands shot from my ass to the sheets, fisting them in his hands and squeezing his eyes shut. He slammed his hand against the bed and thrust so hard up into me that I nearly fell off. The climax smashed into me like a freight train and my fingers dug into his chest. My thighs quaked and my pussy clamped around his cock as it swelled, the pulse of his orgasm setting off another for me.

I slumped forward, falling onto his chest, my heart pounding so hard I swore he could hear it too.

"See, what'd I tell you? You're a dangerous woman."

22

SEPH

The small wooden staircase was full of people. Berk and LJ stood in the middle of the snow-covered backyard in snow boots, shorts, and jackets, crowded around the grill, which was billowing smoke into the air.

I crossed my arms over my chest. Being there with just the guys was one thing, but the house felt different with other people in it. These weren't strangers at a club or a bar. These were people in his house, his other friends. Their opinions had to matter to him too, right? What if they found me lacking?

The volume increased as more people came in through the front door. I was surrounded. I kept expecting someone to show up and tell me it was time to leave.

Reece carried a keg out of the kitchen, and we backed up against the railing to let him and Nix past. The corners of his mouth lifted higher as he passed. "Don't even think of bailing, Wild Child."

"How'd you get roped into all this?" The girl beside me

leaned over and talked out of the side of her mouth, lifting her chin toward the backyard grilling and snow-diving. She had bright blue eyes and curly black hair. "Is Reece black-mailing you with unseemly pictures?" Her eyes glittered with mischief.

"No, I think we're kind of dating." It was the first time I'd said those words out loud. Was that what it was? Was he my boyfriend? "Is that how LJ got you here? Sexy blackmail pics?"

She snorted into her beer, spraying foam over the rim of her cup. "Not unless they're our bathtub pics from when we were five. And good for Reece. LJ said he had a rough year last year. You seem like just the kind of person he should be dating."

"We met like two minutes ago. How can you tell?"

"I just can. I'm Marisa, LJ's best friend, whether he likes it or not."

"Seph, Reece's...girlfriend?" My voice went up at the end like it was a question.

I glanced up and watched him helping LJ build a wall of snow around the keg. That was one way to handle it. We'd spent every night together since that night in the pool house. Usually we stayed at his place. It was a chance for me to get out of my apartment, and his house was closer to campus anyway. We'd watched movies with the guys, made dinner together, and fallen asleep in each other's arms. That was kind of like a girlfriend, right? Or maybe I was getting ahead of myself. I nibbled my bottom lip, thinking I shouldn't have said it until I'd asked him.

"Are you heading home for Thanksgiving?" She brushed her hair back from her face. Sticking her hands into her pockets, she glanced up at me, waiting for my response.

The break was something most people looked forward to, but not me. The coil of dread at the thought of heading back up to Boston sat deep in my stomach.

"Yeah, I leave tomorrow."

Marisa cupped her hands around her mouth. "L!" She pointed to her head, gathering up her hair in her hand. Her glossy curls tumbled everywhere.

His head snapped up and he rolled his eyes before tugging something off his wrist and shooting it at her sling-shot style. Her hand shot out and she snagged the light blue circle from the air.

"Thank you," she shouted over the din of the party chatter and music, putting her hair up in a bun. "It's getting hot, right? Or is he slipping extra shots into my drink again?"

"No, it's definitely hot." I tugged my shirt away from my chest as sweat trickled down my back, even standing in freezing temperatures. Body heat from the people pouring out of the house and into the backyard melted the snow around us.

My phone vibrated in my pocket. After taking it out and glancing at the screen, I shoved it back into my pocket. Could he read my thoughts now? The crush of bodies spilling out into the small space made the freezing temperatures tolerable.

"Where's the hot tub? I can't believe they got rid of the Brothel fan favorite." A girl behind us walked down the steps, her nasal voice reminding me of Alexa. I was sure they'd be best bitch friends. She laughed with a girl in a bright pink sweater, weaving their way through the party.

"The Brothel?" I mouthed to Marisa.

"This place used to belong to a frat, as LJ explains it. The nickname for it was the Brothel." She rolled her eyes. "Unfortunately, the name stuck when the frat got kicked off campus for hazing and the Trojans took over. It's probably the first time actual Trojans have outnumbered the used rubber kind hidden around the place. You wouldn't believe the disinfecting they had to do when they moved in." She waved her arms up at the house and over the crowd of people milling around below. The bright pink sweater and friend made a beeline straight for Reece and LJ.

"Does it get weird being friends with him when he gets so much...attention?" There had to be a better word for it, but I wasn't sure what it was.

Her lips slammed together and she took another gulp from her cup, finishing it off. "He's a big boy. He can do what he wants." There was an edge to her voice, equal parts disinterest, anger, and sadness. "Let's get another drink. I know where LJ keeps the good stuff." She grabbed my hand and tugged me along with her through the ever-growing party. People streamed in through the doors like ants over a lollipop.

She slipped the key to LJ's room out of her pocket and dragged me inside. His room was neater than Reece's—well, neater than it used to be. The pile of clothes that migrated around his room had been successfully banished into his drawers, neatly folded. There were framed pictures on LJ's desk, one of him with his arm around Marisa and another where they looked like they were in elementary school.

I picked it up. "Is this you two?"

Bottles clinked against one another as she rifled through the booze stash in his closet.

"That's us. I still can't believe we've known each other since we were that little." She stared thoughtfully at the frame. "He's my oldest friend." She said it more to herself than to me. There was a thump out in the hallway. "Anyway, let me have your cup."

With our cups filled to the brim with "the good stuff," as she called it, we headed back downstairs. There were even more people, and the volume and heat levels had increased exponentially.

The glowing screen of her phone lit up her face as we battled with the crowd. "LJ said they saved us some burgers, but he won't be able to beat off the marauding horde for much longer."

We pushed our way through the sea of people. A pair of arms wrapped around me and I jumped, my head whipping around.

Reece smiled back at me. My heart raced even faster and I held on to his arms as everyone gave him a wide berth to make our way to the back of the house. "You almost missed the food. I thought you'd left." He tightened his arms around me.

"Marisa took me upstairs to get some of 'the good stuff.'" I did air quotes. The wintry air from the open kitchen door was a welcome reprieve from the packed house.

"You keep stealing his booze during parties and he'll open a tab," Reece called back to Marisa.

"He won't miss it. He's too busy entertaining guests." She lifted her cup in his direction from the bottom of the steps. Pink sweater and her friend had cozied up to him as he shut down the grill.

"Finally! People have been trying to steal these." Berk rounded the grill as LJ's head popped up and his gaze shot to Marisa. He jumped back from the girls like they'd become radioactive.

"Here you are, my lady. Your burger awaits." Berk handed us plates with burgers oozing with loads of cheese.

My stomach growled and rumbled. Even over the ungodly loud party inside, everyone's eyes widened at the kraken awakening in my stomach. Reece let go of me and I took a bite of the burger—juicy and delicious, just like a burger should be. I finished it in record time, leaving Berk in my dust. He threw his burger down onto his plate as I licked the last bit of ketchup off my thumb.

"You really know how to give a guy a complex." He picked up the juicy patty sandwiched within a potato bun and stared at it like it had betrayed him.

"Next time, I'll let you win."

"It's not the same."

I pouted like a kid finding only clothes under the Christmas tree. Sighing, he took another bite.

"Only two more games this season—you ready man?" LJ squeezed Reece's shoulder.

He stiffened beside me. "I'm ready, but my parents are bummed I'll miss Thanksgiving. At least the hotels are usually pretty good about having enough food on hand for a ravenous bunch of football players."

"Thanksgiving in Boston," Berk grumbled.

"The game's in Boston?" My head shot up and I wiped my mouth with a napkin.

Reece's fingers crumpled the edge of his paper plate and he exchanged a look with Berk.

"Why didn't you tell me the game was in Boston?" I turned to face him. Berk rushed off as Reece shot an intense glare at his retreating figure.

He shrugged. "It's not a big deal."

"If it wasn't a big deal, you'd have mentioned it."

"I thought you'd see it on the schedule. It's not like it's a state secret or anything." He shrugged, and I felt a small sting. "We're there for a game and we fly out the next day. It's not like we have time to see anyone or meet up with people." He took a gulp from his cup like he hadn't had a drink in years. His Adam's apple bobbed.

"Did you not tell me to make sure I didn't invite you to meet my family?"

"No." It was the least convincing no in the history of nos. He'd asked me if I'd watch his other games, but he hadn't mentioned this one. I'd thought he figured it was over Thanksgiving and didn't want to put that extra burden on me, but now it seemed he hadn't wanted me to realize he was in Boston.

"I met your family." Maybe I had been wrong. We weren't dating. We were sleeping together, killing our time until we both left. I'd known that was the case but had thought maybe things had changed over the past week or so. The stinging pain spread, seeping deeper into my heart.

"It wasn't planned."

"So if your mom hadn't spotted us on the bridge, you wouldn't have had me meet her?" The easy acceptance from Mary and John and the rest of the family felt hollower. I'd probably never see them again.

"Did you plan on meeting my parents? You wanted to have sex with me, put a check next to that line on your list, and move on." He slammed his food down.

"Things changed."

"Yes, they did." He dragged his hands through his hair. "You're a genius, Seph." His shoulders sagged and he peered over at me.

"What does that have to do with anything?"

"Your parents are also crazy smart."

"Again, why would that make you not want to meet them?"

"Because they'll take one look at me and know I'm a jock nowhere near on your level."

Relief washed over me and my lips curved up into a small smile. "You're nervous?" The sadness radiating off him stifled that relief.

"Of course—who wouldn't be?" He stared down at the ground.

I wrapped my arms around him and squeezed him tighter. Damn, he sure knew how to make himself even more endearing and adorable. "You don't need to worry about that. They'll love you." *At least Mom will.* I swallowed past the lump in my throat.

He pulled back and stared into my eyes, running his knuckles along my chin. "Really?"

I breathed past the churning knot. "Really."

I'd flown up to Boston on the ticket my dad had bought me. Of course, it was the earliest ticket in. The sterile quiet of my house didn't make it feel like the home I'd once lived in. It felt like I was a guest even after two days back. I checked the score on my phone. They were heading into the last quarter. The game had started late because of the weather. There'd been a break in the snow, but Reece would be over an hour late as it was.

"Persephone."

I dropped my hand under my desk and turned off the screen so the light didn't give me away.

"Yes, Dad."

He stood in the doorway to my room like a harbinger of

bad memories. "Dinner will be ready in twenty minutes. You should get yourself ready." He looked me up and down, and I had to stop myself from cringing. I kept my chin raised. Apparently my cream tights, navy skirt, and cream sweater weren't a dead giveaway I was ready and had gotten myself together over the last hour. My hair was braided tightly against my head in a way I hadn't done in a while. Never a hair out of place or a stray piece of lint, but no matter what I did, he'd find a reason to pick, to try to make me feel smaller.

"Thank you for letting me know."

"What time will your friend be arriving? We won't be holding dinner for late arrivals."

Why had I wanted Reece to come here and be subjected to my father's withering scrutiny, knowing Reece was already feeling insecure? *Because we don't have much time left.* Every minute we had together was a minute I wanted to hold on to with both hands, but by the time the game was over and he did the press conference thing, it would probably be at least another hour until he arrived.

He was already nervous about meeting my parents; how would he feel if he walked in and we were finishing up Thanksgiving dinner after I invited him? Like he was an intruder barging in. I couldn't do that to him after how amazing his family had been with no notice at all.

My heart squeezed at the idea of cancelling the invitation so late, but it was better he had the hotel Thanksgiving with the rest of the team rather than showing up here, even though I'd been using looking forward to his visit to keep me going since I stepped on the plane.

"Actually, he won't be able to make it. His event is running over and he doesn't want to disturb us." It would be nothing like what he thought a family Thanksgiving should be. His family was probably all crowded in the kitchen, laughing and joking. I'd be lucky if I made it through dinner without frostbite. What had I been thinking? So selfish about wanting to see him that I'd subject him to this? I was so used to it, I'd forgotten what it was really like to be back home.

Dad's lips tightened and the corners turned down.

"I can go help Mom." Closing my book, I set it on the desktop beside me.

"She can handle things on her own. We have a lot to discuss over the meal." He closed the door behind him like he was locking a jail cell.

Had being away for a few months made me forget that my family was nothing like Reece's? That mine wasn't a sitcom version of a family, but the cold shell of what an alien might think a family looked like?

Grabbing my phone, I sent Reece a message. The wood of the steps creaked under my feet as I walked downstairs. My dad's office door was closed and I tiptoed into the kitchen. Mom stood in front of the stove, mashing potatoes in a pot.

"Mom." I touched her arm.

She jumped and turned. Her smile for me was always real, always there, and sometimes it was the only thing I had to cling to for warmth.

"Come to help me?" She bumped me with her hip.

"If you need it."

"I'm sure I can find something for you to do. What time is your friend arriving?" Lifting the pot, she gently trans-ferred the potatoes into a serving bowl.

I cleared my throat. "He can't make it."

Her face fell. "Oh, that's a shame."

"It might be for the best. Aunt Sophie mentioned coming up for Christmas. Has she talked to you at all?"

She froze, spatula in hand, a lump of potatoes on the tip of it. "No, I haven't heard from her."

"It's hard to get past the gatekeeper." I glanced over my shoulder.

She did the same and went back to the potatoes. "You know how your father is once he gets something in his head."

"How did you two even meet? Aunt Sophie said you were a free spirit like her growing up."

Her cheeks pinked up and she set down the pot. Letting out a sigh, she covered the bowl of mashed potatoes in foil and opened the oven. "I was. Your father was my tutor in college. My parents were always trying to get me to settle down. They always wanted me to get serious about my studies so I could find a nice, responsible college boy to marry."

"And that boy was dad?"

"Not at first. Can you cut these for the salad?" She set the cutting board and an assortment of vegetables in front of me. "I was on the verge of academic probation and he was my assigned tutor. I was still dragging your aunt out almost every night." The faraway look in her eye didn't match the bland tone in her voice. Her eyes sparkled while her words told the tale of a girl making every mistake in the book.

"So how did you end up together?" The peppers crunched as I sliced them under my blade.

"My dad died of a heart attack, and I took that to mean life was short. I barely slowed down. I couldn't, because that would mean facing what had happened. Mom kept telling me it was a sign, said I needed to start taking things seriously." She wiped her hands on her apron. "Even Aunt Sophie tried to rein me in, but I didn't listen.

"And then my mom died three months later. That was when I knew it *was* a sign. I was the one Aunt Sophie looked to. I was the big sister. I didn't have a choice. Your father found me crying in the library trying to sort through the life insurance documents and other things I needed to figure out. He sat down with me and handled it all. He was so sure of himself, the even-keeled kind of boy my parents would have approved of, so when he asked me out, I said yes. And the rest, as they say, is history."

"You never told me any of that before."

"Not much to tell. We met in college, got married, and then we had you." She pinched my cheek.

"Do you ever wonder how your life would have turned out if your parents hadn't died?"

She stopped in front of the oven with a tray of rolls midway out. "I try not to." Shaking her head, she quietly closed the oven door and gave me a small smile that didn't reach her eyes.

My fingers tightened around the handle of the knife. "Do you think I should go to Harvard?" I let it out in one breath, keeping my voice low.

The spoon she'd been stirring the pot of gravy with rattled against the edge. "You're thinking of staying in Philadelphia?" She shot a glance over her shoulder.

"I've been trying to make a decision."

"Does your father know?"

I snorted and peered over at her.

"Of course not." She wiped her hands on her apron. "Well, you know your own mind better than anyone else." Leaning in, she wrapped her arms around me and squeezed me like it might be her last chance. I held on to her tightly, resting my head on her shoulder.

Mom poured wine into the glasses in front of her.

The doorbell rang and my head shot up right alongside Mom's. My phone, which was in my pocket, hadn't buzzed since I'd come down. I sent up a silent prayer. *Please tell me Reece got my message.* Maybe this was someone whose car had broken down on their way to their own warm family Thanksgiving. *Just please not Reece.*

23

REECE

S tanding on her doorstep, I rang the bell. The guys had thought I was crazy when I'd told them where I was going, Reece Michaels pulling a *Meet the Parents* without a gun to his head, but they hadn't had to look into her eyes when she found out I hadn't told her we'd be only a few miles apart today. It was a barb straight to the heart. I'd have to suck up my fears about not measuring up and do this for her.

On the bus ride into the city, I felt like I should have been cramming for a big exam. What was I supposed to say to the parents of a genius like Seph? How many seconds would it take for them to realize she was way out of my league?

My level of concentration during the game had been absolute shit, and Coach's growl had shot straight across the field, his face a heart attack-inducing crimson as he'd stood with his hands on his hips.

I'd dropped my head and jogged off the field.

He'd stalked right over to me and grabbed me by my facemask. Shaking the white bars in front of my face, he'd *thunked* the top of my helmet. The vibrations had gone straight through my skull.

"What in the hell are you doing out there?" His voice had been low and level.

"Sorry, Coach." I'd dropped the ball—again. Unsnapping the chin strap of my helmet, I'd tugged it off my head. The warm sweat warred with the freezing air and they'd fought it out on the tips of my ears.

"Do you know how many scouts are here watching you tonight and you pull something like that?" He'd jabbed his finger out toward the field where I'd lost all ability to perform.

"A lot."

"You're damn right it's a lot. Are you sick or something?" Concern had shone in his eyes.

Standing out in the middle of the field with the eyes of thousands of screaming fans and rival fans on me, scouts taking notes about my every move, I hadn't been fazed. However, knowing I'd be sitting in Seph's family's house in less than a couple of hours meant the spikes of anxiety hadn't stopped.

I'd tugged at the neck of my jersey, shifting my pads on my shoulders, the newly exposed skin tightening in the freezing weather. I couldn't wait for the pros where the sidelines were dotted with heat cannons to keep players from freezing their balls off in the winter.

It had been two days since I'd seen Seph. How had she so quickly become someone I looked forward to seeing almost every day? We'd fallen into a routine of almost daily meet-ups without even realizing it. I wiped my hands on the legs of my pants and bounced in the cold Boston air. Tiny flurries drifted down from the sky.

I'd have to be on my best behavior at her house, but I'd

still get to see her, and that was good enough to tide me over until Sunday when her flight landed.

The second the post-game press conference had finished, I'd bolted with my button-down, sweater, and ironed pants. My black shoes were shined and I'd jammed my hands into the pockets of my slacks, waiting for the door to open.

All the other doors on the street were red, blue, and some even yellow. Decorative wreaths made of fall leaves or other seasonal decorations dotted each one, their shutters painted to match, or sometimes covered in designs. Seph's house had black slatted shutters, no flower boxes or wreath.

Inside my pocket, I wrapped my fingers around the gift I'd gotten her. It wasn't Christmas yet, but there didn't have to be a reason to get someone something special. She deserved it, and she needed it. There were only so many ways I could tell her she wasn't like anyone else I'd ever met. She needed to believe that.

The doorknob turned and Seph's head popped out. Her eyes widened and she glanced over her shoulder.

The happiness I'd thought I'd see on her face when I showed up wasn't even close to the look she gave me. This expression verged on fear. Stepping outside, she pulled the door behind her, leaving only a gap.

"What are you doing here? Didn't you get my message?"

"Yeah, I saw it. Did you think I'd chicken out or something?" I searched her face for clues about what had changed between yesterday and today. "I wanted to spend Thanksgiving with you."

The tightness in her shoulders relaxed and her lips parted.

"Persephone, who is it?" A loud voice came from behind her then the door opened fully.

Her back went straight and she sucked in a sharp breath. She darted a look over her shoulder, and her jaw tightened.

"Dad, this is Reece." Her words were tight and brittle like they might crack at any moment. "The friend I invited to dinner."

"I thought you said he couldn't make it in time."

"His plans changed." Each of her words was like a carefully plotted course. She stepped back into the house, her father backing up, giving me enough room to enter.

I stepped inside the townhouse's dark brown door. Some of the food was already out on the table. I glanced at Seph.

Her head dipped. "Sorry, when the game went into overtime, I knew you'd be late. I didn't want you to rush to get here." Her hands were clasped in front of her.

"We value punctuality greatly in this family." Her dad stood behind Seph like four hundred pound linebacker out for blood.

"I apologize for my lateness." I stepped forward and extended my hand. "I'm Reece Michaels. I had a game that ran late."

He stared down at my hand like I'd offered him an old shoe before begrudgingly shaking it. "Dr. Alexander. So you're an athlete?"

"I'm a football player."

I hadn't thought the deep set of his frown could get any lower, but it did then. He looked like one of the grumpy Muppets from the balcony.

"I see."

A door swung open and a woman came through the doorway between the living room and the dining room. She was an older version of Seph.

"You must be Reece. It's so nice to meet you." She held out her hand and shook mine. "I'm Helen."

"Nice to meet you, Helen."

"Let me get your coat."

I unbuttoned it and handed it over to her. She stashed it in the closet beside the front door. The entire time, Seph stood there with her hands clasped in front of her like she was a cadet in etiquette school.

Her father spun on his heels and disappeared from the room.

Only then did Seph reanimate, lifting her head and looking at me.

"The next course is almost ready. I can put some of it on your plate, if you'd like." Her mom wiped her hands on the spotless apron wrapped around her waist.

"I'm sure there's more than enough food coming. It smells wonderful."

Helen's cheeks pinked up and she nodded, heading back into the kitchen.

I took Seph's hand and threaded my fingers through hers, the soft warmth of her hand melting the winter chill I'd felt being away from her for the past few days. "What's up with you? Are you okay?" I needed to soak up as much of her as I could, but she was so jumpy.

Her gaze darted to the open doorway. "I want to apologize in advance." She nibbled on her bottom lip.

"Stop, or you won't have any left." I smoothed my thumb across her lip. "I'll be fine. How bad can it get?"

"Persephone," her dad called from the other room. Her entire body went rigid and she squeezed my hand before relaxing.

"You're right. Let's get in there."

We sat at the table, and the ticking hands of the clock made the only sounds other than silverware clinking against plates. Every sound was amplified by the fact that no one spoke. Each wipe of my mouth with the cloth napkin on my lap sounded like I was shattering glass against the wall.

Even I jumped at the shrill ping of someone's phone. Everyone stopped.

Her dad picked up his phone and shoved back his chair. "I need to take this."

"Arthur..." Her mom glanced to me, her dad shot her a look, and she clammed up. *What the hell is going on?* As he left the room, it felt like the air flowed back in.

Seph and her mom were no longer as careful with every movement and every word. A sinking pit formed in my stomach as the pieces of what was going on fell into place. I wanted to be wrong. *Please let me be wrong, because if I'm right, I'm not going to be able to stop myself from kicking Dr. Alexander's ass.*

"Reece, tell me more about yourself." Her mom leaned forward.

"I'm a senior and a football player."

"He's entering the draft. He'll be a professional player, and he's been instrumental in getting our team to the championship." Seph's pride made my heart swell. She wasn't embarrassed by me. She was proud of me, and I didn't take that lightly.

"There are other people on the team too. It's a group effort. Everyone's worked really hard to get us to this point."

"That's wonderful that you're all doing so well."

My phone vibrated in my pocket. I took it out to silence it.

"Who is it?" Seph leaned over.

"It's my dad." I moved to turn off the ringer.

"Please take the call. It's your dad and it's Thanksgiving. I'm sure he wants to make sure you're okay." Helen shooed me from the table.

I smiled at her and got up from my chair, walking into the living room.

"Hey, Dad. What's up?"

"How are you?" It was the question he asked after every game. He'd know if he watched even one.

"I'm fine."

"No hard hits out there?"

"Nope, not one. I did drop a pass though."

"Why? What happened? Is something wrong with your hands?" His voice was part worried, part hopeful.

"I had a lot on my mind and my head wasn't in the game. It's nothing."

"It's quiet for a team Thanksgiving dinner."

"I'm not with the team. I'm at Seph's house." Staring out the window, I watched more flurries float down, a barely there layer coating the ground.

He made a knowing and pleased humming sound. "Pretty serious."

"She invited me and since I was in town anyway, it would have been rude to turn her down." A few people walked down the street and knocked on the door of the house opposite Seph's. Someone threw the door open and tugged the other person into their arms, their laughter filling the air. I wanted to hold my hands up to the warmth of their embrace. A little different from what I'd been greeted with at the Alexander house.

The call was quiet, the background noise of Mom and Ethan arguing over the next movie and the sound of the TV filtering through the speaker. "I'm glad you're safe. We'll miss you today."

"I miss you guys too."

He cleared his throat. "Your mom wants to talk to you."

"Save me a piece of fudge pie," I called out, trying to catch him before he handed over the phone. There was no way Mom, Ethan, or Becca would save me a piece if I left it up to them.

Their muffled voices and a scratching sound filled my ear, like he had the phone pressed against his chest.

"You're with Seph at her parents' house!" My mom's squeal nearly blew out my eardrums.

"Jesus, Mom. I don't think they heard you across the entire tri-state area."

"Here I was worried you'd be missing us for Thanksgiving, but you're with Seph. I'm sure we're the last thing on your mind."

"Of course I miss you guys."

"Aww, we miss you too, but that's not enough to butter me up to save you a piece of fudge pie—although I will set one aside for Seph."

"That's mean." I laughed and turned, my muscles tensing at the figure in the doorway.

"Now you've got an incentive to bring her by again. Maybe she'll share her piece with you."

Seph's dad gave me a disapproving look. I swore it was the only expression he had. "The next course will be ready shortly."

"I'll be right there, just wishing my family a happy Thanksgiving."

He gave a curt nod and disappeared from the room. Mr. Sunshine and Happiness over there. It was a wonder Seph could speak to anyone at all. If her mom hadn't been around, Seph would have been like those lab monkeys raised without human affection or comfort.

"We're eating soon, Mom. I've got to go."

"Love you, sweetie. Great game." At least Mom checked

the scores, although they didn't watch the games. "We'll see you soon." Her voice pitched up at the end.

"Yes, I'll stop by soon. Love you."

Ending the call, I walked back into the dining room. Seph sat with her back so straight and pressed flush against the chair. She looked a lot like she had the first time I'd seen her, not a hair out of place.

I dropped my hand onto her shoulder. She jumped and her head snapped up, eyes softening when she saw me. I ran my thumb over her wool sweater.

"Is everything okay?" she asked.

"Of course. My dad was checking in on me like always, and they wanted to tease me about eating all the fudge pie."

"It was so good." She got the dreamy look in her eye that everyone got when remembering the dark, rich flavor.

"She said she'd save you a piece for the next time you came by."

Seph's head jerked back a little. "Am I going by again?"

"We're not leaving a piece of pie unclaimed. Yeah, we'll go." I bumped my shoulder against hers and she smiled at me. Lifting her hand, I threaded my fingers through hers. Her pulse jumped wildly under my touch.

The door from the kitchen pushed open and her mom stepped through with two dishes in her oven mitt-covered hands.

Seph released my hand and scooted her chair back. "Mom, you were supposed to let me help you." She jumped up and grabbed one of the dishes from her mom's hand, slipping the mitt onto hers.

I stood and moved the wine glasses to give her a landing pad for the piping hot dishes.

"There are plenty of other dishes to bring out."

"How can I help?"

Her mom smiled at me and the corners of her eyes crinkled. She looked so much like Seph. Other than the small streaks of gray in her hair, it wouldn't be hard to imagine her as Seph's older sister.

"Can you open the bottles of wine on the table? There's a corkscrew on the bar cart in the corner."

"On it."

The two of them disappeared into the kitchen and I grabbed the corkscrew. Twisting it down into the cork, I popped open the bottle of white wine. It was one I'd seen in Nix's parents' wine cellar, which meant it couldn't have been cheap. I opened the other bottle and set them both on the table.

"Persephone is quite an exceptional talent."

I winced, the muscles in my body tightening. Was he a freaking vampire or something? What was with sneaking up on people like this?

"She is. I've never met anyone like her before."

"And you never will. Her potential for growth is above and beyond what she's already accomplished." He lifted the bottle of red and poured a small bit into the glass, swirling it around.

"I'd say she's already accomplished a lot."

He shot me a look over the top of the glass. "She can do more. She can do better."

My teeth clenched tightly and my hands tightened on the back of the chair in front of me. "She's always trying her best. I've never met anyone who works harder."

He made a noise in the back of his throat.

The kitchen door swung open and Seph and her mom walked in, pausing for a second when they spotted her dad and me in our mini standoff.

I plastered a smile on my face. "Let me help with those."

Her dad didn't make a move to help, just sat in his chair at the head of the table and scrutinized every move everyone in the room made. Once all the food was out, Seph sat beside me and I took her hand under the table, running my fingers over her knuckles.

"I'm glad you came." She placed her hand on top of mine.

"I'm glad you invited me." Even if only to be there to run interference for a little bit. Her hesitancy about coming back for Thanksgiving and about moving back to Boston permanently made so much more sense now. She didn't think I wasn't good enough; she was terrified of her asshole father. With each passing minute, it got harder and harder to hold my tongue. He was still her dad, and knocking him out on Thanksgiving Day probably wasn't what she needed right then, even though I was jonesing to do just that.

I'd do whatever I needed to in order to prove to Seph that she didn't need to prove herself to anyone, least of all the pompous asshole at the end of the table. *Do this for Seph. Just get through the night.*

I laughed and rested my hand on Reece's arm. My mom struggled with the overly large platter of sliced meat. He and I both rose out of our seats to help her, and my hand knocked into an object right in front of me. The white wine glass teetered on its edge and crashed down onto the table.

The wine sprayed all over everything. Reece laughed. "Wild Child strikes again."

I laughed along with him; wine glasses and I did have a rather terrible track record. Then it registered that we were the only ones laughing. I wasn't at his parents' house or at the Brothel. I was home. Every muscle in my body tightened and I cringed, grabbing a napkin.

"Persephone Elizabeth Alexander, it seems your time away has made you careless. Can't you see what a mess you've made? You invite this *friend*"—the word was a sneer with disdain dripping from his lips—"and have lost all sense of how you should behave."

He pointed at the alcohol pooled on the dark wooden table like I'd gotten out a can of spray paint and tagged it.

The carefree air that had invaded the house was quickly suppressed. I'd forgotten where I was.

"Get a towel." He slammed his hand down on the table and the glasses rattled.

"Arthur, it's—" Mom put her hand on his shoulder, but he shook her off.

Reece's hands balled up in his lap. His jaw was so tight, I swore he'd crack a tooth.

I ran my hand over his. "It's okay. I'll be right back." Hopping up from my seat, I rushed into the kitchen and grabbed a towel from under the sink along with a bottle of disinfectant spray. Raised voices came from the other room. I made it two steps when there was a bang so loud the plates in the china cabinet rattled. Rushing back into the dining room, I saw Reece's seat was empty.

"Where's Reece?" My head whipped back and forth.

My mom opened her mouth. Her eyes darted to the front door.

My father stood at the head of the table with his hands pressed into the wood. "Your friend needed to get some air." He said *friend* like it might as well have been a dirty word and sat back in his chair so hard it shot back a foot.

I dropped the bottle and towel and ran out after him.

"Persephone, get back in here." My father's voice followed after me as I rushed out of the house without even closing the door. Snow crunched under my shoes, and the freezing air sliced right through my sweater. Wrapping my arms around myself, I looked down the street. Panic rose in my chest, barely ebbing as I spotted him halfway down the block.

I called out his name.

He stopped mid-stride. His hands were shoved into his pockets, and he'd left without his coat. Turning, he wore a look of misery so strong I could see it from this far away. It was one I'd worn often, growing up in my house.

"What happened? Why'd you leave?" Like I didn't already know. Like I didn't want to run away down the freezing, dead-quiet street with him.

His gaze darted back toward my house. "I couldn't breathe in there. I needed to get some air." His jaw worked overtime, the muscle and sinew bunching and relaxing.

"My dad can be a bit of a control freak sometimes."

"That's beyond control freak, Seph." He jabbed his finger toward the door.

"It's how he is. He's always been that way." I shivered. Small flakes floated on the air around us; we were in a snow globe with the tiny pieces of ice suspended inside our bubble.

"That doesn't make it right. He shouldn't speak to you that way. No one should."

"I'm used to it." Shrugging, I ran my hands over my arms. "Let's go back inside. You forgot your coat."

His shoes crunched on the newly formed ice patches on the sidewalk. "You shouldn't have to get used to it. That's not how someone who cares about you talks to you. I'll go get our coats and we can go." He grabbed my hand, massaging his fingers along the back of mine.

"I can't leave. My mom's still inside. I haven't gotten to spend much time with her or even talk to her since I left." Dad had been running interference almost like he knew that would get me back there to see her, and it had worked. Abandoning her with my father after leaving unannounced —no, I couldn't do that to my mom. "This is my family."

"Persephone." My father's warning tone sent another shiver through me and my back went straight. My hand slipped from Reece's hold.

Reece stared over my shoulder. His hands bunched in front of him. "Let's go. We can find a place to get some food. You can ride the team bus back with me, or if Coach won't let you, we'll take the train or I'll rent a car. I don't care."

He reached for my hand, but I snatched it back. "I can't leave." Leaving Mom was hard enough during the school year; I couldn't abandon her to having Thanksgiving on her own with him.

"The hell you can't." His hand touched the back of mine, but I took a mini step away. Hurt flashed in his eyes. "I walked out because I was a split second away from jumping over that table and knocking your dad out. He's an asshole."

"Persephone." I glanced over my shoulder. My dad stood on the front step of our brownstone with his arms across his chest. His gaze locked on the two of us with his disapproving glare set to stun.

"He only wants the best for me." It was the same excuse I'd said over and over on the nights I cried myself to sleep because of him.

"He's the reason you made your list, the reason you feel like you're never good enough." Reece jabbed an angry finger over my shoulder.

"You don't understand, Reece." He didn't. He couldn't know when he had the perfect family. "We don't all get to have a Disney sitcom family."

"My family has their problems too, but I always know they'll be there for me."

"Everyone doesn't get that funny, affectionate group that loves them no matter what. Sometimes things like that come with conditions." He was so lucky. He didn't even realize it. That kind of family was one in a million. Yes, my family was different, but every family was. I wanted to go with him, wanted to say screw it and leave without my coat too, just jump in a cab and go wherever he wanted me to go—but I couldn't.

He shook his head, and the sadness in his eyes brought tears to mine. "But they shouldn't."

"That's not always how it is. Yes, going to Fulton U was my bit of rebellion and so was my list, but this life was never one I thought I'd be able to escape forever. It's not a life I want to escape. You're going to have your big shoot-for-the-stars-life too, and...well, this is mine." Anger bubbled under the surface. He got to do whatever the hell he wanted and answered to no one. Not everyone lived that kind of life. Some of us had people to protect and expectations to fulfill.

He stared up at the sky, a snowflake landing on his cheek, soaking up his warmth and dissolving into him like I wanted to. I wanted to run into the shelter of his arms and never look back. More snow gathered on his lashes and his head dropped, his gaze locked on mine.

My throat tightened at the emotions swimming in his eyes. Resignation? Disappointment? Hurt? Maybe a bit of all three.

"Please, Reece, come back inside. It'll be okay." We didn't have much time left. I wanted to spend this time with him, even if it was under the cloud of my father. We could salvage this. Dad would head into his office not too long after the meal and we could all relax a bit more. It had already been two days without Reece, and that was two days too many. What happened when I wouldn't see him again? My chest tightened, and it was hard to suck in a full breath with Reece in front of me and my dad's oppressive gaze on my back. "Please." I held on tighter to his hand.

"I want to, but I know what'll happen if I go back in there." His jaw clenched. "I can't, Seph."

I nodded, blinking back my tears. "I understand."

"I don't think you do." He shoved his hand into his pocket. "This is for you. I thought I'd save it until Christmas, but I want you to have it now." With his fist wrapped around whatever it was, he placed it in my hand, his warm touch melting away some of the biting cold. He pulled me against him like a final touch standing on a train platform.

Kissing the top of my head, he rested his cheek there for a second before letting me go. I watched him walk away, the stark silence of the street punctuated by my name being called out every few seconds. I stared down the street until Reece's retreating figure disappeared from view.

"Persephone." I jumped at my mom's hand on my shoulder. "Let's get you inside." She draped my coat over my shoulders and spun me around toward the house. Reece was gone. That was what I'd wanted, right? I hadn't even wanted him to come, so why had I burst out the front door and chased him down the block?

Inside the house, she took the coat off and hung it up in the closet right beside where Reece's hung. My nostrils flared and I let out a slow deep breath. *Get ahold of yourself. Calm down. It will be okay. Yes, he left—that's fine. He was going to leave anyway. This is just a little earlier than expected.*

"I'll get you some tea to warm you up." And then she was gone like a ghost in her own house. The perfectly straight picture frames lined the walls, each one of our family looking like a sad Victorian-era transplant. White walls, beige carpet, beige furniture. The walls of the box were closing in with each passing second. *I can totally still breathe just fine in this beige prison. I don't need the distractions anyway. I'll be fine.*

"These are the kinds of friends you make at school down there? And you wonder why we want you back home. You can't be trusted to make important decisions on your own."

He must have kept talking because the drone of his voice and the barbs he slung kept coming, but I couldn't hear him anymore. There was only the pounding of my pulse and the shallow breaths I gulped down.

A thin chain slid out of the death grip I had on what Reece had passed to me. Opening my hand, I stared down at the silver jewelry. A circular pendant lay in the middle of the tangle of the chain. Flipping it over, I sucked in a shuddering breath and read the words: *You are enough.*

They slammed into my head, so hard I was surprised I managed to stay on my feet. And then I did something I'd never done before. I left while my dad was in the middle of one of his diatribes. I grabbed Reece's jacket out of the closet and climbed the stairs two at a time. Closing my door, I sat on the edge of my bed.

With my knees pulled up to my chest, I stared out the window. The snow was picking up even more now. Was he warm? Had he gotten a taxi? They'd be hard to come by on Thanksgiving. How long was it until he left the city? Why hadn't I gone with him?

The gentle knock on the door took me out of my contemplative spiral. Mom poked her head in, holding a tray with a single-serve teapot, milk, and sugar.

"Sorry I didn't get up here sooner. Your father needed a little calming." Her small smile didn't reach her eyes. It almost never did when it came to anything to do with my dad.

"Was it always like this, Mom?"

She put the tray down on my desk and went about making the cup of tea. "Your father has never been a warm man, but brilliant men seldom are."

"Was he like this when you met?"

She turned, and this time the smile did reach her eyes,

but it was still tinged with sadness at the edges. "He was absolutely amazing in classes. He looked so nice in his blazers, and all the girls had crushes on him." Her spoon clinked off the side of the cup. "I was a bit of a wild child at times, like your Aunt Sophie. All the girls wanted his attention, but for some reason, he chose me. It's only natural that you change yourself somewhat for someone you care about." She held out the teacup on a saucer for me.

"But if they care about you, wouldn't they want you to be who you are?"

She tucked a lock of hair behind her ear, a testament to just how frazzled she was. A hair out of place was a massive breach of the Alexander family expectations. "Sometimes they want to make you better." The corners of her lips turned up, but I couldn't even call it a smile. "I need to go clean up downstairs."

"I'll come help."

"No, you enjoy your tea. Let me know when you're finished and I can come get that."

I took a sip of the scalding hot tea. "I'll bring it down."

"No, don't do that. I'll come get it. Your father's still downstairs."

She rearranged the items on the tray.

"I see." Ah, so this was her way of telling me I'd effectively been banished and had to stay in my room. It was like when I was little and they'd send me up without anything to keep me occupied, all the books and paper taken out, my violin locked up. It was the worst thing you could do to a kid with an overactive mind, trap them in a space with nowhere for their energy to go, nowhere for their mind to wander or escape. That had been when I'd started the braiding.

She closed the door behind her, whisper quiet, the same

way she always did everything, never making a sound or disturbing anyone.

Even with the heat turned up, my room felt colder than ever. I expected to see my breath suspended in the air in front of my face. Setting my tea down, I picked up Reece's coat from the edge of the bed. I should have left. Why had I stayed? I didn't want to leave my mom, yes, but more than that, obeying was ingrained in my brain, seared in through years of always doing what was expected of me. Going behind their backs—behind my dad's back—to do anything that went against his vision for who I'd become was simply out of the question.

Putting on Reece's coat, I lay down on my bed, the quilted blanket on top cool against my cheek. I shoved the arms up so my hands were free. Sticking my hand in the pocket, I pulled out his gift.

I stared at the pendant in my palm. The cool metal heated in my hand and I closed my fist around it, holding it up to my mouth. My shoulders shook and I didn't even try to blink back the tears. What would be the point when I'd broken my own heart? The words inscribed on the tiny silver circle were ones I'd never believed, and I didn't know if I could now. *You are enough.* So simple, just three little words.

Was that what he thought of me? There were so many things I'd always felt were lacking, so many ways I'd never measured up. What if he was wrong? What if I wasn't and never would be? That fear ran strong within me, but there was also a smaller thought in the back of my mind: what if he was right?

25

REECE

I slammed my hand into the punching bag in the gym. Icy Hot, sweat, and disinfectant melded together into a smell that only lived in a place where people threw heavy weights every day, but the place was empty now. The heat kicked on, but it wasn't enough to warm the space when it was empty.

Each punch I landed echoed up to the steel beam rafters with peeling white paint above my head. I'd been seconds from laying her dad out. I'd never wanted to slam my fist into someone's face more. The way he spoke to her—how could a father speak to his child like that? My parents and I had our arguments, but every word out of Seph's dad's mouth mouth was yet another dig at her, another thing she was doing wrong in his eyes.

How had she even managed to think she could do *anything* right with someone like that constantly berating and belittling everything she did? Seph was ten times stronger than any guy on my team. Sure, we'd all had coaches yell and shout at us, had them make us run drills until we puked, but it was never because they thought we couldn't do it. They were always trying to build us up. After a couple hours around her dad, I admired that she'd even taken the chance to leave.

My fingers ached and throbbed. I imagined her dad's face at the center of the bag. The flag the ref had thrown the day before when I'd charged one of the defenseman had come when I'd only let out about a tenth of the anger still pounding in my veins.

She'd stood there and let him talk to her like that. Even her mom had looked like she was afraid to make a wrong move. The sometimes embarrassingly, over-the-top way my parents were together didn't seem so embarrassing anymore, and Seph's reaction at their house over a spilled glass made so much more sense now, the way she'd stared at me like the world was about to explode. I wanted to wrap my arms around her and make sure she knew everything would be okay.

What would it have been like, growing up in her parents' house? No wonder she was so cautious and didn't know how to interact with people. How could you when you were worried every second that you might make a mistake?

I didn't care if he was her dad or not, but laying him out wasn't going to win me any points in her book. My dad and I hadn't always seen eye to eye, but there was never a doubt in my mind that he wanted me to be happy. It was why he'd let me play football in the first place after years of giving me a resounding no.

One of the double doors to the gym swung open, creaking like it had never met a can of oil in its life. It banged closed, and I went back to punching—not a smart move considering my whole future rested on keeping my hands protected.

"Want to talk about it?" Nix grabbed the bag, hanging on to it as I landed another five punches.

"Not really." Sweat poured down my face.

"It's either that or fuck up your hands for the game next weekend."

I threw another punch, but he moved the bag out of the way, making me miss and stumble forward. "What the hell, man?"

"You've been unusually quiet since Thanksgiving. You said you were going to Seph's for dinner, ditching the team, and then you're on the bus the next morning looking like you want to bite someone's head off. Meeting the parents didn't go well?"

"No." Using my teeth, I ripped at the Velcro on the base of the boxing glove on my hand. The satisfying rip filled the air. Tucking the glove between my legs, I grabbed the other one, taking it off as well.

"You're going to have to give me more than that."

"Why?" I spun around, throwing my gloves down. "Why do I have to give you anything? You're barely around. You keep disappearing. I'm not the only one with secrets." Grabbing my towel, I clenched my hands around it.

"Mine aren't affecting my game play."

I ran the towel over my face. "Always the perfect player." I threw it down on the bench and brushed past him, knocking into his shoulder. He'd lived the life most people dreamed of. He would get a first-round pick in his sleep and had a legend as his dad, a man who had three championship rings and even more records to his name.

He grabbed my arm and jerked me back. "Fuck you, man. I came here to help you, to let you vent to someone off the field so you don't screw up the future you've been killing yourself for, for how many years? But if you want to be an asshole about it, that's on you."

Spinning on his heel, he stomped away.

"Wait," I called out, and my shoulders sagged as I sat on the workout bench. "Just wait."

He stopped and turned, walking back to me. Dragging a bench press bench over, he sat across from me.

"I'm sorry, okay. I went to Thanksgiving at Seph's house with her parents."

"I take it things didn't go well."

"If you call almost beating her dad's face in and storming out not well, then yeah. It was a clusterfuck."

"What happened?"

"He was being such an asshole, constantly picking her apart. Everything she did was wrong. Every move she made should have been faster or slower. I told you about what happened at my parents' place when she knocked over the glass of wine."

He nodded.

"Man, with the way her dad laid into her when she spilled white wine on the table, I'm surprised she didn't bolt straight from the house."

"That bad, huh?"

I punched my fist into my open palm. "Worse. It was horrible, and I knew if I didn't get out of there, things were going to go sideways. I just left. I stormed out of the house and left her there."

"What were you supposed to do?"

"She ran after me and stared back at me like that was just how it was. I asked her to come with me."

"I take it she didn't."

I shook my head. "No, and I left."

"When it comes to family, stuff gets complicated. You

know that just as well as anyone else. We all have our issues when it comes to family, some worse than others. Some we can outrun, and others we can't." His lips pressed together in a grim line.

"I'm pretty sure she hates me for walking out on her like that." Running my hands over my face, I let out a growl. I should have thrown her over my shoulder and taken her out of there. We could have gone back to my hotel room, taken a shower, had overpriced drinks from the mini bar, and watched movies together. "She probably feels like I abandoned her to her executioner."

"She doesn't." He dropped his hand onto my shoulder.

My eyebrows furrowed. "What makes you say that?"

"Because she'll be here in about two minutes." He cracked a smile. He'd had this up his sleeve this whole time.

I shot up from the bench. "What?"

"She sent me a message and I said I'd help her find you. When I spotted you in here, I told her where you were." He clapped me on the shoulder. "You can thank me later."

"What were you going to do if I'd let you leave before?"

He shrugged. "Let you wallow in your misery a little longer."

I chucked my sweaty towel at his head. "Asshole."

The door to the gym swung open. Seph stepped inside with her hands clasped in front of her against her calf-length coat. She tugged at her thumbs, biting the lips I'd been deprived of for days.

"I'll leave you two to it."

"Thanks," I said absently, my full attention riveted to Seph.

Nix walked out the door, pausing beside her. "Told you I'd find him for you." He threw a look over his shoulder.

"I appreciate it."

He walked out. Her gaze lifted to mine, and she still nibbled on her bottom lip. When she let it loose from between her teeth, it was fuller and glistened in the light. I wanted to run my fingers across it.

Her hair was half up and half down. Her crown of braids was still there, but the gentle waves settled around her shoulders like they had when I'd run my fingers through them, like I wanted to right now.

She stepped forward but stopped halfway across the room like she wanted to be able to make a fast getaway. "I came to say sorry."

I wiped the sweat off my face with a towel. "Why are you sorry, Seph?" It seemed like she'd spent her whole life being sorry and apologizing for shit she didn't need to.

"For Thanksgiving. I shouldn't have invited you in the first place. It was a mistake."

That stung. Like a ninety-yard pass thrown from ten feet away, it slammed straight into my chest. "You didn't want me there?" Why did I sound like a needy little kid who'd been disinvited from a party?

"No." Her voice rang out in the rafters of the gym and she shook her head, taking a step closer. "I wanted to see you. I wanted to spend the holiday with you. I wanted it to be as warm and inviting as when I got to meet your family, but—" Her chin dropped. "My dad doesn't make that easy."

My fists clenched at my sides.

The overhead lights caught the thin silver looped around her neck and disappearing down into her shirt. Moving forward, I lifted my hand and slid it under the chain. The backs of my fingers skimmed along her chest, and she didn't step away.

Running my hand under the metal, I lifted the charm I'd gotten for her out from under her shirt. It was warm in my hand, heated by her skin. "You're wearing it." I stared down at the inscription on it. When I'd seen it, I had picked it up without a second thought. After spending that dinner with her family, I'd realized how much she needed to hear those words.

"I haven't taken it off since you gave it to me." Her words were barely above a whisper.

My throat tightened. I ran my thumb across the inscription. My knuckles brushed against her chest right at the base of her throat.

She swallowed, the hollow of her throat jumping. "It's the best gift I've ever gotten. Thank you." Her hand covered mine, so soft and delicate, long and slender, refined just like her. They contrasted with my rough and overly large ball-catching hands. We were opposite in so many ways, but we fit.

"It's one hundred percent true, all the time."

Her head dipped. My lips ghosted against her forehead as she spoke. "It's hard to believe it when you've never been enough, when no matter how hard you try, you're always lacking." Her whispered words sent that old anger pulsing through my veins, but that came second to making her see the truth.

I tipped her head up and gazed into her eyes. "You're the most amazing person I've ever met."

She rested her hands on my chest, her thumbs tracing a small circle over my sweaty shirt, which clung to my body.

"You're just saying that because I'm the only person you've ever met who put out an ad for sex." She tilted her head to the side, and the corner of her mouth lifted.

"You're right there. I can't imagine I'll run into someone else like that in my life." I tucked a strand of hair behind her ear and cupped her cheek.

What would have happened if I'd been five minutes late? If Coach had set up the meeting at another coffee shop or the PR person had been five minutes early? I swallowed past the anvil-sized lump in my throat. She was the first thing I thought about in the morning and the last thing on my mind as I closed my eyes, hoping my dreams would be filled with her addictive kisses and gentle touch.

The fall was long and hard, so hard I'd have bruises on my knees for months, but she was still leaving at the end of the school year. The time we had left ticked away second by second. I captured her lips with mine instead of saying the words that threatened to make a break for the surface: *I'm in love with you.*

Her hands tightened on my shirt, pulling me in closer, not wanting to break our connection. Coming up for air, we both stood in the middle of the weight room, panting.

"I'm a sweaty, disgusting mess. Give me three minutes and I'll take a shower then we can head to my place."

A small smile curved her lips. "I'll be waiting."

26

SEPH

We burst through the door of his house, and Berk shot forward with an eyebrow lifted. Reece took the steps two at a time, tugging me behind him.

"Hi, Berk! Bye, Berk!" I managed to squeeze the words out before he disappeared from view as we made it to the top of the staircase.

"Have fun, you two crazy kids," he shouted from downstairs.

Reece threw open his door and pulled me inside. The lock had barely clicked before his hands were on me, sinking into my hair, the carefully done braid unraveling as his fingers sank into my scalp, raking across the sensitive skin. His mouth marked its scalding touch on my skin and my body vibrated with desire.

"I missed you." His fingers toyed with the end of my braid. Working like he had all the time in the world and my body wasn't about to combust from his touch, he loosened my hair. Strands fell in front of my face, covering my eyes like a curtain. His gentle touch did just as much to me as the rough pads of his fingers scraping across my skin.

He gripped the hair at the base of my neck and stared down into my eyes. My hair fell around my face, newly loose from the crisscross braid I'd put it in. "I like watching you come undone." He slipped his hand under my chin and kissed my lips until they were throbbing and swollen. The TV volume increased downstairs, vibrating the floor.

"I think Berk is feeling a little resentful." He laughed against my lips and pulled me away from the door to the bed.

Sinking to my knees, I unbuttoned his jeans. He eyed me from the bed like I was a burglar asking to hold his wallet. He lifted his hips and I dragged them down his legs. His cock sprung up, tapping against his stomach.

I hadn't seen it this up close and personal before. The light from outside came through the slatted blinds. I ran my hand up and down his length, spreading the pre-cum collecting on his thick mushroom tip. His fingers sank into the bedspread. It bunched under his hold and he sucked in a breath.

Reveling in the silky smooth feel of his skin and the reaction to my every move, I leaned in closer.

"Seph." My name was a hoarse whisper that spoke of his restraint and closeness to his breaking point. My head swam with the power and pleasure bouncing between us.

"Don't worry, I've read up on this a bunch."

He barked out a laugh. "I can only hope this ends up better than our pool adventure." His last word was cut off as I wrapped my lips around the tip and swirled my tongue around the base of the head.

He groaned and his head shot back. "Fuck, you could have warned me." His body shuddered.

Breathing through my nose, I swallowed more of him. My mouth stretched to the max to take all of him. I'd missed him too. The springtime smell of his skin fresh from the shower brushed against the side of my face. He shot forward, hunched over. Curled over on top of me, his chest brushing against the top of my head, he sank his fingers into my hair, pulling at the roots each time I swiped my tongue across the crown of his dick. His hard length pulsed against my tongue.

His raspy groans sent shivers down my spine. "Stop, Seph."

But I didn't want to stop. The silky smoothness of his shaft, coupled with the urgency of his fingers in my scalp, made me feel like I was flying. My pussy clenched with each tug on my hair.

"I'm going to come." His harsh whisper made my stomach flip.

Tightening my lips, I hollowed my cheeks and sank as deep as I could. He yelled and his dick pulsed in my mouth. Ropes of cum spilled down my throat and I swallowed all of him.

Slowly, he lifted my head away from his dick. The tip came free from my mouth with a pop and he shivered. His panting breaths joined the sounds of my deep inhalations.

"Was that seriously your first time?" His eyes were wide as his chest rose and fell. He kept his hands on my cheeks, holding the sides of my face.

Worry crept into the back of my mind. "I told you I read up on it. It was okay, right?"

He held my chin between his fingers and lifted my face toward him. "If you think that was just okay, next time you might blow my brain out the back of my skull." His lips met mine in a soft, almost reverent way.

My hands ran along his legs. His muscles bunched under my touch. Wrapping his arms around me, he lifted me from the floor and pulled me up onto the bed beside him, never letting his lips leave mine. He delved between my parted lips, stealing away a little bit more of my breath until he was the air I needed.

His hands worked feverishly, lifting my shirt up and over my head and dragging my pants down off my legs like they were on fire.

"I've been dreaming of you every night, and if I'm still dreaming, I don't want to wake up. I need you." That was the only warning I got. He knelt on the bed. The heavy weight of his erect cock jutted out in front of him. His recovery time was nothing short of spectacular based on what I'd read. Staring down at my body, his eyes raked over me.

"I need you too. More than my next breath, I need to feel you."

Exposed and open to him, I'd never felt more alive. He spread my legs, letting my knees fall open. Parting my pussy with his fingers, he pressed a kiss against my clit and sucked it into his mouth. Pulsing electric pleasure shot through my body. My back arched off the bed and I yelped. Painting my pussy with his tongue, he slipped it inside me. I smacked my hand down on the bed beside me. My orgasms slammed into me in rapid succession.

"It's unfair how good you taste, Wild Child. Making me choose between eating you out all night and watching you ride me is almost too cruel." He grabbed a condom out of the pocket of his jeans and ripped it open with his teeth. Rolling it down his length, he hooked my legs behind the knees and rested them on his shoulders. "But I've got to have you now."

He ran his dick along my soaking wet opening, teasing

me with a gentle tap of his head against my clit. I grabbed a fistful of blankets under me. Moving closer on his knees, he plunged into me, one long, slow, forward movement, stretching me with every inch.

With my legs over his shoulders, I was impossibly open to him. His half stroke seemed to never end until the fronts of his thighs settled against the backs of mine. I writhed against him, gasping and sucking in short breaths against his delicious invasion.

He dropped his head, nearly resting it on mine. I'd never thought being twisted up like a pretzel could feel so good.

"You okay?" He swallowed and stared into my eyes, the connection between us tugging me forward like a string was lassoed around my heart.

I nodded. No way were any intelligible sounds coming out of my mouth at this point.

"Good, because I want you to come on my dick so I can make you come again." Leaning in farther, pushing himself deeper than before, he kissed the tip of my nose before beginning his retreat. My walls clamped around him, not wanting him to leave, slow and steady strokes with both of our gazes locked on the apex of my thighs where we were joined together.

"More, Reece. Give me more."

He looked up at me, his eyebrows furrowed in deep concentration. Holding on to my knees, he slammed his hips into me.

I screamed—at least I was pretty sure I did. The windows rattled. He did it again and again, each stroke bottoming out and hurtling me toward the edge of the orgasm I'd been balancing on. My toes curled and I slammed my heels into his back. The orgasm rushed at me like a charging bull, and if I hadn't already been on my back,

I'd have been flat on my ass. I smacked my hands down on the bed, trying to hold on as Reece fucked me harder. My fingers tightened around the sheets and I took them with me as his never-ending advance stole my breath away. The headboard banged against my head and my hips shot off the mattress as he tapped on my clit in time to his thrusts.

The second brutal climax ripped through me, my muscles tightening like I was attached to a live wire. My walls clamped around him. He shouted, his fingers digging into my thighs. His cock expanded in the latex prison, triggering another orgasm that had me banging my hands against the headboard. My eyes fluttered closed and I tried to remember my own name. The warm cocoon of my orgasm and Reece's body made my skin hum.

Falling forward, he caged me under him. He peppered my face with sweaty, half-delirious kisses. "Did I already tell you I missed you?"

"At least once." I ran my hand along the back of his neck. Sweat clung to the hair there. "I got you all sweaty after your shower."

"Any time, Wild Child. Any time at all." He grinned at me.

I pulled him in for another kiss. I hadn't had a thing to drink, but I was definitely drunk on him, and I was more than happy to drink in as much of him as I needed for as long as I could, for forever. My heart stuttered. What if we couldn't have forever? He had been clear about what this was and what it wasn't. He'd be drafted at the end of the year—what then? Even if I stayed, that didn't mean he could.

He hopped off the bed and got rid of the condom before diving back in beside me.

The TV noises from downstairs transformed into a

thumping bass that vibrated the bed. Voices sounded in the hallway.

"Were you supposed to be having a party today?" I propped my head up on my hand.

He threw his arm over his face. "No, but that doesn't mean there isn't one going on downstairs. We don't have to join in. I'll lock the door and they'll leave us alone."

"You don't want to go?" I didn't want him to miss out on a party because of me. I wanted to go down there, but the old insecurities came creeping back, the ones that snuck in whenever we were around people he knew. Would they look at us and ask how the hell it had happened? Would there be looks and snickers? Should I suck it up and go out there anyway? I thought I should add it to my list; then I could feel accomplished for doing it and give myself the excuse to not give a shit what anyone else thought. "We can go, if you want. I haven't been to many parties—scratch that, *any* parties other than the last one you had here."

He set up in bed and gawked at me. "Ever? The grilling we did in the backyard was the first party you'd ever been to?" His eyebrows shot up.

I nodded. "I don't count academic mixers with people almost forty years older than me as parties, per se."

"What about your birthday parties?"

"I never had any. It wasn't like I had friends to invite. My mom would make my favorite meal and sometimes a cupcake, but that was it." I lifted the sheets over my chest, feeling even more naked than in just the physical aspect. The kids on the street always tied balloons around their mailboxes or taped them to their front doors whenever there was a party. I'd sit on the wingback chair in the living room, my knees sinking into the hard leather cushions as I watched them stream in and out of the houses, laughing, playing, and chasing each other.

Reece pounced, caging me under him. "You've never had a birthday party?" He said it like I'd told him I'd never breathed air.

I shrugged. "They weren't really a priority in the Alexander household." I parroted back my dad's words.

He pulled the sheets off me. "Then we're getting in all the partying we can. Come on, Wild Child. Get dressed." Scooping our clothes up off the floor, he piled them onto the bed. I leaned back on the mattress and watched him. His tanned, muscled ass disappeared under the dark blue denim. *Damn shame.*

Glancing over his shoulder, he stared back at me with his jeans unbuttoned. "Is there something on my jeans?" He spun in a circle, trying to check out his own butt.

I held back my laugh, smiling wide at him. I crawled across the bed and tugged him forward by his belt loops. "No, I was admiring the view. The only better one is when you're taking them off."

He smirked and let me have my way with him, stepping to the edge of the bed. Rising up onto my knees, I traced my finger along his abs, trailing it down. He caught my wrist and lifted it up, kissing the inside of it.

"Get dressed. I'm showing you off." He pressed my shirt and pants against my chest.

"I don't really think these are showing-off clothes." I dangled them in front of my face.

"That's what you think." He grinned and tugged his t-shirt over his head.

I shook out my clothes, trying to find the one missing piece. "Where are my underwear?"

"Wouldn't you like to know?" He winked and tapped his naked wrist. "Chop, chop."

27

REECE

S printing as fast as I could, I made it away from the line of scrimmage. There were two seconds left on the clock. Nix's head whipped back and forth, looking for a way to end this. We were down by three. I jumped up, waving my arms in the air as I streaked down the field.

Keyton, a couple yards ahead of me on the other end of the field, had half the number of defenders on his heels. Nix's gaze locked with mine. Linemen rushed at me and I raised my arms, waving them to my left. *Pass to Keyton! He's wide open!* Nix shook his head and launched it at me.

The ball sailed through the air. The stadium was dead silent, thousands of people on their feet and not a sound in the entire place. It would have almost been eerie if the blood pounding in my ears hadn't been such a roar. The ball flew through the fingers of the defender, nearly knocking me off my feet. I recovered, spinning backward and dodging another defender, and the ball slammed into my chest with a satisfying smack.

Pushing off the still slick grass on the field, I pumped my

legs. My muscles strained and I ducked around one block. Spinning around another, I shifted, changing directions, and sprinted into the end zone. The silence of the crowd transformed into an ear-splitting rumble that shook the ground beneath my feet.

The entire team crowded around me, piling on top of one another. Keyton jogged over, his smile wide even under his helmet.

"I tried to get that one to you." I slapped him on the shoulder pads.

He smiled wider and shrugged. "Don't worry about it. A win's a win."

We rushed off the field, the fans chanting my name. This was what I'd always wanted, but on this night, something was missing.

"Two more games!" The voices and screams bounced off the closed tunnel walls on the way to the locker room as I followed the rest of my teammates toward the door. I wanted everything ready for Seph's surprise. She had tutoring to do tonight but had promised she'd make it to one last game before the season ended. There was a ticket at the will call office with her name on it.

"Michaels, what are you doing?" Coach stared at me like I'd grown a second head.

My eyebrows scrunched down.

"Press conference."

I shook my head. "Right, sorry Coach." I jogged after him. Nix stood at the door of the small conference room already. My leg bounced under the table as the reporters went through their questions.

"It was a good game, a nice team effort. Keyton could have made that touchdown just as easily as I did."

The heads from everyone on either side of me whipped around. A pin drop would have sounded like a bomb going off in the room. I ducked my head and waited for the next question.

"Will you be attending the scout training in the lead-up to the championship?"

"He'll be there." Coach leaned into his mic, the feedback sending a squeal ricocheting in the small space.

We made it through the rest of the press conference with minimal effort from me. The reporters had to ask every question twice. I ran through the checklist in the back of my head. I wanted tonight to be perfect for her. Even more than the night in the pool house, I wanted to do this for her, to show her that it wasn't just me who cared about her. She'd need that when I was gone, when she was gone. There were less than six months until the end of the school year—until we'd have to say goodbye.

I froze in the middle of the locker room and Keyton knocked into me.

He grabbed hold of my shoulder, steadying me. "Hey, man, you okay?"

I nodded, shoving myself out of the temporary paralysis that had taken hold of me. The rest of the locker room buzzed with the energy that always came after a game, especially a win. What would she do up in Boston? Find some other super genius to date? They'd go over equations and theorems together and laugh at weird math-related inside jokes.

Or maybe she'd hook up with someone who played in an orchestra and they'd create music together. The ticking clock only got louder the more time I spent with her, and I didn't know how to slow it down. Sometimes I'd wake up at night, run my fingers through her waves, and watch her sleep until it got too hard to breathe. Then I'd have to slam my eyes shut and let her steady breaths calm me.

"Why are you so quiet? The press conference wasn't that bad." Nix sat beside me and rubbed a towel against his hair. "Nervous about tonight?" He tugged his shirt over his head.

I nodded. Better that than let everything running through my head explode all over him. "I think she'll like it."

"Of course she will. If you haven't already noticed, she's really into you. If you planned a sock puppet show, she'd be into it." He laughed and grabbed his stuff.

All my worries about her getting too attached and I was the one finding it hard to catch my breath when I thought about never seeing her again. Getting out of there, I texted the guys to make sure everything was ready.

Jogging up the steps to her apartment, I tried to calm the nerves ricocheting in my stomach. I knocked on the door and bounced from one foot to the other.

Dan opened the door and let me inside. He seemed like a nice enough guy, but based on the tight-lipped responses from Seph, things hadn't thawed out between her and her roommate.

Reece pulled up in front of his house. The street was quiet. Finals, studying, and the weather had finally driven everyone indoors to hibernate.

"I hope you left room for dessert."

He picked up my hand off the center console and laced his fingers through mine, kissing the back of it. The way his lips danced on my skin sent a zing up my spine. He stared into my eyes, the light from the street catching the green and brown swirl of his. Dropping my arms to my sides, I curled my fingers into the sides of my leg to pinch myself.

He ran his hand down my arm and held on to my wrist, bringing it up to his mouth. His lips pressed into the thin skin there, sending my pulse through the roof. He dropped another kiss onto my open palm and I covered his hand with mine. If this was a dream, I didn't want to wake up.

He was all mischief and sweetness, like a candy holding a yummy surprise.

"What's up with you tonight?"

"Nothing." His grin widened, and I had no doubt in my

mind he was up to something. "Let me get the door for you." Inside the silence of his car, I tried to figure out how I'd gotten here. He jogged in front of the vehicle. His button-down shirt fit him perfectly, like it had been tailored. The sleeves were rolled up to his elbows, and his jeans hugged his trim waist and strong thighs.

The December air was crisp and freezing. Every time I stepped outside, it felt like I was attempting a polar plunge.

Closing his car door, he grinned over at me. "What?"

We climbed the steps to the porch. The house was totally dark. "Are we home alone?" My stomach flipped. With him living with three other guys, it wasn't often we had the house to ourselves, and my apartment wasn't exactly the most inviting.

He threw a look over his shoulder. "I love the way you think."

The L word made my heart race. He wasn't saying it for real, but if I mentally squinted a little, I could imagine he had. Slipping his key into the lock, he opened the door and let me walk in first.

Shapes and shadows moved on the other side of the living room and I backed up, wondering if someone had broken in. My pulse raced.

"Surprise!" A chorus of what seemed like a hundred voices all screamed at once and my eyes adjusted to the light. There were at least fifty people inside the house. Rainbow streamers hung from the ceiling. Balloons were taped to the walls and covered the floor. Everyone had on little party hats with elastic straps tucked under their chins.

LJ and Berk stood in the doorway of the kitchen, balancing a huge cake between them. It was a white unicorn with a rainbow mane, and sparklers streamed out of the unicorn's horn. I glanced back at Reece. He wrapped his arms around me from behind and walked me forward, never letting go. Marisa stood beside them with a party blower that curled in and shot out straight with a whistling noise.

"Happy Birthday, Wild Child."

If my heart hadn't already belonged to him, it would have been wrapped up with a bow and presented to him on a rainbow platter at that moment. "But it's not my birthday," I whispered over my shoulder.

"It doesn't matter. You deserve a party." He nipped my earlobe and buried his head in my neck, nuzzling my skin. I laughed, tilting my head to escape his tickle assault.

"Come blow out your candles, Seph. This thing is heavier than it looks." Someone grabbed a lighter and relit some sparklers and the candles along the front. Most of the lights were turned off again. There was a countdown and everyone sang "Happy Birthday" in a mottled mess of a chorus, but I'd never heard anything sweeter. How was I supposed to leave all this at the end of the semester? My first real friends, the first time I felt like I belonged.

Blinking back tears, I blew out a breath and laughed at the *cha, cha, cha* Berk added in at the end of each line. The glow of the candles lit up the room and I took it all in. Everyone was there for me—well, maybe not just me. I was sure when Reece asked people to come to a party, there was no shortage of those wanting to stop by, but still, he'd planned it for me.

Tucking a loose bit of hair behind my ear, I leaned over and closed my eyes. A wish didn't come to mind because I'd already gotten it. I blew out the candles, and the room broke out into applause.

The guys set the cake down on the table and handed the knife to me to make the first cut. Apparently fondant was harder to cut through than it looked. Reece covered my hand with his and helped me cut the first piece, his body against my back. I peered up at everyone around the room, waiting for someone to start asking questions, like *What the hell are you two doing together?* Lifting it out, there were layers of rice crispy treats, chocolate cake, chocolate frosting, and rainbow layers.

"Wow, you went all out for this." I grabbed a fork and took a bite. The chocolate was heavy and rich, so thick I needed a glass of milk.

"Nix got it from that bakery I got the cupcakes from, Bread & Butter."

"Where is Nix?" I craned my neck, scanning the party.

Reece shrugged.

As if on cue, the front door opened and a blast of cold air blew in with the man in question. Nix closed the door behind him, turning off the glowing screen of his phone. He shrugged off his coat before joining the rest of the party.

"Thanks for the cake, Nix." I pulled him in for a hug.

"It was no problem. I got a good deal since my dad's assistant uses them a lot for their charity and corporate events."

Metal clattered to the floor and I turned around. Berk stood a couple feet away, mouth hanging open with his plate teetering in his hand and his fork on the floor. "He gets a hug and I don't? I think I should be offended." He tilted his head to the side dropping his chin to his shoulder with a dramatic sigh, biting his knuckle. The rainbow and unicorn hats everyone else had discarded had been added to Berk's head, so he had a mane of pointy party hats around his face.

"You might want to give him a hug or he might go into full baby meltdown."

"I'm sorry, Berk. Can you ever forgive me?" I held out my arms and he set down his plate, running to me in slow motion. Lifting me in his arms, he spun me around.

"Happy Birthday, Seph. Did you like the unicorn?" He set me down. "That was my suggestion." Of course it was.

"It's the best birthday cake I've ever had."

"You're not just saying that because it's your only one?" Reece took me out of Berk's hold and I rested my hand on his chest.

"No, not because it was my only one. Any other ones I have after this will have a lot to live up to. Thank you everyone. I can't tell you how much this means to me." My throat tightened and I pressed my lips together. I'd lost out on having people like them in my life before, but now that I knew what it felt like to have friends, there was no going back.

"Enough of the sappy stuff. Let's play pin the tail on the donkey. If you miss, you have to take a shot." LJ cupped his hands around his mouth and broadcast the rules and line-up to the party.

"I had to call off The Pink Menace again next door," Nix grumbled and massaged his shoulder.

"You did hit her in the face with your balls." Reece shrugged.

My head shot up.

Nix's mouth thinned into a line of annoyance. He turned to me. "Ball—singular. A football. Not that I only have one ball or something." His cheeks brightened like he'd been on the beach all day and had forgotten sunscreen.

"It was at the beginning of junior year. I apologized a million times."

"Maybe she wants you to do it again." Reece chuckled and his arms tightened around me.

Nix pulled his phone out of his pocket and wandered off.

I wrapped my hands around Reece's arm and buried my face in his shoulder. "So you did have something up your sleeve." Grinning, I pulled him down for a kiss.

He slipped his hand along the back of my neck. "I've got to have some secrets."

"Enough sucking face, you two. You're first up." Berk waved us over.

Someone cranked up the music and everyone dug into the pizzas in the kitchen. A pizza party birthday complete with kids' party games, a delicious cake, and the guy who'd stolen my heart—there hadn't been a better night ever.

Berk chucked a fork at Nix, who looked up from his phone. "Get off your phone, man. You've been glued to that thing since you walked in. You didn't even have any cake."

I cut a piece of cake for Nix, who kept his eye trained on his phone like it might make a break for the door. Walking over to him, I stood in front of him.

His head popped up and I sat beside him, giving him the plate and the fork.

He took the plate from my hand and shoveled a chunk of the cake into his mouth with his eyes still trained on his phone screen.

"Is everything okay?"

His head snapped up and he stared at me. "It's fine. I'm waiting for someone to respond, and I don't want to miss the message."

"Is it someone you're seeing?" I tilted my head and stared at his hands.

He squeezed his thighs just above his knees and one leg bounced up and down. The phone rocked from side to side.

"No, but I'm not her type."

"Does she have a pulse?"

He barked out a laugh and looked at me. Some of the tension in him relaxed.

Nix was crazy handsome in the stereotypical college movie star kind of way. The rest of the guys were more thrown together, Reece included, while Nix was put together. Still, I smelled the hallmarks of the pressure a person is under when they feel they always need to look a certain way. I ran my hand along the herringbone braid draped over my shoulder.

"Last I checked, yes, she does have a pulse." He slipped his phone into his pocket. "And she hates my guts."

"Get your ass in here—it's me and LJ against you and Berk for beer pong." Reece waved him into the dining-room-turned-tournament-zone.

Nix shoved off the couch and walked over to them. "You know he loses on purpose just to drink more."

"I play better when I'm buzzed." Berk downed his cup.

"If they weren't so hot and lovable, they'd be annoyingly obnoxious." Marisa leaned against the wall beside the couch, shaking the ice in her cup.

"You think LJ's hot?" I didn't even try to beat down my creeping smile.

Her eyes got wide and she sputtered. "What? N-No, not him. I meant the other guys." She upended her cup, gulping down the contents.

The crowd of people watching the game cheered, and the satisfying *thunk* of the ball hitting the side of the cup made its way into the living room.

"I mean, I've known him since first grade. He tried to steal my scissors from my table, and I may have stabbed him with them to teach him a lesson. He's still got that scar. We've been best friends since." She shrugged.

"And you followed him to college."

"What? No, I'm only here because of a financial aid situation and this place always finds a way to FU." She shook imaginary pompoms in her hands. "Do you want another drink? Let me get us another drink." Without waiting for a response from me, she plucked my cup from my hand and rushed into the kitchen.

Other people at the party kept wishing me a happy birthday, and I felt the tiniest bit bad for Reece lying to them. But, with the laughter, music, and dancing all around me, the people hanging out and having fun, I didn't think they minded another reason to have a party.

Marisa walked back from the kitchen, balancing two cups and two plates piled high with even more cake. My stomach was near to bursting, but I wasn't going to turn her down.

"Seph, I've got to have you over to my place. You can meet my roommate, Liv. She's awesome. Maybe I can cook you dinner."

"NO!" The shout came from all the guys in the dining room and Marisa jumped, nearly spilling the drinks and the cake. All four rushed to the doorway, shaking their heads and slicing their fingers in front of their throats.

Marisa turned around and they all stared up at the ceiling, whistling before wandering back to their game. She sat beside me and handed over my drink and a plate. Reece caught my eye and mouthed, *Don't do it*.

I laughed into my cup and winced at the straight vodka with a splash of cranberry juice.

"How's the drink? I hope it's strong enough."

"It's totally fine." My words came out half wheeze and

half cough. Reece made another shot and looked over at me. He winked and my stomach flipped. There were five months left until he left or I left or both. How would I get through the day when I knew a man who lit my soul on fire was out there in the world and I'd left him behind? How would I pick up the pieces of my broken heart when he left me?

29

REECE

Snow came down, blanketing the streets, transforming the city grime into a living Christmas card. The campus was quiet now that classes and most exams were over. The shuttles from campus to the airport had been running non-stop as the quad, dorms, and apartments emptied.

"Anyone have socks? I have about eight different sizes and colors and no matches." Berk leaned out of his door, swinging from the doorjamb.

Tugging open my sock drawer, I smiled, grabbing a handful of the neatly paired socks. The great senior year sock war had ended up with the five of us guys, Marisa, her roommate, Liv, and Seph splitting into teams for a battle that saw many casualties, mainly anything breakable in the house and a dented shin when Marisa tripped LJ up the stairs before beaning him with a sock straight to the eye. We'd left our poor Nerf guns behind because we didn't have enough for everyone. A shopping trip was in order. I walked past our stash tucked into a laundry basket in the hallway.

"Next time." Ducking around the corner, I landed next to LJ.

"Here." I threw three pairs at him and he disappeared back into his room. "Next time guard your artillery better."

"We can't all have a tactical expert on our sides," Berk grumbled under his breath, referring to Seph and her wealth of historical knowledge.

I flipped through the stack of freshly washed clothes in my drawers and pulled out what I'd need for the next couple of days. Packing for away games was always a pain in the ass, but as much as I'd fought her, Seph's folding method helped me keep everything organized. She'd even bought me a basket for my laundry so I didn't leave a trail of dirty clothes when I took them to the washer and dryer.

Even studying was easier with her around. The rewards for getting through my work were so much better than the satisfaction of a job well done when her arms were wrapped around my neck. I'd weathered the finals storm and come out mostly unscathed, although it wasn't like anyone cared about my grades as long as I stayed eligible to play. Coach has us doing drills and studying tape, trying to keep us out of trouble now that he owned us 24/7 in the lead-up to the end of the season. When the next semester started, we'd do it as champions or as the team that had fallen short.

It was time for the bus ride to our last game before the championship. I'd miss the guys. There'd be other teams, but not like them. Two more games to cement my future. Sleeping on the bus usually sucked, but I'd do whatever I could to keep myself from focusing too much on the game. Overthinking things led to mistakes, and mistakes lost playoffs.

I shoved my headphones into my duffel as a notification

popped up on my phone. Diving across the bed, I scooped it up and unlocked the screen to read the alert about a sneaker sale at the mall. I flipped to my texts. My last message to Seph from a couple hours ago still showed as unread.

Me: I wish the season was over already. I'm going to miss you.

We hadn't seen each other much since Coach decided he needed to dictate everything in our lives in the week leading up to the game. He'd be riding our asses after this win too. I couldn't even let myself think not winning was a possibility. Two more weeks and the pressure cooker would finally be turned off. Two more weeks to become a first-round draft pick.

"We need to get to the bus in twenty or Coach will skin us alive," LJ called out from across the hall.

"Or maybe just you," Nix shouted. Berk barreled down the steps like a kid chasing after the ice cream truck waving a twenty stolen from his dad's wallet. The front door banged open, sending a blast of winter air blowing up the stairs. I swore I saw snowflakes swirling in the air.

"Close the freaking door, jackass. Wait until we're all down there," Nix shouted after him.

"Okay, very funny. Who wrote this?" Berk called out from the bottom of the steps. "This is the second one I've gotten."

I poked my head out of my bedroom door. "Who wrote what? And second what?"

Berk climbed the steps with a folded piece of purple paper and a green envelope in his hand. His eyes scanned the paper and he tripped on the last step, nearly face-planting on the landing. I reached out for him and grabbed his arm.

"Can you not bust your face open before the game tomorrow? What is that?"

He stared at the piece of paper clutched in his hands like he'd burn a hole through it, laser vision style.

"What is it and why do you think we wrote it?" I tugged on the corner of the colored paper.

He snatched it back. His cheeks were flushed, and it wasn't from the ten seconds out in the cold. Now I had to see what had actually made Berk blush.

"It's—it's a love note." He said the words like they were foreign and he was testing them out on his tongue. "Who's fucking with me?"

"Sounds like someone wants to fuck you if it's a love note."

"A love note?" Nix came out with his duffel over his shoulder. "Let me see." He snatched the paper out of Berk's hand.

Nix's eyes widened and his cheeks reddened as he made his way through the words. Berk grabbed for the paper, but Nix planted his hand in the center of his chest, keeping him back.

"What does it say?" I moved to block Berk and tried to get a look over the top edge of the note.

"Dude, if you think this is a love note, I feel bad for your grandkids when they find your old 'love' letters tucked away in an old hat box in your attic." Nix held it out to me. Berk's hand grabbed for the edges of the paper.

His name was neatly written at the top. Loopy feminine handwriting scrawled across the paper, perfectly straight even though it wasn't lined, detailing the scene they wanted to play out with Berk.

You'd sink between my thighs, slamming your cock into me, and

I'd be so wet for you. My screams would be the only thing to drown out the sound of our bodies slapping against one another. And your groans as you came harder than you ever thought possible.

My eyebrows shot up and my mouth hung open. The rest of the note went into even more detail. The back of my neck heated up. Nix blocked Berk at the top of the steps, not letting him pass.

LJ came out of his room. "You guys ready? I don't need Coach riding my ass about being late." I handed the note to him.

He dropped his duffel and took the paper from my hand with a suspicious look in his eyes. Flattening the paper, he started reading. He made it halfway then sucked in a sharp breath, choking on his own spit.

"Why in the hell would you think one of us wrote this?" LJ waved it in front of Berk, who broke past the Nix blockade and grabbed the note from LJ, then slipped it back into the envelope.

"I was caught off guard. That's all. None of you wrote this, really? Or put someone up to writing it?" He focused on each one of us like he could break us under his scrutiny.

"I don't even want to think about you and some of those words in the same sentence, let alone combine them into a note like that, but this is the Brothel, so we know people have some fucked-up ideas of what happens here."

"You're right. Probably some crazy who's going to try to jump me at the next party." Berk didn't trash the note, though, instead slipping it into his back pocket before he jogged downstairs.

～

I tapped my phone against the side of my leg. Someone behind me snored and probably needed to get a doctor to check that out. There might as well have been a foghorn on the bus, which was filled with the familiar smell of game equipment, convenience store microwaved food, and soda. Most of the guys had headphones on, played on their phones, or tried to sleep. We'd won another one, another step closer to the championship. Just one more game to go, but the win took a back seat.

I stared up the aisle at the highway off-ramp. We'd be back on campus soon. Seph hadn't responded to any of my messages. My leg bounced up and down. She never ghosted on messages. It was always a prompt reply as soon as *Read* appeared below the message, but none of my texts had been read since I'd left on Thursday.

Two days of agony, trying to figure out why she hadn't replied. It wasn't like I could call up her roommate. Had the birthday party been too much? Was she pissed I was traveling so much? The end of the season always got a bit more intense with practices, traveling, and games. I'd make it up to her.

I was tempted to call Marisa and have her check on Seph, but that seemed a little stalkerish. It wasn't like her roommate would leave her dying in the middle of the floor...*would she?*

"Matthews, don't forget the scouts are coming to practice tomorrow." Coach leaned over the seat in front of me on the bus, bracing his hands on the seat backs.

LJ tensed beside me, his hand tightening around his phone. The glow of the screen lit up his face.

Coach's gaze darted to him and his screen. The creases in his forehead deepened. "LJ." His name might as well have been a rival team's from the way Coach said it. "They'll be there by ten. Make sure you're not late." He tugged on the brim of his hat and went back to his seat.

"Think there's any chance he'll get hit by a bus in the next year? If not, I'm screwed when it comes to getting scouted. I ride the bench more than I ride this bus."

"Have you told Marisa about him taking whatever's going on between them out on you?"

He stared at me like I'd lost my mind. "She's got enough to deal with. What am I supposed to say? *Yeah, Risa, I know he abandoned you and your mom when you were little, but how about you get along with him for the sake of my career?*"

"Sounds reasonable."

He looked over at me like I'd suggested he set himself on fire and race around the field to get the scouts' attention.

"You don't know what it's like for her."

"Does she know what it's like for you?" I lifted my chin toward our coach, who was crouched down a few rows up, talking to another one of the seniors. "You have a year left. This is make or break time. If you're not on the field and you're not being seen by scouts, none of this matters, unless you don't want to go pro."

"Of course I do, but she's my best friend."

"And wouldn't a best friend want what's best for you?"

He leaned back in his seat and stared down at his phone. Without another word, he dragged his headphones up onto his head and stared out the window.

This was what happened when you put people ahead of your career. These were the types of hard choices I'd done my best to avoid—until Seph. I dragged my fingers through my hair. I'd never expected her. *Why hasn't she answered? Did something happen to her?* We'd never gone this long without talking.

Ten minutes until we got to campus. I wasn't even stopping at home first. I'd get in my car and go straight to her apartment. What if she needed me and I hadn't been there for her? Shit, I was already a goner and I hadn't even noticed it. I loved her, and that scared the shit out of me, more than I'd even thought possible.

30

SEPH

"We know you can go anywhere you choose, but we'd like you to know the offer for the PhD program still stands. There's a lot of exciting work we're doing here, and we think you'd make a great addition to the team."

The wood-paneled office in the math department didn't make me feel like I was walking into an early grave like some did up in Boston. This room felt full of the history of those who'd come before me, brimming with the possibilities of what I could do in the future. Maybe it was because it was a few hundred miles away from the weight of the expectations and rigid requirements I lived under up there.

"I thank you for your kind words, and I'll have a decision by the beginning of the new semester. Would that be too late?" Once I went home for Christmas break, I'd tell my dad in no uncertain terms: he either did things my way in Boston, or I'd stay in Philadelphia.

Reece was gone for another away game. The last before the championship. It sucked that he was away, but I'd kept track of the score online.

Turning the corner, I slammed into someone. Earth to Seph, pay attention. The two of us were sprawled out on the floor. Lifting my head, I cringed. Graham.

He picked himself up off the floor and offered his hand.

I hesitated.

"Don't worry. I won't bite. You're not the first girl to blow me off and you won't be the last."

Cringing intensifies. "I'm sorry I didn't return your texts." God, I was an asshole.

"You were...busy." His voice is light and not the least bit biting, like I'd braced myself for.

Nodding, I cross my arms over my chest before switching to setting them on my hips, then drop them at my sides. What even are hands, anyway, and why's it so hard to figure out what to do with them in awkward situations.

"I can't say I'm surprised. I'm sure you're not bored out of your mind wandering around museums with him."

My jaw fell open and I snapped it shut. "I wasn't bored."

"You were practically sleepwalking." The corner of his mouth lifted. "I've got class, but I'm glad you found whatever it was you were looking for. You look happy."

I smiled wide like a dopey idiot. "I am."

He squeezed my shoulder as he passed and a little twinge that I hadn't even realized had been there in my chest released. Asshole-ishness avoided.

My fingers itched to check the score of the game. I'd buried my phone in my bag to make sure I didn't accidentally answer a call from my dad. I needed to get my head on straight about how I'd break this to him and Mom. She was looking forward to me coming back home, but I couldn't live under the same roof with him again. No one should have to.

She'd let him make all the choices, let him completely run her life, and she wasn't happy. How could she be? It was like she thought of being with him as the universe's way of punishing her. That was no way to live your life.

Snow crunched under my boots on the walk back to my apartment. How long could I hold out on my own? I'd never flown completely solo, and when I did, it led to things like the sex ad. I'd tasked Reece with helping me navigate normal college life, and my only guide would be gone.

Kicking the packed white snow off my boots, I opened my apartment door.

Alexa yelped and fell off the couch, tugging her shirt back down over her breasts.

I did a double take. That wasn't Dan zipping up his jeans like I was an angry dad coming home to find his daughter banging away in the living room.

"You could knock," she sneered.

"Isn't this my apartment too? I'm pretty sure I pay half the rent." *And maybe if you're cheating on your boyfriend, you might want to be a bit more discreet about it.* I shook my head, grabbed a carton of Chinese food from the fridge, and trudged into my room. After shoving a forkful into my mouth, I changed into my pajamas. It had been a while since I'd stayed in my own bed. The default was to sleep over at the Brothel. That wasn't a sentence I had ever thought I'd say, but that place felt way more like home than this apartment ever had. I glanced around at the bare walls and sterile feeling.

What was Reece up to out on the road? Probably enjoying adoring fans screaming his name. I flopped onto my bed, my stomach queasy. He loved life in the limelight. He thrived on it. Even if I wanted us to be something more after the school year ended, how could I ever compete?

~

I doubled over, clutching my midsection. My stomach was in a vise and it wouldn't stop. The only thing worse than dying right then would be surviving. I supposed that takeout had been a bit older than I'd thought. Lying in my bed, I clutched my stomach and prayed it would be over soon, either my sickness or my life. My stomach cramped up again. I wanted to shout at the sky, *I have nothing left to give*, but I couldn't, my head buried too far in the trashcan.

"Are you okay?" Dan pushed open my door.

"She's fine. Let's go. Her barfing is getting on my nerves."

Always the caring maternal type. I'd never wanted to puke on someone more in my entire life. If I could have dragged myself across the floor to her, I would have.

"She doesn't look so good." The worry in his voice made me feel even worse. How had a kind person like him ended up with her? My mental musings over how people end up in relationships with shitty people were cut off by another round of puking. I shoved my head in the trashcan. At this point, I was seriously worried I might not live through the day.

Feeling around on my nightstand, I grabbed the bottle of water and squirted some into my mouth. The front door closed and I hung my head, resting my cheek against the cool bedspread.

"Do you only puke when I'm in your apartment?"

I jumped, nearly falling out of my bed. Reece shot across the room and grabbed hold of me, helping me back into the bed.

I groaned. "Why are you here?" I pushed him away and rolled across my mattress.

"The team bus just got back to campus. You didn't answer your phone, and I was worried." The bed dipped and he rested his hand against my forehead. "You're burning up." The mattress shifted again. His footsteps faded and the sound of running water filled the room.

He came back and laid a cool washcloth on my forehead.

"How long have you been like this?" He ran another cloth over my neck and shoulders.

"A day or so. I don't know, they're kind of running together." I closed my eyes and rolled to my side, resting against him. He brushed his hand along my hair. Slowly, his fingers unraveled what was left of my braids.

"Why didn't you tell me?"

"While you were two states away? There was nothing you could do." I cracked one eye open and gave him the best smile I could muster, somewhere between a grimace and a wince.

He stared down at me and brushed the sweaty hair off my face, moving the cool washcloth to a different spot. "Don't worry, Wild Child." He dropped a kiss onto my forehead. "Sleep now. I'm here."

The pain in my stomach eased and my eyes drifted closed. Reece was there, and it would all be okay.

I eased my eyes open slowly. My muscles ached like I'd been out running all night. I lifted the blankets and glanced down at my body. New clean pajamas had replaced the sweat-soaked ones. Reece shifted under me, his arms tightening around me. He rubbed his hand over his nose and turned his head on the pillow. He was still there. Sitting up, I braced myself for the dizziness and clenching pain in my stomach. None came.

An empty bowl with a spoon sticking out of it sat on the

nightstand. Flashes of Reece feeding me chicken noodle soup and hot tea came back to me. At one point, I'd told him to go, but he'd said, "I'm staying until you're better. Get over it." And that had been the end of that conversation. I placed my hands over my face. So much puking.

Looking over my shoulder, I got a flutter in my stomach, but this time it wasn't the relentless assault of food poisoning. His jaw was covered in scruff, and I resisted the urge to run my fingers through his disheveled hair. He had to be wiped after taking care of me for...how long had it been?

A phone buzzed. I searched around the room. I had no idea where my phone was. The glowing light of the screen was a beacon, but it was Reece's phone. The light shut off before I could see who'd called. I nibbled on my lip. Wake him and let him know or let him sleep?

Spotting my own phone, I scooted over and grabbed it from the edge of the bed, plugged in and fully charged. Nearly forty-eight hours since I'd first been stricken down with the plague.

There were missed messages and calls from my dad, my mom, and Aunt Sophie, along with an invite from Marisa to go out dancing with her and her roommate. I replied to Mom, Aunt Sophie, and Marisa.

My first girls' night out invite.

Me: *I'm back from the dead and I'm in.*

Marisa: *Awesome!*

I sent off a message to my aunt and mom, responding to my dad's question last. The more time I put between our little talks the better. Reece's phone buzzed again.

Strong arms wrapped around me from behind and he buried his head in my shoulder. "You're awake."

Leaning back against him, I soaked up his warmth. "How are you?"

"Relieved. You scared the shit out of me." He turned me in his arms. His eyes searched my face as his fingers brushed hair back from my face.

"Sorry."

"If you hadn't gotten better by this morning, I was taking you to the hospital. You sure you're feeling okay?"

"Better than okay. I feel like I slept for a month. My muscles are achy, but other than that, I feel back to normal."

Reece's phone vibrated across the table beside my bed.

"That's the third call you've gotten since I woke up. You might want to check it."

He groaned and let go of me, leaning back to snag his phone off the table. Unlocking it, he flicked his finger across the screen. His eyes widened and he shot straight up out of bed. "Shit! What the fuck is wrong with me?" Grabbing his folded jeans off my dresser, he shoved his legs into them. "I'm sorry, Seph. I totally forgot about the scout practice this morning."

My stomach dropped. "What time does it start?" I checked the time. It was nine forty-seven.

"Ten." He jammed his feet into his sneakers.

"S—" The apology died in my throat when his eyes narrowed.

"Don't say it." He slipped his hand around the back of my neck and held me still. "You needed me. That was all that mattered, but I've got to go now." His lips landed on mine, hungry and sweet at the same time. My chest heaved and my head swam. "I'll come back as soon as I'm finished. I l—" His eyes widened and he froze. "I'm glad you're feeling better."

"How about I meet you at the Brothel? I need to get out of this place after being trapped inside for a few days."

"Okay, message me when you get there." He pulled open

my bedroom door. "The key's inside the light beside the front door." His gaze raked over me and he rushed back in, kissing me on the forehead before disappearing like if he didn't do it quickly, he wouldn't be able to go.

Stretching my sore muscles, I headed out of my room and into the hallway. Alexa's door opened and she stared at me. "Oh, you're alive. I had to stay at Dan's because your retching nearly made me puke."

"Sorry for the inconvenience," I grumbled under my breath. She followed behind me as I walked to the bathroom, still squawking about something.

Turning once I was inside, I closed the door in her wide-eyed face with a smile on mine. Adrenaline surged through my veins. Damn that felt good. Hopping into the shower, I rested my head against the cool tiles. I wouldn't have thought Reece would be the kind of guy to hold back a girl's hair, but I'd underestimated him from the beginning. He was so much more than most people thought he was. He was a protector, loyal to his friends, accepting of me with all my flaws and ability to get myself and him into trouble, and he spoke to my body, igniting a fire I hadn't even discovered yet. Was it any wonder I'd fallen hopelessly in love with him?

31

REECE

Her legs bounced on the bed, her toes dancing with joy as she scooped up the last of the chocolate ice cream in the bottom of the bowl.

I grabbed hold of her and lifted her shirt, blowing raspberries on her stomach. She yelped and shoved at me, spilling some of her ice cream on my shoulder.

"Stop it, you're making a mess." I flexed my fingers along her stomach.

She twitched and tried to push my hands away. "You're going to make me pee—stop tickling me!"

I blew on her stomach again and she let out a breathless laugh. Her eyes glittered with a love I'd never experienced before, the kind I'd run headlong away from even the hint of, but with her, I wanted it all. I wanted even more, and that scared the ever-loving shit out of me.

Resting my chin on her stomach, I stared up at her. She balanced her bowl of melted ice cream in her hand. Chocolate covered her fingers and was splattered all over her shirt.

"We should probably get you out of this so it doesn't

stain." I bunched her shirt in my hand, lifting it higher and exposing more of her skin.

"Was that your plan all along? To get me out of my clothes again?" She set the bowl down on the nightstand and slid one of her fingers into her mouth, licking off the ice cream.

Lifting my head, I nodded. Why lie? "I'd keep you out of your clothes until the end of time if I could."

"You keep feeding me like this and it's only a matter of time before I have no clothes left that fit and people start asking when the baby's due." She laughed and rolled over.

A bucket of icy water ran down my spine. My mouth went dry and my heart tried to brute-force its way out of my chest. Flashes of the end of last year bombarded me: the accusations, the smug looks from so many people like they'd just been waiting for me to fuck up, the inevitable whispers even after I'd been vindicated.

Not a single word when my name was cleared. Not a single apology when they found out Celeste was a gold-digging bitch. I couldn't go through that again. My hands went numb and it was hard to focus. The lights dimmed, winking in and out as the blood rushed to my head.

"What?"

I shot up, my back banging against the window blinds. They shook and rattled with a shrill clatter. Everything around me was too loud, like it had been the first time the accusation was leveled at me, microphones shoved into my face with people questioning what I planned to do and if I was going to take care of my responsibilities.

"It was a joke." Her eyes widened and she sat up, wiping her hands on her pajama pants. "I'm sure my clothes will still fit. I'll stick to these—they've got some room." She tugged at the waistband of her bottoms, smiling at me.

"I need to go." I shoved my legs into my jeans, trying not to look at her. I couldn't stay. All I could see was Celeste. I needed to get out of there. *Where the hell are my shoes?* I spun in a circle in her room, scanning the floor. The whole place was a blur.

"Go where? We were going to watch a movie."

"I've got to go. I forgot I need to be somewhere." A streak of red caught my eye. I crouched down and freed my sneakers from under her bed, my numb fingers dropping them twice before finally successfully retrieving them.

"I can come with you." She swung her legs off the side of the bed.

"No." The word came out too forcefully.

She jumped and froze, half on, half off the bed.

I wasn't trying to scare her. I shook my head and sat on the edge of her desk, shoving my feet into my sneakers.

"Reece, talk to me." Her hand landed on my arm. I dropped my shoulder so her hand fell free, and snatched up my shirt from the desk chair. It was getting harder to breathe.

We'd always used protection, but what if Seph did get pregnant? What then? It wasn't that it scared me; that wasn't what was making me run. It was that it *didn't* scare me. I was twenty-two and way too young to have kids. I'd be drafted and away from her and our child. My lips thinned to a grim line.

Stop talking about your hypothetical children.

Stop thinking about how much it would suck to be away from her and them when you're on the road.

Stop thinking this is more than we both agreed it would be. My dad was fucked up, and her dad was beyond fucked up —how would I even know how to be a dad? The same room-dimming, hard-to-breathe panic slammed into my chest. Before, with Celeste, I'd known it was bullshit, but with Seph, it was different. What if she did get pregnant?

I nearly dropped to my knees. We had no idea what it took to be parents. Seph's psycho dad had her afraid to make a single mistake. My dad made me feel invisible. I needed to get out of there.

"This is all too much. We set ground rules in the beginning. You're leaving at the end of the semester. I'm headed into the draft." My head pounded as blood rushed through my veins and made it hard to focus. I buttoned my jeans and grabbed my coat off the back of her door. "Now is not the time for me to get distracted."

A gasp shot through her parted lips and she jerked back. "Are—are you breaking up with me?" Her voice cracked.

"I just think we both got so wrapped up in everything, in your list and having fun that we're not thinking clearly and rationally."

"You sound like me." Her small laugh held no humor and couldn't cover the tightness in her voice.

"I've got the Championship game and then it's the draft. I've been dreaming of this my whole life—starting on a professional team, winning a championship—and getting sidetracked will only screw things up. I'm not letting anything get in the way of my plans."

"Including me." She stood in the center of the room with her arms wrapped around her waist.

I wanted to claw back everything I'd said at the stinging pain in her eyes. Every fiber of my being shouted that I should wrap her up in my arms and tell her I was sorry, the same voice telling me this was a mistake and I was an idiot. What did any of that matter? The cheering stadiums, the fans, the draft. This was what had stopped my dad dead in his tracks. I wasn't going to live a life of regret. I couldn't do that to myself, and I couldn't do that to her. This was for the best. This was what we'd both decided in the beginning.

Her lips tightened into a thin white line, all the color draining out of them. Those pink, soft lips I'd trailed my thumb across so many times, the same ones I'd tasted like they were my last meal on earth.

She blinked, staring at me like she was seeing me with new eyes, maybe for the first time.

I clenched my hands into fists at my sides to keep from reaching for her.

"Of course." She shook her head like she could knock the thoughts from her mind, the silly thoughts of me and her. Reaching behind her neck, she tugged on the silver chain draped down over her collarbones, the same ones I'd had my lips on minutes ago. "You should have this back."

"Seph, no. I gave that to you." I stepped forward, reaching for her hand.

She stepped back, evading my grasp. I swallowed the lump in my throat. She undid the clasp and let the chain and pendant fall into her hand.

"Keep it," I said softly.

Staring up into my eyes, her tears caught on her lashes like rain. "Why would I want to keep when it's not true?" Her voice cracked.

"Of course it's true." *Fuck.* This wasn't about her. If it were, I'd have never left her bed, but I didn't want to wake up in ten years resenting her because I'd held myself back to be with her. Did Dad ever feel that way? No, but how could he not feel it? How could you give up something you'd worked for your entire life just to be with someone?

Her nostrils flared and she shoved the still warm metal into my hand. "You can go now." Her throat worked up and down, tightening like she was holding in a scream.

Everything I'd thought this was and everything I'd convinced myself it wasn't evaporated. "Seph..." I reached for her. She brushed past me, storming to the door and wrenching it open.

"Please leave." Her voice quivered and I squeezed my eyes shut, dropping my head.

Turning to her, I closed the gap between us. "I didn't mean for this to happen."

"And I was just looking for a first fuck, remember?" She pushed on the door, banging it into my shoulder until I was completely locked out. The latch clicked as she shoved it closed all the way.

Her roommate stood in the kitchen. The clink of her spoon against the side of her mug ticked away each second, a smug look on her face as the weight of what I'd just done sank down onto my shoulders. It was heavier than any drill, any tackle, any loss.

I bit out a curse. This was exactly why I needed to end this, why I needed to not get sidetracked. I banged my fist on her door and bolted from the apartment. I was going pro. She was going to Harvard. It was as simple as that. Who knew where the hell I'd end up? The draft might send me to Seattle or Miami.

Inside my car with my hands wrapped around the steering wheel, the cold metal pressed against my palms. I needed to focus, to get paid and live the life my dad should have been living. So why did I feel like I was adrift? Like I was freefalling into an abyss I'd never be able to pull myself out of? I rested my head on the steering wheel and tried to remember what it was like to breathe, what it was like to live a life without Seph.

32

REECE

I dragged a chair out of the corner of the garage and stared out the open door at the snow drifting to the ground. Two days until the championship game. Two days until what I'd thought was the most important moment of my life, but I hadn't even returned the calls from any of the agents who'd contacted me. It had been nine days since I'd last spoken to Seph. I'd escaped the prison-like surveillance Coach had us all under and was at my parents' house.

Mom's face had dimmed the second she'd pulled into the driveway and spotted me.

"Is everything okay? Is everyone okay?" She'd hopped out of the car and crouched down, resting her hand against my cheek.

My lips tightened.

"What's going on with you?"

"Nothing."

"You can't tell me nothing when you've been walking around here since yesterday like someone killed the dog and we've never even had a dog."

"Let me help you with the groceries." I loaded up my arms with bags and took them into the kitchen. Mom whispered with Dad in the living room before dropping her hand onto his arm and disappearing upstairs.

"Reece, can I talk to you for a minute?"

After setting all the bags down on the counter and table, I walked into the living room. Dad ran his hand up and down his arm. "Your mom said you were out in the garage staring at nothing. Is everything okay?" The corner of his mouth lifted. "Is it about football?"

"No, but of course you'd want something to be wrong. You'd love for me to fuck this up, wouldn't you?" I jumped up from my spot on the couch and rounded on him. "You can't stand that I'm going to go pro. I'm going to stay in as long as I can, and letting someone get in the way of that—letting someone distract me from being the best wide receiver in the game isn't happening."

"That's what you think? That I want you to screw up?"

"Why else wouldn't you come to any of my games? You didn't even want me to play in the first place. If I hadn't forged your name on my permission slips, would you have let me play?"

"Absolutely not." His voice was hard, and there was an edge to the glint in his eye.

I threw my hands up. "Exactly. You left because you couldn't hack it. You missed Mom and gave up the glory for what? To be a pencil pusher at Grandpop's office? I'm not doing that. I'm not going to live my life regretting it and keeping my kids from living the life they deserve."

He dropped his head. Running his hand along his neck, he squeezed it. The light from the lamp reflected off his wedding ring. "Is that what you think?"

"It's what I know."

His head rose like he had a hundred pound weight around his neck. Standing, he walked closer and stood in front of me.

"I didn't stop playing because of your mom." Dad clamped his hand over my shoulder. "Not only because of her, I never wanted to stop you from living your dream, but I didn't want you to make the same mistakes I made."

"You don't need to worry about that. I made sure I didn't." The sadness in Seph's eyes when she'd handed me back the necklace I'd given her flashed in my mind.

"And from the look in your eyes and the way you've been moping around here, you might have missed out on the best thing that's ever happened to you." He gave me one of those annoyingly sage Dad looks.

A flare of anger broke free. "Like you don't wish you hadn't left and played one more season."

"I couldn't take one more hit, Reece." His tone was shrouded in grimness.

"No one likes taking hits."

"It wasn't just being taken out by a defenseman. Maybe I wasn't as fast as you, but those hits came often, and when my bell got rung, it stayed rung. That last season I played I had three concussions. It wasn't until the last one that I found out how high the price was."

"But you're fine." Wasn't he? He'd been healthy as a horse, running five miles most mornings before going off to the office.

"I'm okay now, but..." He shook his head and held his fist up to his mouth.

Fear prickled the back of my neck.

"I wasn't fast enough, and I wasn't smart enough to quit while I was ahead."

"Dad, you're freaking me out." I searched his face for answers.

"I almost lost you all. That last season I started losing time. The doctors said it was temporary, that it would all straighten itself out, and maybe if I hadn't gotten hit, it would have, but I did."

He looked up at me with tears welled up in his eyes. He held on to my shoulder and squeezed.

"I lost your first three years, everything from right after your mom told me she was pregnant"—he snapped his finger—"gone. I didn't remember resting my head on her stomach like I did with Ethan or holding her hand in the delivery room...the first time I got to hold you in my arms... you smashing your face into that sugar-free cupcake she made you on your first birthday."

A tear slid down his cheek.

"All your firsts were wiped away. The coaches wanted me to keep going. The doctors were willing to sign off on me going back to playing, but I couldn't take the chance. I was so ashamed that I'd even considered it, but I kept wondering what else I would lose. I didn't want to lose any more of you, your mom, or Ethan, so I quit. I walked out of the coach's office and left. I didn't look back, and I've never regretted that decision for a second.

"When you wanted to play, that was hard for me. I knew you'd be a star. There wasn't a doubt in my mind. You loved the game and loved the crowds, even when you were in high school, but I didn't know if, presented with that choice, you'd make the one you wouldn't regret the rest of your life. Sometimes memories are all we have, and there's no amount of money in the world that can get those back."

My dad stared at me with tears in his eyes. His hand closed on my shoulder. His nostrils flared. So many of the things my dad had said growing up finally clicked into place.

"The photo albums?" I stared into his watery eyes. He never looked at my childhood photo albums. Ethan and Rebecca's, he'd pull out every so often and look at, but mine gathered dust on the bookcase.

He jerked back. "You noticed that?"

The weight pressing against my chest intensified.

"After the first few times I looked them over, there was nothing, not even the slightest flicker. The guilt was too much. Looking at them reminded me of the trade I'd made. My stupidity robbed me of that time with you. Every so often I'd check Ethan and Rebecca's as a test for myself to make sure it hadn't progressed and become even worse. For you, I was determined to build new memories I'd treasure."

"You made me think you didn't believe in me." I jumped up, knocking his hand off my shoulder. "For years, I wanted you to just watch me play, and you refused." The crushing waves of sadness that had overwhelmed me now let a ray of sunlight break through the raging storm.

"I couldn't watch, even for you. I love you and to know you might go through what I went through...I tried to save you from that."

"By not telling me? By lying to me? You could have told me." Tears burned the backs of my eyes. All this time, I'd thought he didn't believe in me or he was jealous of what I'd been able to do. "I just wanted you there to support me and be my dad."

He shot up and wrapped his arms around me, holding on to my shoulders. I buried my head in his shoulder, and the wave of emotions poured out of me.

"I know, son. I'm sorry. I messed up, but I've always been proud of you." He shook me with his words. "I've never been prouder, and I'm sorry I ever made you feel that way. I'll do better." He held on tight, patting me on the back.

With a shaky breath, I let go of him. My head pounded and I used my shirt to dry my face.

My dad clapped his hand on my shoulder. He squeezed it, staring back at me with red-ringed eyes. "How about I get you a slice of fudge pie?" The corners of his mouth lifted.

"You think you can make everything better with a slice of pie?"

He shrugged. "How about two?"

I shook my head at him. "Deal." Everything I'd known in the world was turned upside down and I didn't know how to make any of it right, but I'd start with the pie. His memories of me and the family had been the most important thing. He'd given up the fame and the glory to keep the ones he had and make new ones. If someone had told me all the memories I had of Seph would be wiped away tomorrow and I'd be none the wiser, I wouldn't have even toyed with the idea.

I'd been trying to fight what she meant to me, and only now that I'd lost her did the truth come out. I'd figure it out over fudge pie. I couldn't leave things as they were. I couldn't let her believe I didn't care, couldn't let her believe I didn't love her.

My gaze ran over the crowd and stopped on the red coat in a sea of navy. Her hair stuck out of the red knitted hat, blowing in the wind. My heart ached like it was caught in a vise.

Bodies slammed into me, this time in celebration. The Gatorade dumped over my head blinded me for a second.

Wiping the sugary drink out of my eyes, I caught the red disappearing up the steps of the stadium and out the tunnel as everyone else celebrated. She was leaving.

"Coach, I've got to go." Pulling my jersey off, I dumped it on the concrete floor of the tunnel. The cheers and roars from everyone and some jackass with an airhorn nearly blew out my eardrums.

"What, son?" He leaned in.

"I've got to go." I tugged off my pads and dropped them, moving along with the crowd as they pushed us toward the locker room.

"Are you crazy? We just won! Everyone's going to be out there waiting to talk to you. You've gotten on my damn nerves this season with your showboating, but you did good out there, kid." He wrapped his arms around my neck and pulled me in close.

"And now I've got somewhere to be."

"Where could be more important than here?" Someone grabbed him and steered him away.

"We did it!" LJ jumped onto my back, nearly knocking me over. Coach glared at him before stalking off.

I let the celebration drag me toward the locker room. Rushing inside, I bolted for my locker. The place was chaos. Half the team was inside, losing their minds. Pads, jerseys, towels, equipment, and every person imaginable was crammed into the small space filled with overly large people.

My name was called out from every direction, but I was determined. No time for a shower. I kicked off my cleats and opened my locker. *Fuck.* My shoes were gone. It didn't matter. Pulling open the locker next to mine, I glanced down at the gray monstrosities sitting in there.

As I yanked my shirt over my head, it clung to the sweat

on my body. *Screw it.* Grabbing my jeans, I jumped into them, dove for Berk's shoes, and tugged them on. Buttoning my jeans, I held my keys between my teeth and pushed my way out through the crowd.

Bursting out of the locker room, I elbowed my way through the reporters, teammates, fans, and anyone else in my way. I wrapped my hands around the long metal bar running across the steel door at the end of the hallway and threw it open. A blast of wind so cold my teeth ached hit me the second I stepped outside. My feet slipped and slid in Berk's shitty shoes.

Yanking open the door to my car, I revved the engine and threw it into reverse. The traffic on the road conspired against me on the way to her apartment.

33

SEPH

I welcomed the numbness, preferred it to the raw, sawing, can't-think-straight pain detonating in my chest. Reece had walked away—hell, he hadn't walked, he'd *run* away the second I'd brought up something even jokingly close to a future. That had been my answer, so why was I in this taxi? Why was I subjecting myself to this torture?

"They'll want you to start your coursework over the summer, formalities for beginning the PhD program." My dad's voice droned on out of the speaker of my phone.

The back of the taxi was even colder than outside.

Leaning my head against the headrest, I stared out the window, the clear blue sky stretching on forever above me. How could the rest of the world go on like nothing had happened? I'd been waking up with the air trapped in my lungs, clawing at the sheets as I tried to suck in another breath.

This call made me want to jump from the taxi, leave my phone behind, disappear into the city, and become someone else, someone who didn't know what it was like to feel his caress and sweet whispers.

It was so much harder trying to keep myself together after closing the door on Reece. It was like closing the door on the possibility of a future unlike any I could have imagined for myself.

When I showed up at the will call office and gave them my name, I figured there wouldn't be a ticket there for me and I could take solace in the fact that I'd tried to keep my promise, but the woman had asked to see my ID through the crackly speaker. I slipped it into the little well at the bottom of the glass and she slid it back to me with a single ticket.

Fans crowded around the stadium entrance and I found my way to my seat, right behind the Trojan's bench, a few rows from the bottom. The team ran out onto the field and everyone was on their feet. I used their standing bodies to shield me in case he saw, but he was focused on the game, giving it his all like he did for everything. It was my first time watching him on the field. I'd followed the games online with the text stats before, but I'd never sat down to see him play in person. It was bittersweet, so much of his work out there for everyone to see.

By the last quarter, I cheered along with the rest of the fans in the stands. I jumped up and down as the kinetic energy of the roofless building exploded with joy when the ball bounced twice in Reece's hands before he clamped it against his chest. The next pass, Nix looked poised to throw it to him again, but instead he threw it to number 52, Keyton in block letters across the player's back. That catch was clean, without a bounce, and as he crossed the line into the end zone, the place exploded, the noise so loud I was tempted to cover my ears, fearing I'd suffer actual hearing loss. The joy was overwhelming. I'd never been in a sea of people so focused on one goal together.

Sitting in my seat, I watched Reece pile on top of Keyton and scooted along the row until I hit the aisle. He'd played better than anyone else on the field. I had no idea about the rules, but he'd given everything to the game. It was no wonder he'd choose it over me.

Riding back to my apartment in the taxi, I blinked back tears. For a second I had thought he'd seen me, but then he'd gone right back to celebrating with the rest of the team. He'd place well in the draft with a championship and a touchdown in the winning game next to his name.

The apartment was quiet. Walking into my room, I spotted the shiny, silver latches under my bed. I grabbed the case and flipped it open. The same case I hadn't touched in weeks.

I picked up my violin now that I could feel my fingers again. That was one thing stadiums didn't have: great heating. Even packed in amongst thousands of screaming fans, the cold from the night sliced through my coat and gloves, or maybe it was a cold that didn't come from the elements but rather from no longer being in his embrace.

My bow ran across the strings. Closing my eyes, I swayed along to the melody I'd played a thousand times before, still feeling it deep in my bones. This story of love lost was real now. Before they'd been finger positions on my strings; now they were notes on my soul. I poured myself into the rhythm and melody, trying to keep myself together. I was fraying more and more every day, but it was showing me that I could stand up to the pressure. I wasn't going to Boston next year. I'd stay in Philly even if I was all alone. I'd made a life for myself, and even though it had fallen apart, I could do it again. It wouldn't be the same.

There would always be two parts of my life: BR and AR. After Reece would be a little less bright, but I could do it. I'd go to Boston and tell my mom exactly what I planned on doing. Maybe I'd bring Aunt Sophie as backup. My mom didn't have to live under the iron grip of my dad either.

He didn't deserve another word from me or a single thought, but I'd do everything I could to get my mom to see the same went for her. We should both be free.

My bedroom door flew open. I jumped, spinning around.

"I'm home now." Alexa stood in the doorway with her hand on the knob, closing the door.

I lifted the violin back to my shoulder.

"Didn't you hear me?" She opened the door fully.

"I heard you, I just don't care." I was tired of caving to bullies.

"You could be a bit more respectful. We do live together."

I put my violin on the bed and turned.

She seemed to take that as me giving in to her and closed the door.

I flung it open, and it slammed into the wall as I stormed out into the hallway.

"You're a vile person who can only feel better about yourself when you're belittling other people. You don't talk to friends like that." The tension had been building for the past four months and there was no stopping it now.

She crossed her arms over her chest and stared at me. "At least I have friends."

"Do you? It seems to me they all fled the country to get away from you. All you do is browbeat Dan and act like a nuclear bitch to me. All I ever wanted to be was your friend."

"You came in here with your violin and your fucking librarian clothes, and I see the way you look at Dan."

I stared at her and it finally clicked. "You're jealous."

"Hell no."

"Wow, you're actually jealous of me. All this time I thought maybe that was just a personality quirk, but you're actually jealous of me." It was stupid that this hadn't even occurred to me as a possibility before now, but when had I ever been around mean girls before? Living with Alexa was a crash course in hierarchical female dynamics. Her nostrils flared.

The front door opened and Dan stepped in. His gaze bounced from me to her.

"Are you going to let her talk to me like this, Dan?" She turned around, staring at him.

Dan stepped back with a box of pizza in his hands. "Seph?"

"Stop calling her that. Her name's Persephone."

"My friends call me Seph." I stepped closer. There was no backing down this time. Semester break was in a few days, and I wasn't going to let her stomp all over me anymore and treat me like shit. It was her or me, and it sure as hell wasn't going to be me to back down first. Next semester would be wicked witch free.

"Oh, so you two are friends now?" She glared at me. "You're trying to steal him from me."

I threw my hands up in the air. "I don't want Dan—no offense."

He shrugged.

"But neither do you, right?" Her late-night shirtless

sleepover buddies didn't exactly scream, *I'm in a serious and committed relationship.*

Her face dropped and her gaze darted from me to Dan. "You don't know what you're talking about," she said through gritted teeth.

"What?" He dropped the pizza box on the counter and stepped beside her. "What's she talking about?"

"He deserves to know. It's the least you can do to prove you're not a completely horrible person." It was like cauterizing a wound. This would hurt, and Dan seemed so sweet; I didn't want to inflict this on him, but he had a right to know.

"It's none of your business." She seethed at me like a snake eyeing up its prey, but I wasn't scared of her anymore.

"What's none of her business? What did you do, Alexa?" His voice pitched up and tears glistened in his eyes. Not how I wanted this to go down, but it was better it happened now versus later, and how quickly he jumped from the one thing I'd said to accusing her let me know this wasn't out of the blue.

"It was nothing...just a mistake I made." She turned and ran her hands over his chest.

Dan stepped back, staring at her like he was seeing her for the first time. "A mistake. Another one." His Adam's apple bobbed up and down. "You promised it would never happen again." His voice cracked.

"You just *had* to stick your nose into my business." Alexa turned on me, spitting her venom like I'd called that guy over to the apartment and made her do whatever she'd done with him.

I shrugged. "I guess I did, because I'm sick and tired of people like you railroading good people because they are too nice and put up with your shitty behavior."

"We've been together since ninth grade. There's nothing

you can do to break us up. He's never going to find someone who can give him what I can." She grabbed Dan's arm, trying to loop hers through his, but he pulled away, taking a step back.

"You lied to me *again*." Tears welled in his eyes. "Who was it?"

"It doesn't matter," she cooed, like a sweet voice could erase the pain of her cheating.

"Who?" His voice cracked.

"Chad."

I grabbed my coat. They needed to figure this out on their own. Their voices got higher and I dashed into my room to grab my bag. It sucked being the one to push them to this point, but I hoped it helped spare him the years of emotional abuse she'd heap on him. Maybe it would get her to see the error of her ways, to see that treating people like shit wasn't a valid way to live her life.

I walked out of my room and he stood by the front door. Alexa switched between coos to placate him and snapping at him, telling him the horrible lies that had gotten her this far.

With my hand on the doorknob, I stared at him over my shoulder. "You deserve better, Dan. You deserve someone who'll love you and who'll never make you feel like you're not enough. She's out there for you."

His gaze snapped to mine. Alexa shoved at his shoulder, nearly knocking him over. I tried to get him to believe it with my eyes. *You can do it. I can't do it for you.*

He nodded and pulled the door open. Alexa jumped back so she didn't catch a face full of wood, and Dan motioned for me to go through first. "You're right." He stepped outside and slammed the door shut behind him. A loud bang followed us on the way out, but I didn't care. If she wrecked the rest of my stuff in the apartment, at least I'd helped Dan see the light of day, and if I could help him, maybe I could help my mom too. Then maybe at some point I'd be able to help myself. The distraction from the pain in my heart had helped. Maybe that was what I could do to avoid it, to avoid thinking about Reece—just keep pushing forward and helping other people, and then I wouldn't have to stop and think about how I hadn't even been able to help myself.

34

REECE

I threw my car into park near her building after pulling into the first spot I saw. My car hung halfway out, but I'd take a busted bumper if it meant getting to her faster. My heart hammered against my ribs. I'd walked out on the biggest press conference of my life up until now, and that was barely a blip on my radar. That win without her there to celebrate with me was a hollow yawning pit. I wanted her to run onto the field and wrap her arms around me, wanted to plant a kiss on her lips and stare into her eyes. I wanted her.

My dad's words slammed into the center of my chest. A pro career lasted however long it took for my body to fail, but her love...that was forever—at least it would have been if I hadn't fucked it up.

She walked out of her building, but she wasn't alone. Dan stood next to her, looking like he'd walked through a minefield. She turned him and rested her hand on his arm then his shoulder. He nodded along with whatever she was saying.

I couldn't hear the words, but this wasn't a talk about

what they liked on pizza. This was an intimate discussion. Standing on her tiptoes, she wrapped her arms around his neck, and he held on to her like she was a lifeline in a storm. His hands bunched her coat along her back.

Swallowing down the racing bile in my throat, I clenched my fists in my pockets and took a deep breath. My sneakers crunched on the thin sheet of ice forming on the ground.

Seph let go of him and smiled, the gentle, kind expression she had for anyone she cared about. The ice cracked under my feet and I wished I were on a lake that could swallow me up. I'd rather have felt the icy daggers of freezing winter water than watch her with someone else.

Her head turned and she spotted me. I knew because her smile faltered and then fell. The knotted pit in my stomach grew.

Dan turned to follow her gaze and his eyes widened. "Didn't you just win the championship? What the hell are you doing here?"

I lifted my chin, jutting it forward. "I'm here to talk to Seph."

Dan's gaze bounced from me to Seph and back to me. "I—I'll leave you two to talk. Thanks for everything, Seph." He stuck his hands in his pockets and walked over to his car, glancing back over his shoulder before hopping inside.

We stood on the freezing sidewalk, staring at each other. The puffs of air from her lips drifted over my face as I got closer.

"You came to my game." I'd left the ticket there on the off chance she'd show up.

"I promised I would." She shrugged. The uncertainty in her eyes killed me.

"There are a lot of ways I can tell you I'm sorry, but I thought I'd show you. Will you let me?"

She nibbled her bottom lip like she always did when she was nervous or trying to decide the best course of action. It wasn't a flat-out no, so I'd take it.

"It won't take long." I held out my hand. "A ten-minute drive."

She stared down at it and walked past me. My heart plummeted. I squeezed my eyes shut and dropped my hand. I'd royally fucked things up.

"Are we going or not?"

I spun around. She stood beside the passenger side of my car. Jogging over to her, I skidded on the ice and caught myself. She tugged open the door before I could get to her and climbed in.

Bracing my hands on the roof of my car, I looked up at the sky. *Please don't let me fuck this up.*

We drove in silence. I had to take a few side streets to avoid all the post-championship celebrations. People took over the main roads with flags and banners hanging from their cars, cheering and chanting.

Seph craned her neck to check everyone out. "You're missing all the fun."

"I'm right where I want to be." I peered over at her. My fingers itched to reach over and take her hand, to thread through hers and bring them up to my mouth. I wanted to kiss our interlaced fingers in a promise of forever.

Cars dotted the visitor side of the stadium parking lot. Most people from the losing team knew to get out of dodge. Exiting the car, I couldn't stop myself from watching her. Her cheeks glowed with a wintry flush. Wisps of her hair had escaped the red knit hat she always wore. Was her hair braided underneath? Would I get to find out later? Would I ever get to run my fingers through her hair again as she lay on my chest sound asleep?

She looked to me with an eyebrow raised. That snapped me out of my daydream, wanting to both stretch this moment out in case it was the last and move past it with her by my side.

I walked to one of the doors of the stadium and knocked. Winning a championship had its perks, mainly the ground-keepers bending the rules for me just this once to get me inside. The wide hallways were eerily quiet. It was like walking into your childhood home after your parents had packed up for a move. It was just as you remembered it and yet completely foreign. This didn't feel like the same place I'd been a couple of hours ago.

Seph sped up, brushing against my arm. I slowed down, navigating the twists and turns of the place I'd spent my last four years in, and it hit me: this would be one of the last times I'd be there.

"Where are we going?" She sped up to get in front of me.

"Here." I guided her out of the tunnel. Swinging to the left, we went up a few stairs and I sat in the second seat in the first row, right on the fifty-yard line. I patted the hard-molded plastic seat beside me, holding it down for her to sit.

She eyed me and the field before sitting and staring straight ahead. "Why are we here?"

I leaned forward, resting my arms on the steel railings that lined the perimeter of the first row.

"I've played football since I was ten years old. It was flag football, but even then there were people whispering about how good I was. I'm sure there are thousands of kids all across the country who get the same treatment, but my dad was a former NFL player, so it was different."

I tightened my grip. Soon there'd be a championship ring on my finger, clinking against the cold metal.

"But my dad would never watch me play. He didn't even want me to play. For a long time, I thought it was because he didn't believe in me or he was worried about me being better than him, worried I'd surpass his achievements."

Our conversation replayed in my head.

"And what about now?" She leaned forward, her shoulder brushing my back.

"Now I know he was only trying to protect me. It was the only way he could let me do what he saw I needed to do. Stopping me would've been like asking me to stop breathing, so he did what he needed to do to let me play."

She sat beside me in silence. The faraway echoing noises of people cleaning up around the stadium bounced their way across the field.

I took a deep, shaky breath. Turning fully in my seat, I took her hand in mine. "And I'd give it all up for you."

Snatching her hand from mine, she jumped up. Her feet slapped against the hard concrete and my heart plummeted. She stared back at me like I'd told her I was headed to the moon. "Are you out of your fucking mind?"

My head snapped back. "It's true."

"If it's true then you probably need to get a CT scan." She snatched her hat off her head. Her hair stuck up as the static cling supercharged it. "Why would you ever say something like that? Is that what you think I want from you? I saw you out there tonight. You were indescribable. How could you even think for a second of throwing away all that talent? For what? For nothing? To prove a point?"

I stood and braced my hands on her shoulders. "It wouldn't be for nothing, Seph. It would be for you."

She glared at me and crossed her arms over her chest.

"No, it would be for you. Then you get to make this big sacrifice and in fifteen years you're staring at me like some stranger who stole something from you."

"There wouldn't be a day that went by without you that I wouldn't feel that never-ending sense of loss, knowing I gave up something I could never get back, knowing I sacrificed being with the person I love for fame and glory to strangers who could never mean as much to me as you do."

"You're not giving anything up." She jammed her finger into the center of my chest. "I'm not going to let you hold that over my head."

The corners of my mouth turned up. "Does that mean I'll be around to *not* hold it over your head?"

"I'm scared." She nibbled her bottom lip.

I dragged her into my arms. "I'm scared too, Wild Child, but with your brains and my athleticism, we can outsmart or outrun any problem we come up against." Running my fingers along the nape of her neck, I held on tight. Her lavender and library smell was a scent I'd wear any day if it meant I got to hold her. "At least for a few more years until my knees give out."

She pushed against my chest and I loosened my hold on her like a creaky gate that needed oil. I'd never take this for granted again.

"I'm not going back to Boston." She stared up into my eyes.

"I don't care if you're going to Timbuktu—we'll figure it out when the time comes."

Her eyebrows scrunched down and tugged on the buttons of my coat. "Did you just say you love me?"

I waited for the pulse-pounding freak-out or urge to backpedal, but there wasn't any. There was only the bright glow of her smile and the warmth of my hand on hers. "You bet your ass I did, and I'll say it every day for the rest of our lives." I ran my hand along the side of her face and dipped my head.

Her lips parted in the sweetest invitation, and I poured my love into that kiss. The electrifying spark between us grew until I needed to get her to the closest flat surface immediately.

A loud squeal ricocheted from the loud speakers followed by some whoops and cheers. I glanced up and saw the two of us were up on the big screen.

Seph glanced up and her cheeks reddened. She dipped her head, holding on to the front of my coat.

Her head snapped back. "What the hell happened to your shoes?" She stared at them like they were something that had crawled out from the seafloor.

I looked down at the gray monstrosities on my feet and laughed. "After the game, I couldn't find mine, so I stole Berk's."

"If you'd have led with that, we wouldn't even have needed your whole speech." She pressed a quick kiss to my lips, laughing and shaking her head. "Since you wear the same size, maybe you need to let him have a pair. Is that a hole?"

The side of my little toe peeked out of a rip just above the worn-down rubber sole of the sneaker. I shook my head. "He's freaking hopeless." I held on to both sides of her face and rest my forehead against hers. "Let's go home."

"And where exactly is that?" She tugged on the edges of my coat.

"Wherever we are." I groaned. "There's going to be an insane party in our house—hell, all over campus. It'll probably be going on for the next week."

She tapped her finger along her lips. "I might have a spot."

"Where?"

She turned and walked, holding my hand. I rushed to keep up with her as she said, "You'll see."

35

SEPH

Cheers and airhorns blared all over campus. The roving crowds of marauding cheerleaders lurked around every corner. A drum beat banging out the school's fight song got closer. Ducking behind some bushes, we hid as the impromptu marching band passed by, carrying a fifth of rum and their own battery-powered blender in a wagon they towed behind them.

Campus security walked by and high-fived them. If you can't beat 'em, join 'em, right? There probably weren't enough citation notepads to give out to every person on the entire campus.

Pushing the wet, slick bushes aside, we stepped back out onto the path.

"Not that I'm complaining or anything, but where on campus do you think we're going to find a place that's not going insane right now?"

I tugged him forward, turning the corner. He stared up at the gray stone building and his head tilted to the side.

"Trust me."

We walked in through the double automatic doors.

There were papers strewn all over the floor, abandoned backpacks and orphaned coffee tumblers all over the tables. It looked like a zombie apocalypse movie. The circulation desk was empty and it was whisper quiet inside.

"I told you I'd find a place."

He shook his head. "I should've known you'd have the inside track on the quietest spot on campus."

"Where I study, it's like this all the time—not in the post-apocalyptic, people just disappeared in the middle of what they were doing kind of way, but more in the no one has been here for years kind of way."

"What exactly will you have us do once we get to this quiet spot?" His teeth scraped against the skin at the side of my neck.

"It's a good place to talk." I let out a shuddery breath as he sucked on my throbbing pulse point. Squeezing my thighs together, I tried to focus on what I'd been saying and doing. Too many days had passed without feeling his touch.

"All you want to do is talk?" He tightened his arm around me, running his thumb across my shoulder. Even through my coat, I could feel every stroke.

I licked my lips and nodded. "You need to tell me about your Christmas."

"Sure, I've got a slideshow on my phone I can show you." He released me and took my hand.

"Really?"

"Unfortunately, yes. My mom and dad put one together every year, like a little year-end review. They email it out to us and then we go through it on Christmas Day. I always thought it was weird, but it makes more sense now."

"Why?" I searched his face for the answer.

He squeezed my hand. "I'll tell you later."

"I want to see the slideshow. I'm sure it's awesome." I grabbed for his phone.

He lifted it up high. "We're not watching my family Christmas slideshow. Take me to your lair to have your way with me." Reece wrapped his arm around me, kissing the side of my face.

The elevator shuddered, the doors groaning open like they had been asleep for a hundred years.

"What if we make a wager?" I tapped my finger to my chin.

He squinted and looked at me out of the corners of his eyes. "If this gets me naked again, I'm all for it." His grin was as infectious as a yawn.

"After the slideshow."

He grumbled beside me.

The elevator rumbled and shook, carrying us to the third floor. Ancient elevators were par for the course in libraries like these. The back of his hand brushed against mine, my need for him blooming deep in my stomach and spreading throughout my body. Drawing it out, we savored the need to delve into one another like diving headfirst into a surging surf.

"Here's the deal."

"I'm listening." He crossed his arms over his chest. The thermal under his coat stretched tightly across his muscled body.

"Whoever gets to my study room first gets to decide what we do once we get there."

"You want to race me." He shook his head like I'd placed a bet on a horse they'd be putting down after the race.

I stuck out my hand. "Deal?"

His lazy smile was a sexual ambush. My heart flipped

and he slipped his hand into mine, his fingertips brushing against the inside of my wrist. "Deal, Wild Child."

A sizzle of pleasure rolled down my spine whenever he said that. I could be wild with him.

The elevator doors opened. I tugged my hand free from his grip and bolted, clearing the retreating doors before they fully opened.

"But I don't know where your study room is!" he called after me.

Glancing over my shoulder, I laughed at the wide-eyed look on Reece's face. "I know!"

His lips curled up into a happy predatory smile as he took off after me.

I ducked down one of the aisles of the stacks. Our game of cat and mouse was the release we needed. Where else was better to do so than a deserted library? My home turf.

The heavy muted thud of his footsteps on the dull carpet sent a shiver up my spine. I slipped around the far end of a shelf and tiptoed farther back toward my study room. I saw his shadow pass by through the gaps in the books on the shelves as I ducked down lower.

My heart hammered in my chest and I slammed my lips together to keep from laughing. Sliding my coat off, I threw it into the next row of books to distract him and took off in the opposite direction.

His footsteps thudded behind me. "All you're doing is getting yourself less clothed for me," he declared in a singsong voice.

I duck-walked along the stacks, cursing my sense of direction. I was on the wrong side of the wide walkway between the two halves of the room. Peeking out from the end of the row, I made a break for it. I got halfway down the aisle with the door to my study room in sight.

Maybe it was cruel of me, but the thought of getting to take my time flipping through the family slideshow while he came out of his skin beside me made the chase worth it. It would be just as hard on me as it was on him, but who didn't love a little delayed gratification?

Within seconds, like a serial killer in a movie, he grabbed me and lifted me off the ground. I yelped and tried to make a break for the study room. He dumped our coats on the floor. The hum of the fluorescent lighting overhead was our only company aside from the books on the shelves, but a new arrival made himself known, pressed against my back.

"I told you I'd get you." He spun me around, lifting my hands and pinning them above my head.

His hand snaked down between us and tugged up my shirt, exposing my skin to the cool air in the room and his heated touch. My hands pressed against the cool, metal shelves. My fingertips brushed against the spines of the books. A shiver shot down my body as Reece's hand dipped into the back of my pants, cupping my ass.

"I figured a head start would help."

He took his hand out and worked quickly, unbuttoning and unzipping my pants and shoving them down my legs. I broke out in goose bumps as the cross breeze of the room glided across my skin. It had absolutely nothing to do with the crazy amounts of hormones rushing through my body or the six-one football player undressing me in public.

"Not when you're the prize."

His fingers slid along my stomach, sending shots of pleasure rolling through my body. He shoved the front of my shirt up and over my breasts, exposing my bra. Dropping a kiss onto the top of each cup, he stared at me like I was the altar and the service was about to begin.

I glanced over at the closed door to my study room. We were close.

"You're not going to make it. This place is deserted—how about we add another first to your list?"

"Which one?" I licked my dry lips.

He popped the button on his jeans, and their muted thud on the floor sent rippling waves of pleasure shooting through my pussy.

"You'll figure it out."

Dropping his hand from my wrist, he cupped my ass, lifting my legs so they wrapped around his hips. The hard, insistent nudge of his cock against my slit sent a shudder through the two of us. My body was on fire and I ground myself against him.

The two of us froze the second his thick mushroom head pushed inside me.

"Oh shit." I moaned and held on to the shelves behind me.

He squatted down while holding me and shook his wallet free from the back pocket of his jeans on the floor. It dropped to the ground as he freed a condom from the leather confines. Tearing it open with his teeth, he rolled it on, holding me up with one arm. He was raw power and muscle, and I was more than happy to have a front-row seat to his next demonstration of athletic prowess.

In one smooth, solid thrust, he embedded himself in me, stretching me to my limit and stealing my breath away. Reece hissed as I tightened my legs around him and ground myself in small circles.

I looped my arms around his neck, holding on and frantic for the sweet taste of him and the orgasm I teetered on the edge of. The shelves clanked and rattled behind me.

He squeezed and massaged my ass, never letting our

bodies apart for more than a second. Sweat beaded on my skin. Dipping his knees, his thrusts changed direction and he rubbed the spot inside of me that lit me up like a New Year's Eve fireworks display. I bit down on his shoulder. My mouth filled with the salty taste of his skin. My muffled yelp was buried in his shoulder and he kept slamming me down onto his thick cock. He pressed his face against my neck and groaned. He expanded inside me, triggering another wave of pleasure that sent my eyes rolling back in my head.

Panting, he lowered us both to the floor. Our coats made up a makeshift nest for our recovery. He draped my coat over me and laid me down on his chest.

"I don't think I figured out which new addition that was to my list." I ran my finger over his chest.

He chuckled, his body vibrating under me. "I'll have to keep trying until you figure it out then."

I lifted my head. His breathing slowed and he lay back with his eyes closed and eyelashes reaching for the ceiling. I traced my fingertips over his cheeks and eyelids.

He propped his hand behind his head and stared down at me. "I've got something for you."

"The slideshow?"

He shook his head at the hopefulness oozing out of my voice. "Just wait until you have to sit through it next Christmas. Then you'll be sorry."

Next Christmas. I couldn't wait. He shifted me to one side and reached under him. "I needed to return this to you." The long silver chain and pendant swayed back and forth as it dangled from his hand.

My throat tightened and my eyes filled. Blinking them away, I sat up. He draped it around my neck, closing the clasp and kissing the back of my shoulder. "It was always yours and it's always been true, but I wanted you to have this." I glanced over my shoulder and kissed him. Sinking deep into that kiss, I was ready for round two.

There was a faint ding. We both broke apart and stared at each other.

"Was that—" The rumbling rattle of the old door creaking open confirmed my worst fear. We scrambled to get our clothes back on, the muted thud of footsteps getting closer every second.

With my pants buttoned, I shoved my arms into my coat, and Reece grabbed the condom wrapper on the floor, shoving it into his pocket. Holding hands, we walked down the side aisle toward the elevator and nearly ran into the only other guy on the whole campus who thought now was the best time to go to the library.

He jumped and nearly spilled his coffee. I laughed, burying my head in Reece's shoulder, and we ran for the elevator. I could feel the guy's eyes on us as we speed walked to get out of there. Once inside, he looked over at me.

"You know your coat's on inside out, right?"

I glanced down at the lining of my coat, which was, indeed, currently on the outside. Shoving at his shoulder, I shrugged it off and flipped it right side out. "Why didn't you tell me?"

"I was just happy he didn't see your underwear sticking out of my pocket." He tugged at the bright blue edge of the lace poking out of his jeans.

Someone had set a flamethrower to my cheeks. Reece kissed the side of my head. "Let's go, Wild Child. We've got some celebrating to do."

EPILOGUE

REECE

I sat on the bench with my elbows resting on my legs. There couldn't have been a more perfect first season in the pros. The stadium vibrated around us. The stands were a living organism fed by the yardage gained on the field, a sea of green and gold. Sweat dripped off the tip of my nose. Scanning the crowd, I spotted them. No one wanted the sky box tickets; they wanted to be right in the action.

Seph was easy to spot in her red coat, a bold move in a crowd all clad in green. She had her hair up in a crown of braids I couldn't wait to take down later. Unraveling them and letting her smooth, caramel strands run through my fingers was a post-game ritual I never wanted to go without.

Mom and Dad sat beside her, their arms wrapped around each other. After a long talk with my dad, we'd finally started to mend the rift that had been there since I picked up a football. I was lucky they weren't making out. They'd come to every home game this season.

Blinking back the moisture in my eyes, I waved to them.

A sharp call, loud even over the frenzy of the crowd, drew my attention. With his hands cupped around his mouth, Nix shouted down to me, his voice carrying despite the uproar. "It took you three games to make your first touchdown. I'm so disappointed." His wide grin showed he was anything but.

"Why don't you get your ass down here then?"

He shrugged and threw back, "I'll leave that to the professionals."

"Excuses."

The game ended with another win for us. If we kept this momentum going, it could be a banner season with hockey and football each securing a championship for Philly. I darted in and out of the locker room as quickly as I could, no press conference for me. If I never had to do one again, it would be too soon.

My parents, Seph, and Nix waited for me in the hallway.

"You ready?" I slipped my hand into hers. Bringing it up to my mouth, I kissed the back of it.

"Yeah, my mom texted me that they're almost to the hotel. I wish they could've gotten an earlier flight to see you play."

"There's plenty of time for that, and we'll be in Seattle later this season. I can have them roll out the red carpet for them."

"Just make sure you don't eat any of the baked goods Aunt Sophie brings tonight," she warned everyone.

"Sweetie, you were wonderful." Mom kissed me on the cheek and squeezed me.

"Great game, son." My dad hugged me and clapped me on the back. "Keep playing like that and I'll have a steady supply of fudge pies for you at the house."

"I feel like you're trying to fatten me up."

He laughed and wrapped his arm around my mom's shoulder.

"He's trying to get them out of the house. He's been stress baking, so there's about ten in the fridge already—not that I'm complaining."

My gaze snapped to his and he said, "It's my problem, not yours. Keep doing what you're doing. I'm proud of you." He blinked like he had something in his eye and tightened his hand around Mom's shoulder.

His words hit me right in the chest and I nodded.

"Everyone ready to eat?" Nix rubbed his hands together.

"Now you sound like Berk." We walked out of the stadium. Splitting between cars, we got to the restaurant. I slipped my hand into Seph's on the center console. She took her eyes off the road and smiled at me.

No matter how many times she did it, it was like the first time, a feeling like rays of sunlight hitting your face after a dreary day. I loved this woman more than I'd ever thought possible.

"What's up?" She squeezed my hand. That reassuring gesture let me know she was there for me and would always be there for me.

"Nothing, I'm just happy classes are over so you got to come to my game."

"Who'd have thought I'd be busier than you this year, Mr. Pro Football Player?"

"You're lucky I keep a clean house and I'm an excellent cook."

"I am lucky."

~

SEPH

Getting to the restaurant, I spotted my Aunt Sophie right away, and I did a double take when I looked at the person beside her. *Mom!* It was a complete transformation. Aunt Sophie's hair was dyed a light green, almost a teal, and Mom's usually light brown hair was a bold, deep red.

I'd never gotten the whole *Is this your mom or your sister* thing, but I wouldn't have been surprised if people thought I was her mom from the way she looked. When Aunt Sophie and I had gone to my house together, I hadn't known if my mom would come with us. I'd barely convinced Reece to stay behind at the hotel—and by barely, I mean I hadn't. He'd waited in the car outside the house in case there were any issues.

I walked in the front door. "Mom?" I stood in the middle of the entryway, calling for her, which I'd never done before. Aunt Sophie stood beside me.

The hurried but muted rush of her coming down the steps was the only sound in the whole house, aside from the ticking of the grandfather clock in the living room.

"Seph, what's wrong? Are you okay?" She stared at me wide-eyed like she'd expected to find me with a limb hanging off my body. "Sophia, what are you doing here?"

"I'm here to do what I should have done years ago. We're going."

"Where are you two going?" Her gaze bounced between us and she wrung her hands in front of her.

Stepping forward, I grasped her arm gently. "Not me and Aunt Sophie, Mom—the three of us. I'm staying in Philly. I've gone over everything with Dr. Huntsman. I'll graduate at the end of next year and finish my PhD there."

Mom glanced over her shoulder. "But your father—"

"Has no say in what I do, or in what you do." I slid my hand down to hers. "Come with us, Mom. He has no power over you, and I'm not going to let him ruin our lives anymore."

"Helen, what's all this noise?" My father stepped into the entryway, and every muscle in my mom's body tightened like a gazelle caught in the crosshairs.

"Why hello, Arthur."

"Sophia." My mom jumped at his sneer.

"Is that any way to greet your sister-in-law, you insufferable prick?"

My dad's eyes widened and his face turned beet red. "Get out of my house."

"Gladly. Helen, let's go." Aunt Sophie opened the front door.

"Helen." As if the warning tone in his voice that had been ground down into our brains wasn't enough, he dropped his hand onto the back of her neck. She sucked in a sharp breath and I let go of her hand.

Funneling every harsh word, scornful comment, and memory of bruises, I planted both my hands in the center of his chest and shoved him. He stumbled back and banged his back against the ticking clock. "You don't get to do that ever again. You will never lay a hand on her or me again. In fact, after today, I never want to speak to you again."

He stared at me like I was a stranger, which was exactly what I wanted him to be to me.

"Mom, I love you. I love you so much and I don't want to see you unhappy. I don't want you to have to walk on eggshells in your own home. Please, come with us. There's nothing left for you here." I held out my hand, tears welling in my eyes. The outline of her got blurry and the lump in my chest got heavier.

She looked to my dad. He pushed himself away from the clock.

"Helen." The tone was no longer a warning, now a threat.

"Helen, we can do this together." Aunt Sophie held out her hand beside mine.

Mom's throat tightened and she took a half-step forward. My dad's hand shot out and wrapped around her wrist.

"Arthur, I swear, I'll shove my shoe so far up your ass you'll be tasting hemp for the rest of your natural life. Get your hands off her." I didn't think I'd ever heard Aunt Sophie raise her voice, but liquid fire dripped from her every word.

My dad's face blanched and he let go.

"What do you say, Wild One—ready for another adventure?" Aunt Sophie's eyes and voice softened, and Mom took both our hands.

The tears cascaded down my cheeks at the whoosh of relief rushing through me.

We opened the front door and Reece stopped his pacing out on the brick sidewalk. His gaze shot to my tearful one and back through the open door. The muscles in his neck tightened. When Aunt Sophie and Mom came out after me, his entire body relaxed.

He wrapped his arm around me. "Do you need me to get anything from inside?"

Mom looked up at the house. "No, I've got the most important things I need right here." She squeezed my hand and Aunt Sophie's, and that was her new beginning. It was my new beginning too.

I'd never seen this side of her, but I loved getting to know her again as her own person.

"Honey." She wrapped me up in a massive hug. Aunt Sophie joined in too, and anyone watching would've thought it had been years since we'd seen one another, not a single month.

I tried to ignore Berk flirting with my mom and aunt throughout dinner. Heads turned as laughter erupted from our table, and I didn't mind one bit. Every eye in the place was on us, and how could they not be when one of the darlings of Philadelphia football was sitting at our table?

Dinner turned to after-dinner drinks, and we danced on the small dance floor in front of the band that was playing. Reece's arm was wrapped around my waist, and his other hand held mine.

He'd had another heart-stopping game. Watching him out on the field, I didn't know how he could have even entertained the idea of doing anything else.

"You're stiff all of a sudden. What deep thoughts are you delving into?"

I opened my mouth but then snapped it shut. Maybe I didn't want to know the answer.

"Spill it." He spun me and pulled me toward him.

I licked my lips and took a deep breath. "After spending half the season in the pros, do you think you really could have given it up? Like if I lost my mind and told you I didn't want you to play and wanted you to just follow me to wherever I wanted to do my PhD, would you really have done it?"

He ran his hand along the side of my face, cupping my cheek. "In a heartbeat. Football won't last forever. We're forever. You showed me that. And if I'd played without you, I'd have been empty. All I'd have was the game, and then one day that would go away and I'd know exactly what I'd lost. Putting a pro contract up against these hands..." He took my hand in his. "These lips..." Leaning in, he captured my lips with his, drinking down my kisses. "This brain..." He tickled the nape of my neck. "It's no contest. You're more than enough. You're perfect."

∼

Thank you so much for reading Reece and Seph's story! It really meant to much to me in so many different ways. For an extra special day with them, you can check out their bonus epilogue HERE!

The Second We Met - Nix + The Pink Haired Menace

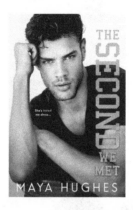

Start reading the enemies to lovers, nightmare neighbor romance, The Second We Met, right now!

The Third Best Thing - Berk + Jules

If you want a sweet and steamy secret admirer, girl next door read, check out The Third Best Thing!

The Fourth Time Charm - LJ + Marisa

My best friend. My new roommate. My coach's daughter.

EXCERPT FROM SHAMELESS KING

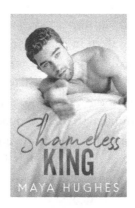

Declan - Prom

The Rittenhouse Prep prom committee had gone all out again this year. Limos and luxury cars lined the entrance to the building. Those cars cost more than my house was worth, but you couldn't tell that from the way people called out our names as we walked by. Me and the guys who'd had my back since our first practice together freshman year, The Kings, were State Champions—again.

I'd been to every prom since freshman year. It seemed even senior girls had no problem being seen on the arm of a freshman, as long as it was me. The thumping of the music guided us through the entrance of the building with a slightly fishy smell. Being right on the water, the building had a distinct salt-and-sea tinge to the air.

My rented tux fit well. Working my magic, I'd done a deal with the shop. Told people where I got mine from, and the shop rented it to me and had it altered for free. It was a pretty sweet deal. I figured if I was going to be uncomfortable in the thing, at least I'd look good.

And from the way heads turned as we walked in, I knew I did. Lots of guys walked in with their custom tuxes, but I didn't care because all eyes were on me and the rest of the Kings. Rittenhouse Prep Kings and state hockey champions in the flesh. People on the dance floor clapped and cheered when we came in through the double doors of the ballroom.

"Declan!" Someone whooped from a few tables away. A bunch of woo-hoos and Kings' chants later and we could finally leave our spot at the door. If Ford got any redder, he'd be ready to explode. He tugged at his collar. They'd had to special order his tux. But he had that strong silent thing chicks went wild for. Jet black hair, serious scowl that melted away in an instant. He hated the attention; that was fine. I could soak up more than enough for all of us.

The warm buzz from the pre-prom drinks we'd had at Emmett's meant I was feeling good. Nothing too crazy. We didn't want to get kicked out, but just enough to kick up the fun a notch.

"What did I tell you? We don't need dates." I grinned, and my eyes swept over a few of the more plunging necklines of some of the dresses our fellow students wore. We moved through the room, and people's heads turned as we walked past some classmates already seated. High fives were doled out for all of us as we strolled by.

"Declan, guys, this way, I'll show you to the table." One of the bubbly juniors rushed up to us and looped her arm around Heath's, tugging him forward. I rolled my eyes. Heath never had to bat an eyelash to get the women to fawn all over him. Blond hair worked for guys as well. He was easy to spot with the surfer look on the East Coast.

"We took the liberty of putting your tent cards on the table already. We didn't want you to have to find your names." She had a mountain of blonde hair piled up on top of her head. The curls were so tight it looked like she could bounce around on her head like Tigger.

Our spot was a prime location in the center of the ten-seater tables dotted around the dance floor.

"I have a feeling we're going to be dancing a lot," Ford grumbled, elbowing Colm as he took his seat. He looked as uncomfortable as I felt. The fabric of his tux was stretched to its limit on his shoulders—if he wasn't a gentle giant, who'd mastered the art of chilling the fuck out, I'd swear he was ready to Hulk out at any second.

"Don't worry, big guy; I'm happy to intercept any dance requests someone might throw your way." I lifted my glass of water to him as a toast.

Colm slid his flask across to my lap, and my eyes got wide. He was our resident mischief maker lately. Having your life thrown into chaos had a way of making people act not quite like themselves. Emmett by far got into the most trouble out of all of us, but with his parents' power and influence he never really had to worry about the conse-quences. Heath, Ford, and I were scholarship kids who knew how to toe the line. "Is this the older brother breaking all the rules?" I covered my mouth in fake outrage.

"Shut up. Olivia's not here, so what she doesn't know won't hurt her." Colm had become the guardian of his younger sister when their parents died earlier that year in a car accident. He'd always taken on the protector role, but that had gone into hyperdrive now that Olivia relied on him.

I drained the water and put my glass under the table, pouring some of the vodka into it.

"Declan, can I have a dance later?" A girl, Hannah—or was it Anna?—asked as she passed by on the arm of her date.

I winced and shrugged my shoulders at the guy. *Sorry, dude.* I'd convinced the guys to go solo. Well, except for Emmett. He'd of course brought, Avery. They'd been joined at the hip since sophomore year. But Heath, Ford, and Colm were by my side at our table. Blue light skated over the room from the massive fish tank that took up one entire wall.

Not many people got to say they had their prom at an aquarium. A group of other students crowded around one end of the tank where a fish that looked almost as big as Emmett hung near the glass. All it was missing was the giant bushy beard.

This was one of our last nights all together. The prom, the big pep rally, a final blow out at Emmett's, and then we were all off to college. Bittersweet in a way. Leaving most of the guys behind. Heath and I would be playing locally at the University of Philadelphia. Colm and Ford would be up in Boston, and Emmett was being cagey with his plans for next year.

A few hors d'oeuvres and a shot from the flask later, and the prom was really in full swing. Emmett arrived with Avery on his arm, beaming like he always was whenever she was near him. Dude had it so bad and he didn't even care. We didn't even give him shit about it anymore, that was just how it was. Avery meant everything to him, made sense when you had parents as shitty as his.

The room heated up, and I shrugged off my jacket, draping it over the back of my chair, ready to get back on the dance floor. While most people would have expected everyone to be uptight, it seemed that the dim lighting and fish as an audience meant everyone was ready to show off their moves.

"Holy shit!" someone behind me said, and my gaze darted all over the place to figure out what they were talking about.

I'd been hit in the chest with a puck before, but nothing quite compared to this feeling. Across the room, standing in front of the entrance, was a breathtaking sight. I don't remember what the hell color her dress was, all I knew was I couldn't take my eyes off her.

She stood there fidgeting with the small bag in her hands and glanced around the room.

"Wow, looks like the Ice Queen has finally thawed out a bit."

A slight murmur rippled through the people around me. My stomach dropped as my mind whirred trying to place her. And like a slow motion reveal, Makenna Halstead slid those horn-rimmed glasses she'd worn every second I'd ever seen her back on.

Avery spotted her and raced across the room, wrapping her arms around an incredibly uncomfortable-looking Makenna. It was like now that she knew all eyes were on her, she couldn't handle the pressure.

It wasn't just the glasses that were missing. It was also the telltale bun and the talk-to-me-and-I'll-kill-you stare.

Normally, she walked with her shoulders square and a stomp that could shatter bone. I'd never seen her look so...nice.

She bit her bottom lip. It was the first time I'd ever seen her look unsure. I'd have never thought her barely strawberry-blonde hair was that long, since she always wore it up. She also swore up and down that dances and other stuff like this were a waste of time, so seeing her here had taken my brain at least a little while to piece it together.

Avery dragged her over to our table. We had a couple seats free. Mak gave the table a small wave.

"No, you're not wearing those tonight. You don't need them." Avery tugged the glasses off her face and shoved them back in her bag.

"Actually, I kind of do." Makenna reached for the bag as Avery smacked her hands away.

"Nope! I'm sure one of these strapping young men would be happy to lead you around like your very own seeing-eye stud if you do need to go anywhere."

The corners of her mouth turned down, but this time her lips were all soft and shiny. Deep pink brought out the fullness I'd never seen before. I shook my head. This was Mak the Ice Queen we were talking about.

She sat on a seat beside Ford, who seemed completely content to be sitting beside someone who was also happy doing her best mute impersonation.

"If you don't dance to at least five songs tonight, I swear I'm tanking our final project on purpose."

Mak gasped, like a real-life hand-to-chest gasp in horror at Avery even suggesting it.

"They would never find your body, Avery." Mak grinned up at her with her arms crossed over her chest.

I laughed into my napkin, and Mak turned her glare on me.

"I'm sure Emmett would. He's like a bloodhound when it comes to me." Right on time Emmett slid his arms around her waist and planted his nose in her neck, letting out a sniff loud enough for everyone to hear.

"I smell someone who needs to get out there and dance." Emmett led Avery away from the table. Avery held out her hand, flashing a five at Mak over and over. I grabbed the flask from the spot Colm had stashed it and had another drink.

A long, slender hand slid its way down over my shoulder, stopping at my chest. "You promised me a dance." The smell from Anna's hot breath against my neck told me we weren't the only ones who'd snuck in a little booze tonight. It was not a good smell on her, and my skin crawled. Out of the corner of my eye, I caught the pissed-off face of her date. I did not want to have a fight tonight.

"Listen, I'm sorry. I would, but I already promised Mak a dance, and you know how she gets when she can't get what she wants, and it looks like tonight she wants me."

Mak's eyes got as wide as saucers, and her mouth hung open. Slipping out of the grasp of the date-ditcher, I rounded the table and held out my hand to Mak.

Glancing behind me at the very pissed-off Hannah or Anna and her even more pissed-off date, Mak perhaps sized up the situation and didn't want to be in the middle of a whirlwind of haymakers or thrown drinks, so she took my hand. A small jolt shot straight up my arm the second my skin touched hers. It was that same feeling you got standing in line for concessions at a movie you'd been waiting for forever. I shook my head. This was Mak we were talking about, and she didn't look one bit affected by my fingers wrapped around her.

"And tonight I want you?" She lifted an eyebrow at me as we walked out onto the dance floor with the corners of her mouth turned up the tiniest bit.

"I improvised. I know how people get when they don't get a piece of me." I grinned at her, but she just rolled her eyes.

"Probably for the best. Hannah can be a real bitch when she doesn't get what she wants, which probably means Edgar is in for a rough night. Poor guy." She glanced back over her shoulder to a very irate Hannah standing with her arms crossed over her chest.

People parted out of the way to give us some room. The moderately fast-paced song switched up to a slow one almost as soon as we found our spot.

We stood there staring at each other. I took a step forward, and Mak hesitated before looping her arms around my neck. The sensation was back now and worse than before. Staring down into Mak's eyes, I really saw them for the first time. They were the brightest blue I'd ever seen. Maybe it was the room or a trick of the lights, but I'd never seen so many blues in one spot.

It was the soft stroke of her fingers along the hair at the nape of my neck that made my hands tighten on her waist. The way she stared into my eyes, I don't even know if she realized she was doing it. Like her hands had a mind of their own, trying to soak up a little bit more of me. And I figured that was how she felt because my fingers had the same idea as I pulled her in tighter against me. Her lips parted, and her eyelashes fluttered.

The thud of my heart pounded as we moved to our own rhythm under the dim lights at the center of a sea of people.

Electricity buzzed through my body, but I knew it wasn't just the vodka. It was all to do with the woman in my arms who usually drove me up a wall.

"I don't think I've ever seen you without your glasses before."

"I don't think I've ever seen you in a tux before." Her pink tongue darted out to lick her bottom lip. The wetness left behind drew my gaze to it, and I wanted to have my own sample of her lips.

"You've never been to prom before." My hands pressed into the small of her back, closing the tiniest of gaps that had been between us. *Why did she feel so good in my arms?* The blues and greens from the fish tank washed over us like a spell had been cast and we were living in our own little underwater bubble.

"Almost didn't come to this one."

"Why not?" I leaned my head back, savoring the trail her fingertip blazed along the base of my neck.

She never let herself have any fun. Normally, it also meant no one else could have any fun and it irked the shit out of me, but tonight I just wanted to hold her close on the dance floor all night.

"It's not really my thing, but I figured it's a rite of passage and all, so I decided to come." She shrugged her shoulders.

"I'm glad you did."

Even with the pretense of her helping me out of a dance with the devil—aka Hannah—gone, we stayed out there through a string of slow songs. At least I think they were slow songs; our tempo didn't change. It was the first time we'd probably had a civil conversation with each other in years. So weird that it would happen now. It was like one of those high school movies I swore I never watched, but I had at least a few times, where the big thing happened between the two nemeses.

My head dipped down slightly. It was like the warning sirens blaring on a submarine. My blood pounded in my veins, and I needed to taste her lips like I needed my next breath. It was an uncontrolled dive, and I didn't know exactly what I was doing, but she wasn't pulling back. She wasn't pushing her hands against me or cocking her hand back for a slap; if anything, she leaned in even more.

Her eyes almost fluttered closed as my lips parted, so close to hers. Her body went stiff, and her eyes snapped open wide. "Are you drunk?" She pushed back in my arms.

I let them drop. "No, I'm not drunk. I've had a couple drinks, but that's it." I took a step toward her, and she took a step back.

Before I could say anything else, a booming voice came out over the squealing PA. "And now it's time to announce our prom king and queen." One of the prom committee girls grabbed me by the arm. "We need you up front, Declan."

With a strength I didn't think someone of her size could possess, she pushed me from the middle of the dance floor. I glanced behind me at a stone-faced Mak with her arms crossed over her chest. She was back at our table and had her glasses back on her face. Things were back just how they'd always been.

The bright lights hanging from the ceiling shined in my face as they went through whatever the hell they were doing up onstage. I kept my eyes on Mak with the corners of my mouth turned down as she slowly made her way toward the double doors.

"And this year's prom king is Declan McAvoy!" Someone placed a crown on my head, and everyone cheered. The doors closed behind Mak, and I couldn't help but feel like that was the end to something. The end of something that hadn't even really started. But I know one thing. If I'd known how long it would be until I got to hold her again, I'd have held on a bit longer.

∼

If you'd love to know more about Declan and Mak's history it all starts in SHAMELESS KING!

Enemies to lovers has never felt so good!

Declan McAvoy. Voted Biggest Flirt. Highest goal scorer in Kings of Rittenhouse Prep history.

Everyone's impressed, well except one person...

I can't deny it. I want her. More than I ever thought I could want a woman. I've got one semester–only four months–to convince her everything she thought about me was wrong.

Will my queen let me prove to her I'm the King she can't live without?

Only one way to find out...

One-click SHAMELESS KING now!

ACKNOWLEDGMENTS

As with every single one of my books, I couldn't have done it without the help of so many people. From my editors to my friends, they are such an important part of bringing my characters to life.

I wanted to give a special thanks for Tamara Mayata and Caitlin Marie! Nikki is there to hold my hand, help me talk through what my characters are thinking and keeps me on track. Najla is an amazing cover designer who always amazes me with what she comes up with.

And I wanted to send out a special thank you to one of my Sirens, Dimaris. It's such a blast to have you in my group and I can't thank you enough to how much you've helped share The Perfect First love.

Last, but never least, thank you to you! Without readers like you, I wouldn't be able to keep breathing life into those stories that only live in my mind. I can't thank you enough and I'd love to hear from you <3

Until next time!

Maya xx

ALSO BY MAYA HUGHES

CONNECT WITH MAYA

Sign up for my newsletter to get exclusive bonus content, ARC opportunities, sneak peeks, new release alerts and to find out just what I'm books are coming up next.

Join my reader group for teasers, giveaways and more!

Follow my Amazon author page for new release alerts!

Follow me on Instagram, where I try and fail to take pretty pictures!

Follow me on Twitter, just because :)

I'd love to hear from you! Drop me a line anytime :)
https://www.mayahughes.com/
maya@mayahughes.com

CPSIA information can be obtained
at www.ICGtesting.com
Printed in the USA
LVHW091112290421
685951LV00002B/11